PRAISE FOR *MIDSUMMER NIGHTS*

"Fans of the Bard, rejoice—Lara Stokes's stellar debut, *Midsummer Nights*, is here to scratch your theatre-and-hijinks itch. When burned-out big-city actor Miranda returns to her childhood small town of North Lake to perform at a community theater owned by her thespian parents, she views the move as a giant step backward. What she finds instead is community, rekindled friendship, Shakespearean magic, and a swoony love story. Stokes has created a hilarious, lovable, wisecracking force in Miranda, a character you will cheer and laugh alongside as she stumbles toward transformation. Highly recommend—*Midsummer Nights* is a pleasurable read from start to finish!"

—Uzma Jalaluddin, bestselling author of *Yours for the Season*

"Put *Midsummer Nights* on your must-read list, and you can thank us later! Lara Stokes brings this moving story to life in the rich setting of a small town and its beloved community theater. Her characters brim with an oh-so-satisfying blend of wry humor, emotional depth, and meaningful reflections on the pursuit of fame—and what that can cost us. *Midsummer Nights* will leave you cheering for an encore!"

—Tracy Dobmeier and Wendy Katzman, coauthors of *Ten Thousand Light Years from Okay*

MIDSUMMER Nights

MIDSUMMER Nights

a novel

LARA STOKES

LAKE UNION
PUBLISHING

Published by Lake Union Publishing, Seattle

www.apub.com

Amazon, the Amazon logo, and Lake Union Publishing are trademarks of Amazon.com, Inc., or its affiliates.

EU product safety contact:
Amazon Media EU S. à r.l.
38, avenue John F. Kennedy, L-1855 Luxembourg
amazonpublishing-gpsr@amazon.com

ISBN-13: 9781662539855 (paperback)
ISBN-13: 9781662539848 (digital)

Cover design by Zoe Norvell
Cover image: © Patrick Guenette / Alamy; © tahir pro, © galacticus / Shutterstock

Printed in the United States of America

For Dad, whose example led the way to the writing life,
and
for Annette, whose many roles brought me through
many stages

No epi[taph], I pray you, for our play needs no
excuse. —*A Midsummer Night's Dream*, Act V, Scene 1

TEMPEST THEATRE PRESENTS

WILLIAM SHAKESPEARE'S BELOVED COMEDY

A MIDSUMMER NIGHT'S DREAM

DIRECTED BY ROSCOE BELMONT
PRODUCED BY WYNNE BELMONT

Featuring our guest artists:

Theo Raye—star of the Stratford Festival—**as Puck**
Arthur Crew—Tempest favorite!—**as Bottom**
and
Miranda Belmont—television actor—**as Helena**

dramatis personae:

The Royals:

Theseus, duke of Athens
Hippolyta, queen of the Amazons, betrothed to Theseus
Philostrate, master of the revels
Egeus, father to Hermia

The Lovers:

Lysander, in love with Hermia
Demetrius, in love with Hermia
Hermia, daughter to Egeus, in love with Lysander
Helena, in love with Demetrius

The Mechanicals:

Bottom, a weaver
Quince, a carpenter
Snug, a joiner
Flute, a bellows-mender
Snout, a tinker
Starveling, a tailor

The Fairies:

Oberon, king of the fairies
Titania, queen of the fairies
Puck, or Robin Goodfellow, a fairy
Cobweb, a fairy
Moth, a fairy
Mustardseed, a fairy
Peaseblossom, a fairy

There will be a twenty-minute interval.
No talking, no texting, no crinkly wrappers, no flash photography.
Behave yourselves! You're at the theater.

ENJOY THE SHOW!

Chapter 1

May

I did this to myself, but I'm going to blame Shakespeare. I'm going to blame the intersection of art and commerce. I blame both Broadway and Hollywood. I could blame my parents, or my ex, or my boss. I'm also inclined to blame Batman. But however you spin it, I did it. I burned my life down.

If I were an optimist, I would describe my present hell with platitudes. Something like, "Everything you think you know needs to fall apart, and then the clarity comes."

That is such bullshit.

I am not an optimist. Instead, I declare the universe to be a wily bitch, an impish fairy who hands you the wrong potion, expecting you to drink it, then watches gleefully as you spiral.

However you look at it, mine is a predicament of epic proportions. Borderline Shakespearean.

It starts with a phone call. As per my nightly routine, I am two glasses of midrange Malbec deep, googling my enemies (perfectly pleasant actresses who are younger and thinner than me), and avoiding learning my lines for yet another terrible scene I am supposed to shoot tomorrow on the terrible TV show I am on.

My phone blares. My parents. I use the most aggressive ringtone I could find for them (trumpet fanfare) to signify their intrusions, which, blessedly, are down to monthly calls that they bray through until I pretend I have a timer going off in the kitchen and we all hang up in relief. My parents share a cell phone, the most obvious sign of their total codependency. I let it ring thrice while I throw back the rest of my wine. I instinctively straighten my shoulders and smooth my hair. They only recently discovered FaceTime and view it as an occasion I should be presentable for.

"Parents," I say, masking the anxiety that always swells at the first notes of their ringtone. Their faces pop up, both of them hovering over the phone like Narcissus over his riverbed.

"Darling!" coos my mother, as though this call is a lovely surprise, even though she called me. "How are you, sweet love?" She wants something. She frowns. "You look tired."

"I'm very well, Mother, thank you." I prop the phone against the wine bottle and continue my doomscroll on my laptop as though the two agonies will somehow cancel each other out.

"It's raining," says my father savagely. His brows pinch as he scowls outside. My father hates rain. Weather reports are his love language.

"What's up?" I'd like to hurry this along; I'm terribly busy googling.

"Well, darling, we have a bit of a quandary." My mother pauses, hoping, I'm sure, to stir my curiosity, but I'm only half listening. "It's about the Season."

The Season. For the last thirty years, my parents have run a theater company in North Lake, Ontario, the small town they moved us to when I was five. Life has always tended to revolve around the Season.

"What about it?"

"It's doomed," my father says.

"It's not doomed," my mother cuts in. "It's just . . ."

"Fucked," says my dad.

"What's wrong?" I ask.

"It's a casting thing."

"Just say it, Mom."

"Goodness! Manners, Miranda."

"Our lead actress bailed," my father says, clearly irritated by whatever scene my mother is setting up. "Our headliner."

Tempest Theatre's success has always ridden on the novelty of its framework. Each season, they do three shows: a Shakespeare, a drama, and a comedy. They source professional actors from all over the country, from the Stratford Festival, from Toronto, and because they have some pretty fancy donors, they can hire a select few for the whole season. Each year, there are a couple of big names headlining, and the real catch is that the rest of the cast and crew are locals. That is, amateurs. It's Broadway-meets-your-basic-ninth-grade-drama-class, but it works. It engages the community, and though I am loath to admit it, they put on great shows.

"Okay?" I still don't see how this is about me. "Who was it?"

"We aren't supposed to say," says my mother.

"Genevieve Chen," barks my father.

"Wow. You guys got her? She's kind of a big deal!"

"Genevieve Chen is going to Broadway," my mother wails. "We lost her!"

My father clears his throat. "Miranda."

I know where this is going. "Father . . ."

"We need your help."

I have no special fondness for my parents beyond requisite familial pleasantries. They have not offered me a role in almost fifteen years, and it's clear I am a last resort. I resent their assumption that I am even free, even though my TV show, *Listings*, happens to wrap in a week, and I will have three months off between seasons. Still, a summer in my hometown holds no appeal.

"I wish I could." I don't.

My mother presses on. "So, it's *A Midsummer Night's Dream*."

Something sparks inside me. I press it down.

"You would be Helena."

"Titania," I say, despite having no intention of pursuing this.

"Dear heart, it's not up for negotiation."

"Is it cast yet?" I ask.

"Well, not entirely."

"I would want Titania," I say.

"Titania has been cast."

"Who?"

My father clears his throat.

"Me," my mother purrs.

Of course. "I'm too old to play Helena."

"You're thirty-four. The lovers can be any age!" my mother says.

"You look younger from a distance," my father adds.

"I don't want to play Helena," I say. "She's so whiny and pathetic. I get that you're in a bind, but there's nothing in this for me."

"There is funding. You would be well paid," says my mother.

"Okay," I say. "But, hey, who are the other headliners?" There are always three. I'm obviously not going to do this, but I'm curious.

"Well, Arthur, of course," my mother starts, and my dad grunts. Arthur Crew comes most summers, his Toronto theater schedule all but dried up these days. He's a Tempest Theatre staple, people love him, and I have a feeling that, career-wise, it's the highlight of his year.

"Okay, Arthur. Who else?"

There's a long pause.

"Well, who is it?"

They smile at each other. "Theo."

And there it is. They know they've got me.

Something stirs in my chest. It's almost too good to be true.

"It's been a long time, hasn't it?" my father continues. "Since you and Theo have worked together? A lot of time has passed."

"Yes," I say, "it's been a long time." They don't know how often I check his Instagram, or how I have Google Alerts set up in his name.

I assume they know that they are playing with fire here. This is fairly juicy casting, especially in our hometown, and here's the clincher for all of us: We know that if Miranda Belmont and Theo Raye are together onstage again, the show will sell out.

Of course, I won't do it.

My parents hang up, my mother sulking, my father grumbling. It's fine. I have an acting career that is so much bigger than hometown Shakespeare. I owe them nothing. I don't need them.

Chapter 2

I am a regular on *Listings*, a soapy drama about shady but incredibly attractive real estate agents who use their properties to conceal their lives of crime. It's a shitty show but wildly popular, in its sixth season, and I got in at the beginning, playing Lilias Harvey, the sexy, mean secretary. Not a huge role, but enough to eventually buy a nice condo and have a modicum of notoriety in the city. It's the biggest break I've ever had as an actor, though not the most artistically fulfilling one. I have been begging the producers to give me more to do, to let me show more range. They are "thinking about it," they tell me.

This season revolved around a new star, Nick Nolan as Ryder Atlas, a real estate tycoon and undercover detective. Nick is heart-stoppingly handsome, built, and blond, with intense blue eyes and rock star vibes. He high-fives every crew member on set; he is magnetic and gorgeous, with that magic capacity for making anything or anyone within his notice feel like the center of his whole world. And as it happens, he noticed me.

We didn't meet until the season Christmas party five months ago, where he caught my eye across the room, strode over to me, and said, "I've been waiting forever to meet you, gorgeous." He does better with a script.

I had only been in love the one time. Considering the string of assholes that followed, this was pretty on brand. It seemed like we might have sex. I liked that idea. We did. After a few too many cocktails, he pulled me into the coat check and hiked up my dress around my waist. He didn't kiss my mouth, which seemed hot at the time, very *Pretty Woman*, then right as I came, he brushed his lips softly to mine, breathing in my cries. And I was his.

For a while, it was fun. I was so his that I didn't care that he didn't want to go public with the relationship. It wasn't *exactly* a relationship anyway. We went to work, we went back to his place for sex. We went to glitzy show events separately, never speaking, never touching, and for a long time, it felt like a thrilling game, our secret. There were sacred, rare dinners in private rooms of fancy restaurants and one perfect weekend in New York, where we only left the hotel room for ice cream and champagne. I felt drunk on him, fizzed up on chemicals that never seemed to land, and for about five months, it was total bliss. At work, we feigned professionalism, but everyone knew. Sometimes he stuck his head into my trailer, and I pulled him in for quick, furious sex that made the hair and makeup team grumble that they didn't have time for touch-ups. No one said much, aside from that. The star can do pretty much whatever he wants. For five months, he did.

It is all good until we are lying in bed the morning of the season wrap party.

"So, I have news," he murmurs into my hair. I know, by now, to wait for him. He hates it when people step on his lines. He takes a dramatic breath. "I'm going to LA for a few months."

"Oh, yeah?" I say mildly, but my mind has started spinning. I was looking forward to our summer off together.

"Babe." He sits up, turning to me. "I booked *Lego Batman*." He beams expectantly.

"Um, what? Wasn't that . . . already made?"

"It's the live-action version!"

"Isn't that just . . . *Batman*?"

"No." He looks disappointed in me, sorry for me, even. "No, babe, this is the live-action version of the Lego version."

"So, live *Batman* . . ."

"With Lego."

"Um, and you are playing . . . ?"

"Lego Batman. Duh."

"Wow. Okay, um, so, congratulations." I pause. "That's . . . creatively . . . interesting to you?"

He frowns. "You don't sound very proud of me."

"I'm proud of you," I say. "I'm surprised you never mentioned this."

"It just happened. I flew out this week." He told me he was in a meeting, but he didn't say for what.

"Okay, well . . . So how long are you gone for?"

"All summer," he says. "I might have to miss a few episodes next season, but the producers think it will boost viewing if I'm in a big blockbuster, so . . ."

"Yeah, sure." I pause, trying to gather my thoughts. "So, all summer. I guess I could fly out . . . maybe even stay with you for a few weeks? I'm free, as you know . . ."

"Oh." He looks concerned. "Oh, yeah, no, babe. That's not a good idea."

"Why not?" But I know.

"I mean, we aren't, you know, public." He looks at me with practiced tenderness. "We aren't even really official. You know that, babe."

I am quiet. He strokes my face, then my hair, then my arm, as though I am some found kitten, as though I simply require a rote amount of pacifying before he gets more sex. "It's been five months," I say finally. I can feel it coming. I know what I have to do.

"I mean, yeah . . . really? Cool."

"It's been five months, and you have all but kept me under a rock, and now you're just taking off for, what? Three months? And you don't want to see me."

"I'm just going to be pretty busy . . ."

I get out of bed and start to put my clothes on from my bag on the floor. I don't have so much as a toothbrush here. "Yeah, okay. I get it."

I go to the bathroom and close the door behind me, angry tears rising fast. I splash water on my face, but they still burn down my cheeks. I stare at myself in the mirror. I'm bed rumpled, my face blotchy, but I am still youngish. I am widely considered conventionally attractive. My body is to die for. I look more closely at myself, suddenly ashamed that my first and only assessment of myself is of my appearance. But it seems that's all I am these days. It's time. The last five months have been nice. Really, really nice, actually. I had hoped maybe we had more in us. But I can see the cracks in the veneer, and it's time to do what I always do. I open the door.

"Yeah, no," I say. He has already moved on to his phone.

"No, what, babe?" he asks absently.

"I'm actually done here."

He barely looks up. "What do you mean?"

"Put your phone down, Nick. I'm breaking up with you."

His head snaps up. "What?" He looks at me, alarmed.

"I don't factor anywhere in your decisions, in your life. You don't care about me."

"I do!" A switch has flipped. Suddenly he is pleading. "I do!"

"You don't." I want to spew a litany of complaints: *I don't like who I am with you. I don't like what you bring out in me. I don't recognize myself anymore.* The person I am angriest at, I realize, is myself. "It's fine. Go to LA. Be Batman."

"Lego Batman." He sulks.

"It's not a big deal. I thought maybe it was . . . more. But thank you, you've helped me see I was wrong, so . . ." I look around, but there is nothing to take with me except my bag and my rage. "I promise not to make a thing of this at work, but, yeah, we're done here."

He looks at me. For a moment, it seems like he's actually surprised, like he's actually hurt, but he covers it quickly with a hard look I've only ever seen on-screen. "Fine." He returns to his phone. "Whatever."

If I know one thing about this man, it's that he can't handle rejection. My only power move here is to end it first.

Leaving his building, walking out onto the street, I feel a lightness. Relief. Agency. It's been five months since I've had to think for myself. *This is good,* I think. The season has wrapped; we have three months for everything to blow over, and we barely worked together anyway. There is an underlying sadness—deep down, I have real feelings about this—but something in me snapped back there. I need to be able to look in a mirror and see myself.

I want to skip the wrap party, but it will raise suspicion, so instead I put on the silver chain mail minidress I bought for the occasion. Nick loved it, and on one hand, I want no further connection to him, but I also want to make him suffer just a little. Just enough to miss me. I do a shimmery, smoky eye and a bright-berry lip. Just for tonight, I still need the disguise.

I arrive late to the party, looking good, feeling increasingly victorious, and I run through the months of nonsense I submitted to. Nick would disappear and not tell me where he'd been for days. He never wanted to confirm our relationship despite plenty of online speculation, and he never, ever stayed at my place. It was always his place, his schedule, his terms. The thought of my parents' offer flickers in me. I am a sought-after actress! I am turning down Shakespeare. I can turn down Nick Nolan.

I feel the party pulsing before I even arrive. I walk in, knowing full well that the party lights turn my dress into a disco ball, that I light up the floor as I walk through to the bar. People separate, some giving me small smiles, some turning conspicuously away, some whispering as I pass. At first, I think it's the dress, but when I reach Nisha, my closest show friend, who plays a lead in the show, at the bar, and her eyes fill with tears, I know something is up. She hands me a drink.

"What's going on?" I ask. "People are being weird."

"There have been rumblings," she murmurs.

"Of what?"

"You need to talk to Jay . . ."

"Nisha, what do you know? Tell me!"

"You might be in trouble . . . I don't know . . ."

"I broke up with Nick this morning," I say. "Looks like he told everyone . . ."

"He wouldn't tell people you were together," she says. "I doubt he's telling people you dumped him. Can you even dump someone who won't admit they're dating you?"

"Wow, thanks." I take a sip of my drink. Tequila soda. I look for Nick, but he isn't even there.

"It's a double," says Nisha. "I had a feeling."

I turn to her, but she is facing out to the dance floor. "Do you know something?" She doesn't look at me.

"No. I know nothing," she says. "But I have a feeling you need to talk to Jay."

I scan the room for our showrunner Jay, a narcissistic man-child who is always half a syllable away from a #MeToo moment. He catches my eye and tilts his head toward the balcony.

It's cold out there, and I feel naked in my little dress. Jay runs his eyes over me out of habit before he clears his throat awkwardly.

"I'm sorry, Miranda. They're not renewing you for next season."

"What? How?" I know, though. Nick.

"Um, we have tweaked the next episode, and your character is going to take a job in LA."

The irony.

"Any chances of a spin-off?" I ask dryly, my stomach flipping.

"Ha! Man, we are really going to miss that wit. Okay, so, of course, you'll be paid for the rest of the episodes we booked you for. We just . . . yeah, this will be your last one. So sorry. You get it."

I do not get it. I do not pretend to get it. "But, Jay, you've got to tell me why."

There is a long pause. "Ah, well, I think it's just, like, the vibes on set?"

"You're firing me for my consensual relationship with my costar?"

"Well, to be fair, you were never, like, a star."

"Jay, for fuck's sake."

"It's just because that relationship . . . ended." He clears his throat again. "Unfortunately, we are sort of tied to . . ."

"Nick did this," I say.

"I can't discuss the details." He pauses. "But between you and me—and, I mean, for real—he said it was him or you. Our hands are tied. Whatever went down with you two must have been . . ."

"What went down between us has ended, but that has nothing to do with work."

Jay purses his lips. "Yeah, so, unfortunately, it does," he says. "Gotta keep the stars happy, am I right? When it comes down to it, you're replaceable." He shrugs, like we are both in this predicament, like it is up to both of us to get through this. "Do you . . . Should I hug you?" he asks, eyeing the dress again.

"You can fuck yourself," I say. I pull open the balcony door, and everyone who was watching us through the window does an about-face, pretending to look at their drinks, their feet, their phones. I throw my shoulders back and walk slowly across the dance floor to the coat check, where a young woman, some aspiring actress, probably, hands me my jacket.

"Have a great night!" she bleats, and I slip out.

Two breakups in one day. I stand out front, waiting for an Uber, alone, shaken, and angry. Nick and I . . . If I'm honest, we were never going to last. He all but made me break up with myself. But the show, however mediocre, has been my livelihood, my life, for six years. Now I have neither. My defining details have all vanished in one day.

Back home, I drink two glasses of wine in my pajamas and contemplate my options. I could call my agent in the morning and set up some auditions.

I could probably book something pretty easily. But would it just be more of the same? Am I willing to put myself through the paces of auditioning again, throwing myself into another role that doesn't matter to me? The idea of those waiting rooms, learning sides, hours of prep for a rare callback, and selling myself over and over feels exhausting. I could find a lawyer and challenge my dismissal, but if I know Nick, he's probably already anticipated that; there was likely some hushed boardroom conversation about me, some found loophole allowing them to fire me.

I did this to myself. I dumped a movie star, and he got me fired from the shitty show I didn't love. And now suddenly, my life is blank and also wide open.

My phone pings. Nick.

I miss you, babe.

I'm sorry.

I stare at the words.

I'm not doing this anymore.

I think again of my parents' offer. Theater. Shakespeare. *Midsummer's*. Theo. It might be good to get out of here. Just a break: a couple of months of rehearsal, a two-week run, then I can come back and start fresh.

I call my parents.

"Okay," I say. "I'll do it."

A week later, I find a subletter for my condo for the summer, the niece of another actor on the show. I'm going to be gone for three months, tops. I pack a couple of suitcases, stuff them into my car, and drive out of the city. I hope it burns behind me.

Chapter 3

June
Eight weeks until Opening Night

It's been a couple of years since I've been back to North Lake. I have a way of finding excuses not to go. I lost touch with most people after high school, not that I was in touch with many people *during* high school. I lost touch with the Tempest Theatre community after that last humiliating summer. I lost touch with the me who used to belong there. My parents usually come to the city to celebrate holidays, getting a hotel room and making it "festive," as my mother likes to say, which just means an excess of alcohol so we can pretend to talk to each other. But really, it's so that the occasions are marked; we can say we did them in style but not run the risk of any kind of familial intimacy.

My parents always judged my TV show as the artistic equivalent of Styrofoam, but at least I was working. At least they could say, *She's a working actor, yes, we're very proud, yes, yes, yes.* But I knew they didn't watch my show. My mother called it "unpalatable." She wasn't totally wrong. But still, the show was my whole life, the people in it my whole community. In their absence, I am realizing how little else there has been, how I have let my parents slip away from me. How, without *Listings,* I am actually quite alone. I am realizing, as I drive closer to a reunion with Theo, how much that isolation is on me.

I'm always surprised at how beautiful the drive home is. It's terrible getting out of the city; you crawl at a snail's pace, red light upon red light, in slow motion as you creep toward escape. It takes an hour just to get onto the highway. Then there's a slog through gray concrete walls with shitty industrial buildings on the other side, then subdivisions full of cookie-cutter houses that cost over a million dollars and all look the same, squeezed so tightly together, you could barely put your foot between them. There's the giant amusement park on the side of the highway, tall neon structures snaking over and around each other, sometimes a flurry of legs swinging as they run, a roar of dim screams as they pass.

But soon there are open green fields, then the pine trees start, and you reach one epic bend in the road revealing lakes and cottages, boats in the distance now in full view, and suddenly you're in Canada again. There are wide, man-made cliffs, the dynamite holes still ridged in little dips along the rock face, but it creates the illusion of high cliffs full of thick pine trees. You cross bridge after bridge, and underneath each is some gorgeous lake stretched out. You pass by small towns, then through marshes, where I always do a quick scan for moose, even though I've never seen one ever. There's something about knowing they're just out of sight: The hope remains that maybe today is the day.

I'll admit it, the drive home makes me feel romantic and nostalgic. It reminds me of somebody I used to be, someone I no longer am. All I know is, she used to be hopeful and happy.

As I drive, I play over last week's chaos. I think about Nick. I knew he was a bad idea from the start: He was too successful, too attractive, too rich. All that was what got me to drunkenly sleep with him at the Christmas party. But the next day, he sent me flowers with a cute note (badly spelled, but I appreciated the effort). He was so much sweeter than I could have imagined. He kept the cool-guy persona up at work, but I got to see the real him, the guy who was insecure, vulnerable, good, under all that bravado. Once he went to this community outreach event to build a new playground in an under-resourced neighborhood. A publicity thing, he told me. I assumed he was there for the photo op of him breaking ground and shaking hands with city officials, but he walked in ten hours later covered in dirt, ball cap soaked with sweat, beaming. It was the most beautiful he ever looked to me.

That night over takeout, he told me how his single mom had raised him, how she sometimes worked three jobs, how he grew up in one of those subsidized apartments like the ones surrounding the playground that day. He told me he'd decided he would get them out of there—he hadn't known how at the time, but the answer was handed to him in high school, when he was spritzing body spray topless at Abercrombie at the mall and an agent approached him. He was in a movie three months later.

"So, you didn't dream of being an actor?"

"I dreamed of being rich. And acting got me there."

I've thought about that line a lot over the past few months, and I think about it now, half laughing to myself. Nick, I always knew, was not an artist. His ambition was never creative, so this, I know, is why *Lego Batman* is a real win for him. On the one hand, I feel smug. I am heading in the opposite direction to do Shakespeare with intellectuals. On the other hand, I had hoped he'd offer to take me with him.

And then he had me fired. This, I know, was simply to punish me. This is the detail that snags in my brain. The fact that whatever sweetness Nick has in him, his default setting is asshole.

A text from Nisha comes through:

You're really leaving?

Just for the summer, I reply, dictating to my phone. But, yeah, I'm off the show.

Fuckers! This is so shitty! I'm going to quit in protest! I promise to come see your Shakespeare play!

She definitely won't quit, and she probably won't come, but I appreciate the sentiment. I mute my notifications.

I wanted to get an Airbnb, but the truth is I can't really afford one. My pay for the show this summer is decent, but not compared to regular TV work, and I have no idea when my next real paycheck is coming. The theater company puts up the guest actors in a rental for the summer, but Theo's family is there, and he actually likes them, so he has opted to stay at home with them. Arthur always stays at one of the small lakeside cottages walking distance from the theater. My parents have given me two options: Stay in the rental or stay at home and take whatever money was budgeted for the rental as an amendment to my salary for the summer. My getting paid is the main draw of the thing. It's awkward, if you think about it, how many people will be involved, will be working hard and giving their time and putting their hearts into something voluntarily that I had to be dragged into and paid to do. I'm taking a real gamble, opting to stay under my parents' twisted roof for another few thousand dollars, because frankly, now, I need it. Luckily, it's a big house. My parents own a gorgeous old home on a large corner lot on the oldest, prettiest street in town, sprawling Victorians with bay windows, towers, curling wrought iron fences. The house is spacious enough that we won't be on top of each other, but even still, I am dreading it.

They are at the theater when I arrive, a note on the door with a cryptic coded message in iambic pentameter, in my dad's tight, slanted handwriting, directing me to the key, which is hidden under the fairy statue in the back garden, his idea of whimsy.

My parents don't cook—they assemble food. My entire childhood was essentially one big charcuterie board, which certainly impacted my disdain for set mealtimes and my penchant for perpetual grazing. My mother has left a dainty saucer of fruit and cookies, an unusually tender gesture for her, as is the small bud vase of wildflowers on the bedside table in my bedroom. My room is at the top of the house, the tower. As a child, I loved it. I pretended I was Sara Crewe from *A Little Princess* and this was my attic. I would sleep on a pile of clothes on the floor, rub brown eye shadow on my cheeks, and mess up my hair so that I looked like an orphan. My mother would come in and look at me. "You'd think you didn't have a perfectly lovely bed!" she'd say, but I'd catch her little smile. She did not want a normal child. She did not want a little girl who would brush her hair and sleep in the pink canopy bed. If she indeed had to endure having a child at all, it had better be an interesting one. Maybe that was when they recognized that I was also an artist and that I wanted to live in another world, even if that world was objectively worse than the one I was currently in. There was romance in it. There was something aspirational, brave, daring to imagine life being worse than it is, and persevering.

The canopy bed is gone, replaced by a queen bed with an upholstered headboard in pink velvet, a weird homage to its predecessor, as if the bed grew up alongside me somehow. I unpack my suitcases, noting that my dresser drawers have been emptied of my high school clothes. I was not consulted on that, but also, I don't care. I have never been attached to objects from the past. My childhood books are in a neat row on a small white bookcase and on my old wooden desk, the one with the lid that lifts, inside which I hid sticker books and diaries and many, many glitter pens. On top is a script: *A Midsummer Night's Dream* by William Shakespeare. I sit down, open it, planning to highlight my lines, but my mother has already done it, as if to anchor me via neon yellow.

My parents arrive home a few hours later with sagging bags from the boutique cheese store and prepare the evening's charcuterie while we have a glass of wine.

"Theo arrived a few weeks ago . . ." my mother says. "He wanted some time to settle in and reacquaint himself with the town." My father coughs, a tell that there is more to it, but my mother hands him a plate and gives him a look, and they say no more.

Theo. There's no denying his success and, though I am loath to admit it, his talent. It's a real coup that they got him. He's one of the biggest stars they've ever pulled, and he's their own hometown sweetheart. It's a marketing match made in heaven. They are graciously concealing their disappointment at losing Genevieve Chen and having to deal with me. My reputation, unfortunately, precedes me in this town. I'm not a sure thing, and we all know it. I think they know that at any moment I could panic, bolt, abandon ship, and then where would they be? I see right through them. The flowers, the tea tray, my favorite cheese . . . They are staging this whole homecoming because that is what they do. They are experts at setting a scene, establishing a tone, and maneuvering human behavior according to their psychotic whims. The director and the producer.

"So." My mother waits until I have tucked into a surprisingly dreamy Camembert and my mouth is full. "We thought we would do your audition tomorrow afternoon after you settle in."

I nearly choke on my cheese. "Audition?"

"Yes, well, you see, it's a formality. It's just really for appearances so that it's all on the up-and-up."

"Is this because of last time?"

"Goodness, no, Miranda, that was a long time ago." It was, but we all know my doing this is a bit of a gamble.

"Would you have made Genevieve Chen audition?" I ask.

My dad snorts ambiguously.

"Well, that was different," my mother says.

I don't bother asking how. "And Theo did?"

"Oh, yes," my mother says. "Oh, he was wonderful. He did that song from *Company* . . . 'Staying Alive'?"

"'Being Alive.' Why did he sing? It's not a musical."

"I forget. Anyway, it was incredibly charming."

"Who is he playing?"

"Puck." She beams. "He's going to be brilliant." *Of course he is.* "And Arthur did his Hamlet."

"Arthur only auditions with Hamlet," my dad grumbles. "He's still hoping we'll cast him in it one day." He shakes his head. "No one wants to see a sixty-year-old Hamlet. The man has no sense."

"Arthur is a dream. I won't hear a word against him," says my mother. My dad shoots her a dark look. She looks away.

"Fine," I say, to break the silence. "Okay, I'll audition. I mean, I don't have anything prepared. What do you need me to do?"

"Oh, just a comic monologue and a dramatic monologue," my mother says. "It'll look like nepotism if we just give you the part."

"You mean I don't have the part?"

"Of course you have the part."

"Isn't that nepotism?"

"Well, it's an emergency."

"Wow, thanks."

"It's more about optics, about what it looks like to the community," my mother says. "We just want it all neat and tidy."

Nothing my parents do is ever neat and tidy. I doubt this will be any exception.

Chapter 4

My parents started Tempest Theatre long before I was born, back when they still lived in their native England. They did shows in rented back spaces of London's independent theaters. They met at theater school there, and from the get-go, Dad was the director, Mom his leading lady and producer. They toured with the Royal Shakespeare Company and came to Canada to do a season at the Stratford Festival, the best classical theater company in the country. They loved Canada and never went back. When I was small, they did a lot of theater in Toronto, individual acting and directing contracts, but always did a summer show with their friends. They called their company Tempest for the Shakespeare play. My father, I think, fancied himself a bit the magician, Prospero, wielding storms and making art. I was born and they named me Miranda, Prospero's daughter. Even in name, I came second to the theater.

My mom came from old money and, being the only child, inherited everything when her parents died. They used her money to move out of the city to North Lake, a small town two hours from Toronto. They purchased our sprawling Victorian century home and the crumbling theater down the road. I think they were tired of the whole city thing. They just wanted to make good theater without all the hassle. It ended up being easier to do it all themselves in a smaller town, in the theater they owned, where they could choose what they wanted to do.

They started Tempest up right away. It was small at first, just one play. A couple of their theater friends came from the city for the summer, led by the appeal of living for free in a lakeside town north of cottage country. They were able to spin it as a professional theater company for the community. Locals were tickled by the fact that they could do community theater with real professional actors. The company gained some notoriety and got people interested. The whole town came out. They drew in some sponsors and some provincial funding, and it grew to what it is now: a major summer event, a centerpiece of our town.

I don't know anybody from North Lake who hasn't been involved in the shows or at least gone to see them. As it happens in small towns, my parents have developed a sort of celebrity that they won't admit to but secretly love. At least my mother does. There is a certain romance to it, I suppose—artists in our midst, having these great creative minds walking among us. It's surprising what is impressive to some people.

I wish I could've resisted out of spite, but the truth is I loved the theater as much as they did. I remember being very small, perched on the edge of the stage during rehearsal, half in the scene, half out, watching my parents mold these ordinary people, turning it all into a world I could lose myself in. You forget the guy playing Horatio is really a local paramedic, the guy playing Rosencrantz a pizza deliveryman. Somehow, they made magic, whatever the materials. Of course, I would never admit any of this to them. It is my role as their only child to roll my eyes at them and express my frustration and disdain at every turn. But the anchor between us all is theater. It's more than in my blood. It *is* my blood.

I am greeted by a small smattering of applause when I enter the rehearsal hall, the black box space at the back of the theater. It's been a long time since I was home, a long time since I've seen these people. They are kind to greet me so warmly, considering my last performance here. The black curtains are open so that daylight shines through, unusual for this room. I can't help but feel that it looks wrong with light. My parents are at their long audition table, and a handful of locals sit nervously against the walls, frantically reading their sides and eager, I suspect, to see me. The thought is both humbling and off-putting.

I have done hundreds of auditions; my agent sent me out all the time before I got *Listings*, but they never stop making me want to puke a little bit. I know that I am already cast, that I have the part. Everyone knows it. It's no secret that I am The Talent this time around, albeit to the disappointment of many; Genevieve Chen was quite the get, and according to my parents, everyone was very excited to see her. I am local and there is a strong sense of community here, and so to that end, I am welcomed with open arms. Or forgiven, at least. Last time I was on their stage, I shit the bed. There is no way people have forgotten. I know we are all hoping that enough time has gone by that we can put that behind us. I do catch one or two people giving me the side-eye. I can't say I blame them.

The stage manager, Sally, gets up to greet me with a hug. She has worked with my parents for years and has known me since I was a child. I recognize a few faces from the past. I am glad to see some of them. You would think I'd feel safe in this room, but the truth is that my parents are the very last people on planet Earth that I would like to audition for. They are absolutely terrifying. It's perhaps worse that I have the role already, because now I have to justify that choice. I have to prove that I am worthy. We all know I am the second choice. We all know I'm not a sure thing. But here I am, and here I'll stay to do this thing. My parents and Sally are sitting at the long table at one end of the room, along with a teenager who eagerly tells me her name is Kate and she is the assistant stage manager. I smile at her distractedly as I hand my mother my headshot. She looks at it, frowning.

"Is this recent?" she asks.

"What do you mean, 'is it recent'?" I ask. "It's me. It's your daughter's face."

"Did you fill out the form?"

"What form?" I ask.

"Everyone has to fill out their form, stating their experience and personal information," my mother says. I search her expression for any glimpse of irony, but she is merely staring at me with her scarily serious producer face on.

"Are you kidding me right now?" I ask my mother. "I can't believe you're making . . ." I stop. I look around and remember there are other people in the room, people who got up this morning just so that they could see me fail, again, in front of my parents, and I am serving up a truly interesting scene here. I pull out my phone and text her my IMDb page. She looks at it and sniffs.

"Not a lot of theater credits," she says.

"Just show us your monologues," my dad says roughly.

I try not to roll my eyes. I step back. "Which one do you want first?" I ask.

"Whichever one you're more comfortable with," my mother says in a pandering tone that I know she enjoys using on the locals.

I shake her off and launch into my comic monologue, Cecily from *The Importance of Being Earnest*, one of three or four monologues I always keep in my back pocket. When I finish, I look at my parents' faces, which are blank. There is no applause, there are no winks.

"Next one," my dad barks.

And again, I take a breath, and I give him Lady Macbeth. I sail through it. I know this like the back of my hand. The words are familiar, like slipping into something comfortable that I am my best true self in. The beauty of acting. The beauty of escaping whatever garbage bag I really am. When I am done, the little assistant stage manager begins to applaud, but my father shoots her a sharp look, and she stops.

"We do not clap at auditions," he mutters. I know she's going to hear about it later.

"Are we done here?" I ask. The whole thing is so awkward. The whole thing has kind of pissed me off.

The only real reason I'm here at all is because of my name, because of my parents, because they are desperate. On merit alone, I am a very underwhelming star for their season. Okay, fine, I didn't have to come, I chose this, but I'm pissed that my parents are making me audition. I'm pissed that it never occurred to them to ever hire me or cast me in anything until the eleventh hour, until they were totally desperate, until their leading lady left and they thought, *Who would be pathetic and available and still have some appeal? Oh, our own daughter.* I am an afterthought. I have always been their afterthought.

I am filled with fury, and I am filled with fire. Fine. I'll do this. I'll do it, and I will be great. I will show them what I can do. I will show them who I really am. I will show my parents I belong here. Theo's not the only star in this town. But life and experience have humbled me. I can't put my finger exactly on why I'm so agitated—it's simply a perfect storm. It's my parents. It's Theo. It's being home. It's me going backward instead of forward.

Back at home, my mother is warm and bubbly.

"You did very well, darling," she says. "Everyone said so, everyone was very proud of you." I know she's making this shit up. I know I did well, and I know I'm better by far than most people who came to audition. I also know they were expecting a diamond and got raw quartz. I know I am no Genevieve Chen, and that pisses me off. My father, as usual, doesn't say much about my performance, but he nods in agreement at my mother's false praise.

"We're going to work on those consonants," he says. "You need to be hitting them quicker." I don't know what to say, and frankly, I am already tired of talking to them, so I go upstairs for a bath.

Chapter 5

The summer I was twenty-one, I came home to play my namesake. I think my parents had been waiting for the right timing: As long as they had a theater named Tempest and a daughter named Miranda, I had to play the role eventually. It was between my third and fourth years at theater school, and it felt different going home to do a show: I was a trained actor now. I was working with professionals and was well on my way to being one.

Our *Romeo and Juliet* three summers earlier was now the stuff of local legend: high school sweethearts playing star-crossed lovers. It was too perfect. We were too perfect—young and open and ravenous for the roles. We had gone on to the same theater school in Toronto, and that summer, Theo had a dinner theater gig in one of the lakeside tourist towns east of the city, so I went north alone. I almost relished it: I was happy to have the hometown spotlight to myself. I didn't want to play Miranda, but I couldn't pass up a lead role, not to mention a chance to show off: I was so much better now. Miranda is the only female role in the show, and I found the character passive, diminutive. I was too young to really recognize her fire.

The show was special because it was the last season with Bill Miller, famed Canadian stage actor and my dad's best friend. Bill was playing Prospero, the magician, my father in the play. Bill was kind, a generous friend to the company, and a gifted actor, but that year he was in the early stages of dementia, and nobody, including him, knew it yet. He dropped lines constantly but was such a natural at Shakespeare that he would riff in iambic pentameter, sometimes adding a little Richard II here, a little Pericles there. To the naked ear, it sounded like Shakespeare, which it sometimes was. I did my best to keep up, to know the beats of the play inside out. I knew my lines and my cues perfectly. I studied them religiously and even memorized his lines too.

We stumbled through most of the run. Bill was increasingly grumpy—his mood had started to change from that of the sweet grandfatherly figure I knew well to someone gruff and sometimes sharp. I had found ways around his mistakes onstage. During our second-to-last show, I saw him getting really derailed, starting a monologue that wasn't supposed to happen until act 2. I took the risk and cut him off with my next lines, which got him back on track.

Backstage between scenes, he snapped at me: "Never interrupt me onstage again, you little bitch. I'm the professional here."

I was stung, stunned, and totally thrown. It happened again in our next scene: He lost his line and started his off-script ramblings. Usually, I could tell when he was off track. I could see his brain working and sense when he might circle back to our scene eventually, but this time he was gone. He was on to *Hamlet* now, booming, *"To be or not to be."* The audience, now totally aware that we were lost, sat in silence—no one dared smile at the scene before them. Finally, Bill trailed off and stared at me. I was so lost in his reverie that I forgot where we were in the scene, and I blanked. I was so swept up in his nonsense that I lost my own lines. We stared at each other in silence for a long time, and finally, without thinking, I did the worst thing an actor can do. I called, "Line."

In rehearsal, when actors are still learning their scripts, it is common practice to call "line" so as to stay in the scene, and someone, usually the stage manager, feeds the line to the actor.

This is not done onstage.

Not during a show.

Never, ever.

Not even in an emergency. Even in an emergency, you are supposed to do *something*, make it up, improvise. Any half-decent scene partner knows how to feed you the line, but in this case, *I* was supposed to be getting Bill on track. My scene partner was long gone in a world of his own, and I was helpless.

As soon as the word slipped out of my mouth, I knew I was done. There was a small collective gasp from backstage, a long pause, and then Sally quietly called out, *"Why speaks my father so urgently . . ."*

I repeated the line, the rest of my speech flooding back into my brain. I got through the show.

Afterward, my parents cornered me. Bill was livid. He threatened to quit, even though there was only one show left. He blamed me for distracting him.

"What were you thinking?" my mother asked. "How on earth are you going to be an actor if you can't even remember your lines!"

"It's unfortunate," my father said. "Most unfortunate."

"I'm sorry," I said, "but you saw—Bill was all over the place! He was doing *Hamlet*!"

"We, ah, know Bill has been a little . . . off," said my father. "That's why we brought you in. We thought you . . . with all of your training . . . Well, we assumed you would be able to keep him on track."

"I've been keeping him on track all summer! He has made dozens of mistakes! I made one! Give me a break!"

"Oh, Miranda. Don't you see that this is different? We really had to advocate to put you in the role, our own daughter, rather than giving a lead role to a guest artist. Having you play Miranda has, well, it's long been a dream of ours."

"Well, sorry for ruining your dream," I snapped. This was so unfair.

"There's one more show. We just need to get through it, and we can put this behind us," my father said. He attempted to pat my arm, but I swatted him away and stormed off.

The local newspaper reviewed us that night. In an act of kindness, they didn't mention my fumble. They didn't mention me at all. But that didn't matter, because the Tempest Facebook page was full of comments:

> That's what you get for casting your
> own daughter.

> Looks like the fancy theater school
> really paid off.

> Bill is a national treasure!

> I knew Miranda in high school and she thought
> she was better than everyone.

There were kind comments too, **Everyone makes mistakes** and **It's just community theater**, but it didn't matter. We got through the last show without incident, but I felt full panic every time I was onstage.

I never acted in my hometown again.

Until now.

The next day is the read-through, when we will run through the script from start to finish, just so we can all hear it. I'm oddly nervous; really, the only other professionals in the room, aside from my parents, are Theo, as Puck, and Arthur, playing Bottom. The last anyone has actually heard from me is *Listings*, which some people seem to think is exciting, so the bar is low. Still, I feel self-conscious. I haven't felt like myself in weeks. Being here doesn't help that.

I have a bath to calm myself before the read-through. I stand naked in the bathroom, assessing myself again. The first hints of aging are starting to reveal themselves. I'm too thin. What used to be kind of perky and lithe now seems a little gaunt. I don't eat as much as I should—occupational hazard. Years in television have cured me of carbs in general, the camera adding pounds that I imagine are there. I drink too much coffee, too much wine, and really only supplement this with protein shakes and salad. My body in real life is not my real body. My real body is whatever I have to look at on-screen, and even she is a stranger. I suppose my body is conventionally attractive, but looking at it dripping wet, it all seems a little limp.

Before leaving the city, I dyed my hair from the platinum blond I was known for on the show to my natural light brown and cut it a few inches below my chin. I needed to return to myself before returning to everyone else. I blow out my hair and straighten it with just a little wave. I put on my new Reformation navy tank dress that swirls around my thighs, giving the impression of a more romantic figure than I have. It's a softer look than I usually do. In the city I wear black, gold hoops, red lips, but if I am to play Helena, I need to look softer, sweeter. Plainer, really. Might as well get in the role from day one. I let my parents go to the theater ahead of me; they have things to set up, and I don't want to establish a pattern of arriving everywhere together this summer. I need to be, in some capacity, an independent agent, and I think they're relieved by that too. Fact is, we haven't been under the same roof in fifteen years, and none of us are super excited about it.

At the theater, people are buzzing. "First day!" a woman says to me. "So exciting!"

I smile too big at her because I don't know what to say. A few people come up to me to say hello, explaining who they are, what their roles are, how they know my parents, how they watch my show. I hate small talk. I try to be gracious. I glance around the room while people talk at me, looking for Theo.

He's hard to miss—he's the tallest person in every room. I spot him in the corner, chatting to some old ladies. It's as if he can feel my eyes on him. He turns around, his smile breaking across his face like the goddamn sun. One long, perfect arm rises in greeting.

"Mirabel!" he cries with pure joy. He lunges toward me like the giant puppy he is. It hurts my heart. It's been so long. It's been too long. I've behaved so badly. No one else has ever called me Mirabel. Just my Theo.

We are interrupted immediately upon contact, Sally calling us to attention just as his arms wrap tightly around me.

"It's so good to see you," he whispers into my hair. "Talk after, yeah?"

I nod dumbly, my mouth dry, my heart racing. I don't know where to begin with him.

"Okay!" Sally, the stage manager, claps her hands. "Let's go, everybody. This is going to take a while."

People hustle to their seats and sit down, a general flurry of excitement. I have to admit, I do love the read-through. It's such a blank slate, you have no idea who is who and how it's going to sound. I'm actually a little nervous. I am one of two people onstage who everyone is going to expect great things from, not counting Arthur, already the darling of Tempest. The town librarian can play a queen, and no one's going to care much how she does, but Theo and I are the big draws. Maybe it is more pressure than I realized.

My dad clears his throat. *I am to discourse wonders—but ask me not what.* A few people laugh, recognizing it from the play.

"That's my line!" Arthur calls out, and my father shoots daggers at him. Weird. I thought they were friendly.

My father presses on. "*A Midsummer Night's Dream . . .*" He pauses and everyone waits expectantly. What will the great Roscoe Belmont have to say about this Shakespearean play? It's all too delicious. ". . . explores realms beyond this world. It asks us what is reality, and what are our imaginings? What is the value of our real life, and what spell does love cast on us all? How can we, in our humanity, explore the nuances and magic of nature as we navigate the confines and structures we have tried to build around it?"

He looks around the room. They are rapt. "The play takes place in three worlds—that is to say, there are three layers to our cast. First, we have the royals and the lovers, as we prepare for the wedding of Hippolyta and the duke Theseus. The four young lovers seek each other in the woods, where fairy magic wreaks havoc on them. Then we have the world of the rude mechanicals, peasant folks, simple, local merchants." There's a small chuckle at the irony. No one wants to say it, but there is an underlying distinction of theater nobility and peasants in this very room. He clears his throat and continues. "The mechanicals are preparing a theatrical to present at the royal wedding, which goes askew when the lead actor is kidnapped by the queen of the fairies to take as her own lover. Which leads us to the final realm, the fairy world, where the laws and balances of nature are at odds, as the fairy king and fairy queen are also at odds with each other. Only as they are restored to each other's arms can the balance of nature realign."

People nod and murmur in appreciation. This is what they're here for. Deep thoughts by the big smart director. "These worlds merge through the mischief of the fairies. As Oberon and Titania wreak havoc on each other, so too do they wreak havoc on the young lovers. It's a challenging play; there are a lot of moving pieces, and we are working with multiple ensemble casts. That's part of the beauty of it, though, too: You will find each world is insular." He shuffles his notes. "Please turn your attention to the cast list. You will note a few amendments to the original. Our guest artists, as I'm sure you already know, are three local favorites, Arthur Crew, Theo Raye, who I'm sure you're all familiar with, and Miranda Belmont." He pauses, I foolishly hope to add some flattering detail about me, but no. "And now, Sally will take us through some housekeeping."

I'm expecting the read-through to be tedious, but I'm pleasantly surprised. I'm quickly humbled by the local talent. Sure, there's the occasional person stumbling through iambic pentameter; lots of people are retired and just want to be part of something social. There is also, very evidently, a strong theater scene in North Lake. I guess I thought I would be able to succeed on my notoriety alone, but I can see that I really have to do a good job here. I know how arrogant that sounds, but it's kind of a relief. It means that, if nothing else, I get to really act. I haven't done that in so long.

There is a lot of laughter. I'd forgotten how funny the play is, and no one laughs louder than my mother when Arthur speaks. Personally, I've always found him a little shrill. Theo, my parents told me, had his pick of roles. I think we all expected him to go with one of the handsome lover types, and he surprised everybody by requesting to play Puck, the mischievous fairy whose frequent bungles wreak havoc on the fairy realm and human world together. You'd think his height would make for a strange fairy, but my mother and the high school drama teacher playing the fairy king are both tall and slender, so they all kind of go together. Theo reads well as Puck. He's funny. I forgot how funny he is.

As Helena, I spend most of the play with three other characters: Helena's friend, the lovely Hermia, who is played by a blond girl named Bailey who seems to be the shining star of the local university theater program. She is pretty, petite, and incredibly good. Lysander is played by another of the theater students, Max. He is conventionally attractive, chiseled, and built in the way that is effortless when you are twenty-four. He seems nice and he reads with great energy.

Then there's Demetrius, Helena's love interest. I don't catch his name, but he seems to be about my age. He is wearing glasses and a slouchy knit cap, which should be douchey given that it's June, but he somehow looks very cool. He is wearing some band's T-shirt, which reveals two full sleeves of tattoos covering his arms. He is pleasant but guarded. When Demetrius speaks, his voice is gruff, raspy. There's an underlying violence to him in the role that surprises me, especially because between scenes I see him soften, share a pencil with the old lady next to him, laugh openly at the funny parts. He seems to be well known, well liked, but as Demetrius, he's menacing. It's weird doing the scene at a table when so much relies on the physicality, but he looks at me piercingly across the table, eyes flashing, voice clipped. He's really good. That excites me. I keep trying to flip to the cast list to look for his name and then lose my place, coming in late for my next scene. When we break for intermission, I make a point of crossing over to him. I put on my most charming smile, my hand outstretched.

"Hi," I say. "I'm . . ." He shakes my hand, a quick, warm, solid handshake, and the instant his hand is on mine, I know I'm in trouble.

"Miranda Belmont," he says. Of course. Everyone knows who I am.

"Nice to meet you," I say. My smile feels 10 percent too strong, but it's too late to dial it back now.

"Nice to meet you too." He blinks at me.

"Sorry, I don't know your name," I say. He blinks again. There is the tiniest flicker of mirth behind his eyes. There is a game afoot, but I don't seem to be playing it. We stand there awkwardly.

"Will," he says. He seems content to let me do the heavy lifting in this conversation.

"So, have you done Tempest shows before?" I ask after a moment. He's very cute.

He nods, deadpan. "Yeah, a couple. I was in *The Crucible* last year; did you see that one?"

I shake my head. A good daughter would come home every season; a good daughter would have seen all her parents' plays and would recognize the recurring actors. I'm not a good daughter. I haven't been home in three seasons. I'm racking my brain for some other piece of small talk, or some idea as to why this guy seems so familiar, when my father sits down, looks meaningfully around the room, and we all get back into place.

After the read-through, there is a general enthusiasm and congratulations; a couple of people come up to me.

"You're really good," gushes a high school kid. "I love your show. I can't believe we get to act with you!"

It's everything my ego ever wanted to hear in this situation, but really, it just embarrasses me. If only this kid knew that she'll never see me on that show again, that this is the current professional highlight of my year: working for my parents. No one knows this is all I have. I remember being that kid; I remember being in high school and in love with theater, in love with actors and all of it. The whole thing seemed so romantic. Now I am booted out of my tower, disenchanted, and turned back into the frog I secretly always was.

The cast is going out for a drink to celebrate the read-through. I'd forgotten about how much self-congratulatory drinking happens in theater. I look around to catch Theo's eye to take cues from him. I'm not sure if it would be good for morale for us to attend, or awkward that we don't have something better to do. I look around for Will. Is he going? He is in the back corner surrounded by a group of older women, who are chattering intently at him. One gestures over at me, then quickly drops her hand when she sees she's been caught. I'm not in the mood for group dynamics. The truth is, the entire thing has been kind of overwhelming. I feel like I've revisited my whole past in a day, and it wasn't exactly the warm, fuzzy nostalgia tour Theo seems to be having. I tell Sally I have a headache and slip out the back door.

The guy who plays Lysander is leaning against the back wall smoking a joint. "Hey," he says warmly. "Good job in there."

"Oh, thanks, yeah, you too." I've forgotten his name already.

"Max." He smiles. "Want some?" he offers, holding out the joint. I'm tempted, I really am. Escape would be nice right now.

I have a sudden flashback to being fifteen years old, out behind the dumpsters after our school production of *Peter Pan*, standing in my Wendy nightgown with bows in my hair, smoking my first joint with all the stage crew boys. Partly because I really liked them—they were fun and sweet and awkward, which was relaxing to be around. But also because I wanted to scandalize the rest of the cast, who didn't believe I was bold enough. It didn't agree with me. I took three puffs, less than the guys, but it hit me so hard they found me wandering the football field in my nightgown.

"No, thanks," I say. I want to add something to sound cool, so it will seem like I just can't 'cause I'm busy or something. I want this guy to think I'm chill, that I totally smoke weed. Except I don't. "Weed doesn't agree with me," I say. "No judgment!" I add quickly. "It just . . . makes me really loopy . . . like it hits me differently than other people. Like, it might as well be LSD." I am oversharing. Wonderful.

"Bummer!" He shrugs amiably and takes another hit. I don't know why I'm being so weird. I feel like an alien. I don't know what my role is, and I don't know how to be. My default is a bumbling idiot. He reaches out a fist, which I take in both hands before I realize it's supposed to be a fist bump. I pat his hand awkwardly and he chuckles. "It's cool," he says kindly, like he knows I know what an ass I am. I laugh awkwardly and immediately walk away, cringing completely and, not for the first time today, hating myself.

The whole year after the *Tempest* production, I was off my game. At school, I was okay in scene studies, in class, even in rehearsals for the big end-of-year production of *The Importance of Being Earnest*, where I was playing Gwendolen, but in performance, I choked every time. There was no rhyme or reason to it; at least once a show, at a completely different spot every time, I would blank on my lines. I kept coming back to that moment in *Tempest* with Bill, the moment that underscored this new, secret truth: Under pressure, I was fallible. It was true. It had happened, and now it was happening again. My body, buzzing from adrenaline, would suddenly go soft, my vision cloudy. My hearing would fade, and the lines were obscured in my brain. My classmates covered for me where possible, but I heard them grumbling about it backstage. My acting prof stopped looking me in the eye.

At the end of the year, there was a big showcase for all the local agents, and all the acting students had a chance to do two monologues in the hopes of getting signed. It was the single most important event of my university career. This was where most people got an agent, and even then, maybe only a quarter of us actually got signed. Up until *Earnest*, everyone, including me, thought I was a done deal. There was no way I wouldn't get signed. And yet when I stepped onstage and the lights dimmed, and I looked out into that darkness that held my entire future, I choked again. I opened my mouth and nothing came out. I stood there for an excruciatingly long moment. Someone coughed in the darkness, jolting me out of my freeze, and I ran offstage, feeling like my throat was closing in. I threw open the stage door and stood in the daylight, gasping for air.

Chapter 6

The theater is within walking distance of my parents' house, the way a rectory is close to a church: We must dwell close to the source. I'm halfway home when I hear footsteps running behind me, and a voice.

"Mirabel!"

Only one person calls me that. I turn around to look. "Theo."

"Hey!" he says. He comes to a sudden stop and nearly crashes into me. He is out of breath.

"Hello," I say, as though I was expecting him to be chasing me all along. Which I was. Hoping, anyway.

"I didn't get to talk to you." His face is wide open, smiling.

"Oh." I pause, my heart racing again. He never used to make me nervous. "What's up?"

"Just, like, hi! How are you?" He looks so genuine. "I was hoping we could talk earlier but . . ." At the break, he was absolutely swarmed by the cast, all wanting to chat with him and remind him of whatever vague connections they claim to have with him.

"Yeah, no worries. You have a lot of admirers."

"I come home a lot," he says. "I've kept a lot of connections here." He means nothing by it, but it stings.

"Yeah. That's nice." We are standing awkwardly on the sidewalk. My parents' house is just another two blocks. I was looking forward to a nice bath and a very stiff drink. "Well, it was great to see . . ."

"You wanna grab a drink?" he asks in a rush. I realize he's also nervous.

"Oh! Um." I glance down the street toward my bathtub. Yes, I want a drink. I was hoping to enjoy it in silence. To be honest, I've been dreading this encounter. Theo is the only person who has always seen right through me.

"I just felt like . . . we should, well, catch up." A gracious phrasing.

On one hand, I have zero energy to catch up with Theo Raye. On the other hand, we are going to spend the whole summer together. Might as well get this part out of the way.

"Yeah. Okay. Sure." I remember to smile.

"Oh, amazing!" This is a guy who the entire town, nay, country, fawns over, and I might be the only person he has had to convince to hang out with him. "Peasants?" he asks. Peasants Pour House, the most popular pub in town. It will be full of people we kind of know. They will all stop at our booth, and I will hate my life.

"Actually . . . my dad has some pretty good whiskey?" He knows. We used to pilfer it when running lines in my bedroom.

"Ah, yeah, classic. Let's do it." We start to walk home. He falls into step with me in the self-conscious way he always did, deliberately meeting my pace. An entire life in slow motion, just because of his height. Another reminder of how we never quite aligned.

At the house, Theo leans against the counter in my parents' kitchen while I get drinks. My dad has an extensive whiskey collection, and I reach for my favorite, Writers' Tears. I pour us modest glasses, instinctively pouring only enough that my dad won't miss. Teenage habit. I remember that I am an adult now—I can buy more whiskey. I pour more generously. Theo seems completely comfortable, smiling as he looks around.

"It's funny, it's like coming back to my own childhood home." We spent a lot of time here in high school. Theo has never been away from home long enough to develop the levels of nostalgia he's talking about, but I know what he means. I hand him the drink. We hesitate, then clink awkwardly.

"Outside?"

"Sure."

My mother pays a local guy to tend to their garden, but takes all the credit, openly bragging about how well her roses are doing. We make our way to the white Muskoka chairs down by the firepit. I switch it on (of course, my parents only *stage* fires). We lean back and sip our drinks in tandem.

"So," we both say at exactly the same time. He laughs and I look down into my drink. There is a long pause.

"So," he says again. "How the hell are you?" He's so open, so earnest. I want to both bury my face in his hair and send him away.

"Oh," I say. "You know."

"I mean, I don't." He looks into his drink, then back at me. "We don't . . . You stopped talking to me."

"I didn't." I did. "Just, I don't know . . . life . . ." It sounds lame, and it's a lie. Not speaking to Theo Raye has been a particular project of mine for at least seven years. "You don't talk to me either!" I try to pass the buck, but he's not having it.

"Can we . . . Look, we can do the whole thing, we can do small talk."

"No, thank you."

"Okay, or we can actually acknowledge the fact that . . ." He looks at me pleadingly.

"That we used to be best friends, and now we are strangers."

Best friends. Yes. But also, more. A small pang runs through me.

"Or we can just be professional and get through this summer without forcing a friendship that ended." The words fall out of me, bitter and biting. I can't stop myself. He looks so wounded. It's a low blow and we both know it.

"I know things ended . . . weirdly. But I thought I'd hear from you. What . . . happened to us?" He got famous, that's what happened. Among other things. He knows. I shrug. "Is that what you want, Mira?" His voice has dropped an octave. "'Cause, like, I can do that. We are both trained actors. We can pretend there's nothing to talk about. For my part, I'm sorry." He leans in. "Really, truly." He stares at me, waiting.

I say nothing.

He shakes his head, downs the rest of his drink. "There's way better whiskey than this, you know," he says.

I shrug, lean back, and take a long, languid pull from my glass to stop myself from speaking more. It burns. I deserve that. I'm being an asshole. I don't know how else to be with him anymore.

He rolls his eyes. "Jesus. You haven't changed." He stands up. "See you at rehearsal, Miranda." He turns to leave, pauses, and turns back. "Whenever you're ready to act like an adult, you know where to find me."

I sit outside for a long time after he has gone. My chest hurts from the whiskey. I hate myself. I have built a whole wall of bitterness toward Theo, and I don't know how to begin to dismantle it. I rehearse ways to tell my parents I can't stay: *A job has come up in the city, I am not available after all, I have to go.* They would be pissed, and these spiderweb-thin strands of connection that we've been forging this week would dissolve back into our usual nothingness. I've lived in that before. I can handle it. It's not even a sense of duty that makes me want to stay. They replaced Genevieve Chen. They can replace me. It's not like I'm a spectacular bit of casting or anything. No. The thing that roots me back into reality is the simple truth that I have nothing and no one else in my life right now except this play. And that feels like shit.

And worse than that, worse than any of it, is the fact that the sight of Theo seizes my heart. It brings it all back, all that happened and did not happen between us. All that did not happen for me. The truth that, in all these years, I never stopped missing him. I've never stopped loving him. I make my way inside to run the bath, bringing the bottle with me.

Chapter 7

I met Theo in ninth-grade drama class. I had gone to school with all the same kids in elementary school. I had enough superficial friendships to get by and pass as socially acceptable, but I had yet to find a soulmate. All along, he had been across town, waiting out eighth grade like the rest of us. Now, here he was, slumped in his chair in the back corner of the room, trying to look cool.

I later learned this posture was the result of extensive rehearsal, modeled loosely on Brando in *Streetcar*. He deemed it the least approachable stance he could take, protecting him from scary football players who took drama for an easy A. I wasn't put off, though. I recognized another introvert. The first few weeks of high school are critical in establishing what social vibe you want to put out. I was very carefully assessing my classmates' every turn, ultimately finding most of them cloying, shrill, and unpredictable. I wanted to distinguish myself from my peers. I was circling the drama club bulletin board for audition announcements three times a day. I had spent the summer reading Strindberg to prepare myself for my real theatrical debut.

I sat beside him without asking, put my bag on the seat next to mine to prevent anyone else from sitting there, casually and instantly creating an island of only us, which was pretty much how it would go for the next four years. I wanted immediate possession of this boy in a way that I had never even been aware of wanting in another person. He was the same height as me, since I was already five nine when I was fourteen. This made him tall. He was the most beautiful boy I'd ever seen. Until then, I wasn't even certain

I liked boys because of how inferior I found them, so smelly and jocular and obnoxious. They were like a bunch of puppies tumbling over each other, sniffing each other's balls. This boy stared moodily over his shoulder until I sat down. Then he looked at me, and I saw the panic in his eyes. His plan had failed—someone had dared to penetrate the fortress. I pulled my book of plays out of my bag and lined it up neatly with my notebook and pencil to show whatever drama master was about to educate me that I was a serious actress, that I was here to learn, that I meant business.

"You read Strindberg?" he asked.

"You *know* Strindberg?" I asked.

"I spent the summer reading a lot of classics," he said, pulling out a gigantic collected works of Shakespeare.

I will admit I was a tiny bit disappointed. It would've been more interesting if it had been Aristophanes or even Mamet. Shakespeare was a bit basic, really. And yet it wasn't hard to notice that nobody else in the room had brought a giant book of plays to drama class. Nobody else but me.

"What's your favorite?" I asked.

"I really like *The Tempest*," he said quickly. That nearly took my breath away. My eyes widened.

"My name is Miranda," I said. He looked at me blankly, instant proof that he hadn't read it. "Like from *The Tempest*," I said.

"Oh," he said. He looked flustered. "I said *The Tempest* because I thought it sounded cooler than, like, *Hamlet*. Like, less basic." That won me back.

"*Hamlet* is cool," I said. "Have you read that one?"

"Just the one speech." He smiled and rolled his eyes at himself. "My name is Theodore Raymond. Yours is better." He smiled again and my whole world began and ended.

There were only three high schools in town: the Catholic, the public, and the French. We were the public. Our drama teacher was twenty-six-year-old Mr. Tomlinson, who taught gym, coached soccer, and had no interest at all in drama. But he was the youngest and the newest and so he got the leftovers. The long-term drama teacher had retired the year before, which was disappointing, but also, I had heard that she was a tyrant.

Mr. Tomlinson used a textbook to teach drama. We spent a lot of time copying diagrams of the stage and the technical facilities, which, I will acknowledge, were state of the art for a small-town high school. Mr. Tomlinson was contractually obligated to put on a school play, which he did with about as much effort as everyone else in the class. He chose *Peter Pan* because they already had the costumes from a production a few years earlier. He assigned older students to direct, design, stage manage, and produce it while he sat in the back of the theater running strategies for that week's game. Still, I took auditions as seriously as if they were for Juilliard. Theo and I rehearsed after school on the back lawn, giving each other notes and animatedly discussing which audition pieces would be best. We shouldn't have bothered. When I got onstage, ready to launch into the first ten minutes of Strindberg's *The Stronger*, Mr. Tomlinson looked up at me.

"Oh, hey, Miranda. What role do you want?"

"Um, Wendy?" I said, not daring to breathe.

"Yeah, yeah, sounds good," he said.

"Wait," I said.

"What?"

"Don't you want to see my audition?"

"No," he said. "I figured you'd want to be Wendy. I'm cool with that."

I didn't know how to feel. On one hand, I was elated. I had scored my first lead without even trying. On the other hand, I was a little disappointed that I hadn't gotten to show off my chops, such as they were. I knew enough not to look a gift horse in the mouth.

"Thank you, sir!" I squeaked and ran offstage.

The same thing happened with Theo, who, being taller than a lot of boys, got Hook. Theo had the gravitas, the elegance, and the fury of the most resplendent pirate villain. When the cast list went up, we went to look together. Even though we knew our roles, it was gratifying to see them in print. An actress! Finally. I went to high-five him, and he hugged me hard, then pulled back quickly, laughing, embarrassed. It was around then that I knew he probably loved me back.

Our production of *Peter Pan* was an absolute dumpster fire. We had no budget for mechanics, flying being a key theme in the play, so we simply stepped in and out of the window, a flimsy, poorly constructed flat built by the woodworking class. It toppled over on me on opening night, and had some quick-thinking stagehands not rushed out and pulled it off me, I could have been really hurt.

The boy who played Peter couldn't sing, which made no sense, since it was a musical, but Mr. T just gave me all Peter's songs, which again, did not make sense whatsoever, but I was a fourteen-year-old with stars in her eyes. I would take any solo I was given. I would make it work; I would make it shine. It's true, those moments when it was just me onstage in the spotlight singing Peter's lullaby to the Lost Boys, a cappella because we had no backing track or musicians, hearing those heartbeats out there. The silence that my voice sent over the crowd. I came offstage after my solo, and Theo was there, staring at me, his eyes shining. Then he would dash onstage, kidnap my brothers, and charm the audience into hysterics. I've never seen anybody so naturally charismatic onstage with such ease and confidence. He was just a kid. He was magic.

I'm expecting rehearsal to be incredibly awkward, but Theo waves at me warmly when I walk in the room, as though we are indeed the friends we have agreed to play. It makes me sad, but it is also a relief. If nothing else, Theo can be counted on to be gracious. My parents set a clear bar for rehearsals. My father comes in with his vision clear and his blocking already complete. I learn that the rest of the cast has been well trained by him, so rehearsal is surprisingly borderline professional.

The difference, I guess, is the range of abilities. There are people who want to be involved in a production but have never really done a play or even seen one. There is the conservatory class from the college acting program, a few of whom—Max and Bailey, especially—make me raise my eyebrows at their potential. I am used to walking onto a set where everyone is a professional. That doesn't mean they always behave like professionals, but there is a union, there are expectations and rules and ways of doing things and the knowledge that we are all getting paid. I am getting paid here, but aside from Theo, Arthur, and my parents, everyone else is volunteering. It's been so long since I've done anything for the love of it. I hardly know what that feels like anymore.

I watch as they run through the main paces of the first fairy scenes.

"The fairy world." My father is doing another one of his speeches. "Where the laws and balances of nature are at odds as the fairy king and fairy queen are also at odds with each other. Only as they are restored to each other's arms can the balance of nature realign."

The fairy queen, Titania, my sixty-four-year-old mother, and the fairy king, Oberon, a booming high school drama teacher named Marcus, are at odds with each other, wreaking havoc on the natural world and generally fucking with each other. My mother is a challenging human, but her talent as an actor is undeniable. She is surprisingly deft and subtle, not the bellowing Titania you often see, not the sexpot either. There is a vulnerability to her, a light-handedness that is very affecting. I'm surprised that my father is already riding her for her performance.

"Projection, please, Wynnie!" he calls out, and she glares at him.

"*These are the forgeries of jealousy!*" she howls back. "*Happy?*" I don't blame her.

Oberon's sidekick is the fairy Puck, played by Theo. Titania is at all times surrounded by a band of fairies. In an interesting bit of casting, my father has made all the fairies in their sixties and seventies, as opposed to the lithe and delicate young beauties that you expect to play fairies. Usually, it's just a bunch of dancers in tulle.

At first, I'm worried that these fairies are going to be caricatures, spoofs, "rude mechanicals," if you will. But I am almost touched by the grace they bring to the roles. They are witty and charming and strangely elegant. They all have white hair, except for Glory, who has pink streaks in hers, and she informs me that she has no intention of changing it for the play and that I can tell my father as much. I do not comment. Among the group is one giant, round, bald man named Ron, who plays his role as fairy with absolute sincerity.

The scene opens with Titania and Oberon fighting. It's interesting watching my father direct. He has each beat blocked, has aerial drawings to scale of each scene, swooping arrows across the page, numbered, as each actor moves. He has a tendency to bark at people—his family, anyway—in real life, but in rehearsals he speaks gruffly but clearly, and he even has moments of levity, though his quips are so esoteric that they go over most people's heads. He rarely sets foot onstage, but paces in front of it, staring. Admittedly, he brings a level of intensity to rehearsal that is not always fitting a romantic comedy, but people are very into the Shakespeare-ness of it all. They feel that they are doing a Serious Play, even though right now we are watching six geriatric fae draped in rehearsal bedsheets, Theo weaving maniacally among them.

It almost hurts to watch him. He has always edged me out, talent-wise, which I guess is why his career is thriving and mine is presently sponsored by my parents. His face makes me ache for the version of myself I used to be. I don't know what to say to him, though. I don't know how to explain myself. I hunker down in my metal folding chair, turn away from them, and go back to my script, looking for anything I have missed that will add to my performance of a character I don't really want to play.

When his scene is done, Theo catches my eye across the room and raises his eyebrows at me, as if to say, *You ready to stop acting like a little bitch?* The door is open. I slam it shut. Being back here, in this room, with these people, brings so much to the surface. I can't handle Theo. This whole thing only works if I keep my head down and don't let anyone get to me. I pick up my script and strut out of the room. I don't look back.

After the break, we start the lovers' first scene.

"Okay, so, recap," shouts Sally. "Hermia and Lysander are in love, but her father wants her to marry Demetrius. Hermia's best friend, Helena, is in love with Demetrius, who has led her on and then dropped her." I relate. "Hermia and Lysander decide to run away together, and Helena decides to warn Demetrius of their departure in hopes of winning favor with him. Got it?"

Hermia and Lysander (Bailey and Max) already know each other; they both just graduated from the acting program at the university. They have the practiced comfort of people who have done many scene studies together, who know what they are doing, and who trust each other. They are the next-generation Theo and Mira, a thought I quickly catch when I remember that, until recently, Theo and Mira were estranged. We still are. Bailey and Max are young, both beautiful, and both technically excellent. They are not magic in the way Theo is. You can't take your eyes off him onstage, but they are smart, present, and entertaining.

My entrance as Helena is a big, whiny monologue at the top after my friends flee to the forest. *Woe is me, everyone's happy but me, I'm as pretty as her, why doesn't Demetrius like me? Love is stupid!* It's not exactly a stretch. It's my first run at it, so I know no one is expecting much, but I have been nervous about it. I spent the last day learning my lines, practicing in my pink bedroom so I would come off well today. It has paid off: It falls out of me, loose and easy, and that feels good. It surprises me, actually. The others applaud when I am done, and I immediately look at my dad, who is nodding, expressionless, which from him reads as moderate praise. I catch the eye of Will, the guy who plays Demetrius, who raises an eyebrow and cocks his head, a small smile. *Kudos.* For some reason, it sends a swell of pride through me.

It's been so long since I've done theater. I am used to lights and cameras all around. Rarely do we have the luxury of running a scene multiple times. Better shows do, for sure, but on *Listings*, we all got pretty used to just figuring it out on the fly. Two hours to rehearse a scene and a half feels luxurious. On tight days on *Listings*, we often skipped rehearsal altogether, hoping for enough good takes to cobble together a passable scene in post.

"We have a little time," announces my father. "Let's just try the start of the next scene. Demetrius and Helena in the woods."

"I haven't learned that one—" I say, but he cuts me off.

"Relax, Mira, it's just rehearsal." Nothing pleases me as much as being told to relax, especially by my father, especially when faced with spontaneous Shakespeare. Anxiety floods me. I know there are people here just waiting for me to fail again.

I grudgingly get up and follow Will to the stage.

"I'm sorry," I mutter. "I haven't figured this part out yet."

He looks at me sideways. "Relax, Mira." He winks. "It's just rehearsal." I almost smile.

"Okay," bellows Sally. "Demetrius is following Lysander and Hermia into the woods; Helena follows in hot pursuit." She looks around, smiling widely, hoping we will admire her flair. We don't.

"Okay," says my father. "Will is going to come in stage right, Helena follows. Helena, just naturally chase him. Will, avoid her, let's just see what happens. Use the space, but can you try to end up on the blocks for *'Tempt not the hatred of my spirit*?"

"Got it," says Will. I nod.

We start the scene. He storms onstage, I follow. Hot pursuit. He shouts abuse at me, I spew platitudes. It's a little choppy; I'm running underfoot like a puppy. There's a line—*"Use me as you would use your dog!"*—where I drop down and bat at his ankles. I feel ridiculous. I wait for someone to call "cut," then remember I am in a world where that doesn't happen. It's not Will's fault. He's good, he's read the scene, at least, and he leads up to our mark at the correct line.

"Dad," I call out. He glances up. "Do you have any . . . like, direction?" He sighs a little, thinking.

"Don't try so hard," he says after a moment. "Don't play it like a comedy."

I look at my script. Right there on the cover, it says *Shakespeare's Most Beloved Comedy.* What does he want from me?

"What genre would you prefer?" I call back. "Horror? Sci-fi?" A few people dare to titter, but my father looks up again at me sharply.

"Think of it as a different genre for each character," he says. "Your work is to figure yours out."

What does that even mean, what genre? It's Shakespeare. That's a whole genre in itself. It's a comedy. God forbid I try to be funny in a comedy.

"Okay," my father calls out. "Let's go a little further: Demetrius will back Helena against the bench, forcing her down, so he ends hovering over her for the next few lines. Give it a try. Mira, take it from the 'spaniel' bit."

I'm flustered. I'm annoyed at my dad. I haven't done a theater rehearsal in so long, I am not prepared. I'm used to being prepared. I drop down to the ground, giving my spaniel speech again. Will turns on me, and I stumble to my feet.

"You do impeach your modesty too much . . ." He backs me up against the blocks. I fall back as our legs meet, and he hovers over me. *"To trust the opportunity of night and the ill counsel of a desert place . . ."* His voice is low, rumbling, but still bounces off the walls. A perfect theater whisper.

"Hold that!" calls my father, whispering to Sally some blocking detail. Will is over me, supporting himself easily on one arm.

"Are you okay with this?" he asks quietly. He smells good, like trees and something sweet I can't place.

"What? Oh, yeah, sure," I say. I'm surprised he asked. I'm a professional. I'm used to this.

"Will, can you get even closer to her?" Sally calls out. Will raises an eyebrow at me, and I nod. He lowers himself until we are inches apart. I can feel his breath on my face. Our faces are close. My heart is racing, and I have the sudden urge to tip my head up and kiss him. The thought snags in my brain, a glitch. I catch his eye and swallow hard.

"Okay, that's fine," says my dad. "Okay. Thank you, that's all for today." I look at Will, who shrugs, raising himself up. He offers me his hand. I get up on my own.

What did I just feel? What the hell was that?

I stand hastily, brushing sawdust from the bench off my skirt. I'm thrown by the unexpected scene, and whatever primal instinct Will just stirred. There is no place for that, not here, not this time. I am here to work. I am here to redeem myself. I pack up my things in a huff.

Will catches me as I'm storming out of the room. "Hey, I know that annoyed you—" I stop short. Was I obvious? What exactly did he pick up on? "Your dad . . . I mean, listen, he's your dad, you don't need me to explain him to you."

"No," I snap, relieved that it's just about the scene. "I don't." Suddenly this guy thinks he knows me. Good, that makes him less attractive. That helps. I pause. "Well, go on."

"This is what he does. He likes to keep us guessing, keep us thinking. So, just . . . don't take it personally."

"I thought the head games would be over in community theater," I mutter. Will steps back.

"You know, some of us are doing it for the love of it," he says. I can't read if I've pissed him off. "For the record, I'm really looking forward to working with you." There's a tightness to his smile that lets me know that, yes, I have, but he's going to be a class act about it. He raises a hand, in peace or goodbye, and walks away. I feel bad. I could have been nicer. I have so much to be defensive about, but nobody is actually holding me to it. I could let go a little.

In the corner, I see the old fairies watching me. The pink-haired one leans into a long-haired one and whispers. There is nodding and murmuring, and furtive glances in my direction, and I wonder, not for the first time, if I am actually welcome here.

Chapter 8

Seven and a half weeks until Opening Night

Rehearsal has put me in a bad mood. I'm annoyed with my dad. I'm annoyed that I'm doing this stupid play. I'm afraid that any faltering in my performance will unleash the wrath of the community. I am terrified that I won't be able to do theater again, that the old panic will rise and render me numb. I push the fear down and focus on my anger. Who does Will think he is, giving me advice? But also, I like him. I can't like him. I can't get involved with someone in the play—that did not go well for me last time, and anyway, it was probably just the scene, so I have no reason to think he's interested. But why *isn't* he interested in me? I'm hot and kind of famous! Fuck. I feel a petulant need to storm off in a manner that can only be achieved by one's old bicycle—vintage, yellow, wicker basket. I drag it out of the shed and mount it: I will embark on an angry cycling montage through my hometown and scowl at my broken dreams as they flash by.

I make it maybe ten feet before I realize that no one has ridden this bike in at least fifteen years. I learn this when the front tire explodes and the chain falls off. I shudder to a stop and fall over. I lie there on the sidewalk for a moment and actively hate my life.

There's nothing worse than having to walk said bike during said montage. This is exactly when someone from high school is going to lean out a window and say, *Wait, is that Miranda Belmont, famed actor, WALKING a bike?* And then probably throw a slushy at me. My relevance in this world is vastly inflated in my head. Still, the bike shop is a half-hour walk, right downtown, and I have literally nowhere to be until rehearsal tomorrow at noon, so I walk. Downtown is a real mixed bag. There's a bougie coffee shop called Has Beans, an even bougier yoga studio; I make a mental note to look into a summer pass. There's the same old gift shop that has been there my whole life, the same pub with the giant wooden booths where we all drank the second we turned nineteen. There's a bra shop I'll never go to because I barely have boobs, a toy store, and five inexplicable credit unions. There're a lot of new restaurants—Indian, Thai, and shawarma. They make me a little optimistic about the town diversifying a bit, finally, and also, they make me miss the city.

The guy at the bike shop tells me the bike is going to take a few days, which feels anticlimactic. I can't bear to pass back through all the misery of Main Street, so I take the longer route along the waterfront. There's a long multipurpose trail that passes the old train station, the water treatment plant, but then starts to wind toward the marina. There's lovely landscaping, a new playground, and a splash pad in the distance, and I am struck by the decline and rise of my hometown within two blocks. The northern lake in question is Cedar Lake, the largest in the area and so big you can only barely see across it to the other side of town. I hate swimming, and my family isn't exactly outdoorsy. My use of the lake has been limited to lakeside patio dining with my parents and, at the end of high school, partying on The Vessel, the large ferry boat turned nightclub, turned popular lunch spot. I am rounding the corner when I am accosted by a stroller.

"OHMIGOD, MIRANDA, ISTHATYOU?!" The wheels stop inches from my feet, and I immediately jump back in defense. I look up at the offending driver. Oh, fuck.

"Kelsie." I am not a good enough actor to feign delight.

Kelsie Smith-Jones was the queen bee of my high school. She was good at nothing except being hot, which, I am relieved to see, motherhood has taken down a notch. Her hair is still very much a thing, blond, unnaturally shiny, and her tiny, pert body looks, well, like that of a woman in her mid-thirties who has borne—I count the inhabitants of the stroller—at least two humans. I'm reaching; she looks great, and I hate it. She pushes her sunglasses up on her head, her pale-blue eyes boring into me.

"I heard you were maybe back in town, but I figured you were busy with all your, you know, drama stuff." She gestures vaguely. "I never expected to run into you heeeere!" she all but squeals. I want to point out that running into someone you know in the most popular place in town is hardly remarkable, but she launches into a whole monologue. "We've all been watching your show, you know. The girls and I used to make it a thing, every Wednesday, but, you know, kids, and then they bumped it to the early slot, which, you know, dinnertime." Pouty face. "It's so cute you are helping your parents this summer. I love that for you! I'm sure you have something super fun lined up for after, right? I mean, who wants to work for their parents at, like, what are we? What are you? Forty?" Highly invasive wink. "Shh, don't worry, I won't tell."

"I'm thirty-four," I say. "Same as you."

She blinks as though I've told her the sun is pink. Which it probably is, in her little world. She blinks again and presses on. "Ohmigod, have you seen Theo? What a dreamboat! Who knew he was such a hottie?" *Me,* I want to say. I knew. I always knew. "Don't tell Mike, but I sort of have a tiny thing for him now, even though he's—"

"Mike Bale?" It's too good to be true. "You married him?" Mike Bale was our star hockey player, a stocky meathead type who was dumb as a brick, but the teachers loved him because he played rep hockey for the OHL and always seemed to get them tickets just as report cards were coming out.

"Thirteen years!" She beams.

She whips out her phone and shows me the screen. A family photo: They are all dressed in white on a beach, trying to make North Lake look like Nantucket. Mike Bale has gone bald and has a definite dad bod, which pleases me, but the worst thing is how happy they look. I smile tightly and hand the phone back to Kelsie.

"Oh, no, it's a whole shoot, scroll, scroll!"

I pretend to admire another forty-six photos while she rambles about her book club and her yoga studio and Mike's landscaping business. "Ohmigod!" I'm developing misophonia just standing next to her. "I didn't introduce you to the littles! This is Emereigh." She adjusts the blanket on the sleeping baby. "And this is Brightley." Brightley is an extremely sticky person who looks about three and, upon introduction, lets out a loud fart.

"I shit, Mama," he says solemnly. Kelsie's face drops.

"Mike taught him that," she mutters. "Okay, babies, I think we need to, um, tidy up!"

"I shit in my pants." He beams at me. "Shit is poop."

I can't help but smile back. I rarely enjoy children, but this one is growing on me.

"Oh my God. Okay." For half a second, she seems like a real person. She pulls down her sunglasses and turns the stroller around. "Listen, Miranda, *so* good to see you! We should totally, like, *do* something!"

I would rather lie in Brightley's shit than ever see her again, but it's a small town, and who knows what report she is going to give to her band of bitches at book club.

"Totally!" My voice sounds weirdly high. "Come see our show!"

"*Ohmigod*, yes! Totally! I'm going to get tickets the absolute *second* I get home!" She won't, and that's cool. "Byyyyyeeee!" She storms off, scolding Brightley the second she thinks I'm out of earshot. She's going in the direction I was going in. I don't want to follow her, and I don't want to turn back. That kind of sums everything up right now.

I sit on the nearest bench; I will wait until she is out of sight. I look around me. It's a nice place, from this view: kids playing, a small line at the vegan ice-cream truck, sailboats out on the lake, a parasailer lifting off. I grew up here. This is my home. I wish it felt that way.

My phone pings. A text from Theo:

So, I've decided we aren't playing cat and mouse all summer. We're going to be friends. Put on something cute. We're going out. Pick you up at 8.

In spite of myself, I smile for real. Who am I to argue? I reply:

How cute?

Then, another text comes through:

You're right. I'm sorry. Come back.

Nick. I want to delete his number, but you should always have at least one celebrity on your contacts list. I don't reply, though.

Chapter 9

Everyone always thought Theo and I were dating, including me. By the middle of high school, I had never kissed a boy, harboring grandiose ideas about setting and romance and perfection, and in the end, I got all three. Theo was my first kiss. It was tenth grade, the spring musical, another terrible production (*Oklahoma!*) that the local choral society had put on the year before, so our school got all their sets and costumes for free. As if any community needs two productions of *Oklahoma!* in a lifetime, let alone back-to-back. Theo and I were Curly and Laurey. It was the first kiss for both of us, which made sense for awkward, misanthropic me, but zero sense for the charming and gorgeous Theo, who was beloved by all in our school, even though theater kids weren't supposed to be cool. Once in the bathroom, I heard some older girls on the soccer team arguing about which one of them should take his virginity. "If he even is one still."

"Oh, he is. You just know he is."

For months we jokingly avoided the kissing parts, doing mocking high fives and exaggerated hugs every time the moment arose. I wanted to. Of course I did, but this was a good fifteen years before I knew I was allowed to initiate my own love life.

Finally, it was tech week and we hadn't kissed. Mr. T pulled us both aside during lunchtime rehearsal break.

"Kids, you need to figure out this kiss thing. I don't care if you do it or not, but you need to decide and then do the scene the way you're going to do it. It's called practice—"

I interrupted him. "It's actually called rehears—"

He cut me off. "Figure it out." He left us alone backstage.

"So awkward," I muttered.

"Totally," Theo said. We both stood there, silent.

The thing was, we were great together. We rehearsed on non-rehearsal days at my house. We sparred with terrific energy—the chemistry was there. I don't think we knew what chemistry even was, but we knew we were good, and that we were especially good together. There was just this one detail that we had been avoiding.

"So, um, I guess . . ." I stared at my shoes.

"Yeah."

"Um."

"Yeah."

Nothing was happening.

"I've never kissed anyone," I blurted out.

He looked genuinely surprised. "Really? I mean, me neither . . ."

"Wait, really?" This felt unbelievable to me.

"Yeah." He looked embarrassed.

"We don't have to," I started. "Mr. T said . . ."

"But, yeah, I mean, for the integrity of the scene . . ." He looked at his feet.

"I . . . like . . . do you . . . like, do you not want to kiss me?"

"No! Yes! I mean, I do!" he said. He laughed nervously, then got quiet. "I just . . . I know this sounds dumb, but, like, it's both of our first kiss. I don't want to . . . Shouldn't it be . . . nice? Like, special?"

I nearly cried with joy.

"Oh my God, yes! It's so weird how he is, like, forcing us." Our teacher absolutely wasn't forcing us, but it seemed like an adversary might really ramp up the stakes.

Theo got serious. "But . . . the show. We have a responsibility to the show." I nodded. "I love this." He beamed. "Thank you, Mira. Can . . . Let me take care of the arrangements, okay?"

"Jesus, kids, it's not a wedding." Mr. T strode by us, the smug stage manager, Jessica, smirking at us.

"Meet me after school, okay? At the church by my house."

"We're going to kiss at a church?"

"No! I just . . . just meet me there, okay?"

I floated through the rest of rehearsal, through science and civics, and practically ran home. I showered and put on my favorite blue dress that was the color of forget-me-nots and had tiny buttons all the way down. I never wore makeup—but I panicked and put on too much blush. I rushed out the door, calling, "I'm going out!" to my parents, who didn't respond.

Theo was sitting on the church steps, wearing a button-down shirt, his hair wet from the shower. He looked nervous. That relaxed me, somehow. I was going to kiss this boy. Finally, finally, finally. All I had wanted all year was to kiss this boy.

"Here." He shoved a bouquet of daisies at me. "Sorry. I don't know."

I laughed and smelled them.

"Daisies don't actually smell that good," he said.

"No, I like them."

"Okay, come with me." He took my hand and led me down the street. We didn't speak, both staring straight ahead, our mission muting us. Finally, we arrived at a hedge with a break in it. "Come on." He smiled, pulling me down a tiny bramble path.

We emerged into a fairyland. There were tall, flowering trees, peonies in full bloom, huge swaths of wildflowers spilling onto the path. There was a tiny pond with a stone bench, but Theo pulled me onward until we stood beneath a huge, blossoming apple tree.

"What is this place?" I could hardly breathe. "I must have passed it a hundred times. I had no idea it was here!"

"It's a secret garden." He looked proud. "It's kind of a neighborhood project . . . These two old ladies put their backyards together, and they have been growing it for years . . ."

"I love it."

"I thought you would."

We stood there, the branches brushing the top of Theo's head. He had grown three inches over the summer and was now taller than me. "Should we . . . Let's sit down?" He took a blanket from his backpack and spread it out.

We sat facing each other. My heart was pounding. I closed my eyes and waited.

"Wait," he said. "Are you . . . ? Is this . . . ? Like, is this a good place for your first kiss? I have a backup if you don't like this."

"I like it so much," I whispered.

"Is it . . . Sorry, I just have to ask. Is it okay with you that I am your first kiss? I feel like it's a lot of pressure, and I don't want you to feel like you have to . . ."

"I want to," I breathed. I sat back on my heels and opened my eyes. "Wait, do *you* not want to?"

"No! Um, yeah. I want to."

"Okay, good."

"Good." I leaned forward again. There was a long pause. He looked pained.

"What?"

"You sure you consent?"

"Theo!"

"Okay, okay, sorry, I just . . . I'm supposed to ask, right?"

"I mean, I appreciate it. But I think consent has been implied for, like, many hours here." Weeks, months, years, if you wanted to get technical.

"Okay." He took a breath. He closed his eyes.

I reached for his hand and gently pulled him toward me. I lifted my face and kissed him. He seemed surprised. We both opened our eyes and looked directly at each other. Our mouths came apart for a second, but he closed his eyes again and kissed me this time, longer, more intensely. His mouth was soft, if a little slobbery, but maybe that was how it was supposed to be? All I knew was the boy of my dreams was kissing me in a secret garden while apple blossoms fell around us, and for the first time in fifteen years, my life was completely perfect.

"Get a room, Romeo!" We were interrupted by an old lady in rubber boots carrying a rake. She chuckled as she passed.

"Actually, it's for *Oklahoma!*" I called after her, indignant. Theo burst into laughter. He hugged me tightly.

"First kiss!" He high-fived me. "Nailed it." I was slightly concerned that we had reverted back to high fives so quickly after such notable progress, but I didn't want anything to ruin this moment, so I smiled and slapped his hand. I wondered if we should kiss again.

"Wanna go get a slushy?" he asked, perfectly normal, as though nothing had happened.

"Oh. Uh, sure."

Oklahoma! went as well as *Oklahoma!* can, especially when directed by a soccer coach. We kissed onstage each night, each night my heart exploded, and each night Theo hugged me tightly backstage.

"You're so good," he would tell me. "You're the best."

At the cast party at Smug Jessica's house, Theo kissed Mel Donovan, the senior who played Aunt Eller but was lethally hot without the wig and the apron. I watched from across the room as my world ended. I chugged a large plastic cup of Goldschläger and warm Mountain Dew and threw up in Jessica's mom's dahlias.

Chapter 10

Theo picks me up in his mom's old red pickup truck.

"Howdy," I say. He whistles. I'm wearing a black bodycon minidress with a high-low gauze skirt overtop, oversize sunglasses, gold hoops, and a red lip. City girl.

"You said look cute."

"Yeah, I wasn't expecting a smoke show!"

"I'm wearing two skirts," I say lamely. "In case I got the dress code wrong. I can do a costume change."

Theo glances at me. "You can always remove the skirt and wear it as a cape . . ." he says in his best Little Edie voice.

I don't miss a beat. "I think this is the best costume for the day," I say in the same voice.

Then, in perfect unison, we say, deadpan, "I hate women in skirts."

We burst out laughing.

"There she is," he says. We both smile to ourselves. Common ground, at last.

"I think a *Grey Gardens* sort of situation is the best I can hope for," I say finally. "The way my life is going."

"I missed you, Mirabel."

"Yeah . . . I missed you too," I say.

He turns to me suddenly, eyes full. "Did I do something? I'm sorry to keep asking, but . . . I just don't get what happened."

Yes. I owe him this. "You didn't do anything, Theo. I'm just an asshole." I'm surprised by his emotion, touched. "I'm sorry. I . . ." I don't know what to say or how to say it. "I'm glad to see you. I do want to be friends again."

"Good," he says. *"Give me your hands, if we be friends."* I had forgotten this little quirk of his: memorizing the whole script of whatever play we're in, using it at every opportunity. On me, it would look pretentious. But everything Theo does is sweet. He grabs my hand and kisses it, and I let him.

After the cast party make-out with Mel Donovan, Theo and I were strictly professional for most of tenth grade. I couldn't be bothered trying to date anyone else. I knew I just had to finesse my craft; he would be dazzled and come back to me.

I was right.

In twelfth grade, we decided to ditch Mr. T and start our own theater company. We wrote a proposal and convinced our principal to direct a portion of the theater budget to our show. We chose a lovely Canadian two-hander, *Salt-Water Moon* by David French, the playwright's parents' origin story set in the 1930s on a key evening of their courtship. It was simple but complex, romantic, and full of delicious banter. We directed ourselves. We designed and produced it ourselves.

We rehearsed more than we needed to, probably, every night after school. We closed the door for privacy, and our parents never seemed to question it. We brought the kissing back early in the process; it was very important that it be authentic, we decided, and there was no time to waste developing chemistry. Chemistry was very important. Sometimes the chemistry made me want more than kissing, sometimes much more, but if ever I slid my hand down, or tried to slide his hand up to my chest, he'd flinch and pull back.

"What?" I'd ask.

"Nothing," he said. "I just don't want to confuse the work." The work. The scene. The characters. I guess I had to appreciate his commitment.

Once in eleventh grade, I'd gotten drunk at a spring break party and made out with Jesse Matthews from the soccer team. He shoved his hand up my shirt, groping at my nipple, twisting it until it hurt, all while unbuttoning his jeans. I knew what he wanted, and in the moment, I felt suddenly very young, very innocent, very unready for this sort of thing. I shoved him off and ran out of the room. What could have earned me a soccer boyfriend instead gave me a chant of "Ice, ice, baby" every time I passed a soccer player in the hall. After that, I was grateful for sweet, gentle Theo and his boundaries. I felt safe with him. I felt like he was protecting me.

Salt-Water Moon won every award at the high school drama festival. We were a triumph. I wasn't sure what else we were. We seemed to hold hands a lot. Backstage at our final performance, Theo kissed me.

"That wasn't rehearsal," I said softly. "The show is over."

"The show is over." He nodded, leaning his forehead against mine. He had gotten taller again, so he had to dip his head down.

"Was that . . . for real?" I asked, my heart barely beating.

"Yeah. I think it was."

For the rest of twelfth grade, we were official. We took a little bit of shit for it—Theo had gotten taller, hotter, more popular. I still dressed in vaguely Victorian funeral wear and had dyed red hair and pale skin and no boobs. Theo said I was hauntingly beautiful, that I was brilliant. That was all that mattered to me. We never said it, but we knew we loved each other. It was the most simple, obvious thing in the world.

I assumed we were heading to The Vessel, maybe, or a patio downtown, but we are on the highway heading out of town.

"Where are we going?" I ask. "Do I need my cape?"

Theo laughs. He laughs more easily than most people, which I used to think meant he wasn't discerning, but after watching him with the locals this week, I realize his laughter is an act of generosity. The ultimate "yes, and . . ."

"My buddy has a cider place down the road. Thought I'd show you."

I am decidedly overdressed for a cider place down the road, or so I think until we pull in. It's a dirt driveway through an orchard, but when we turn the corner, I see a large barn lit up with fairy lights, a patio with string lights and individual firepits, people lounging around in oversize Muskoka chairs. The main building is all glass and wood, and inside I see a bar.

"Oh, wow, this is super chic!" I feel dumb as soon as I say it, but Theo is generous.

"*Oui, très chic!*" he agrees. He holds the truck door open for me and gives me his hand. The orchard still has a few trees in flower, late bloomers. Theo catches me looking at them. "Here we are again, Mirabel, just a couple of kids under the apple trees." He grins, and for the millionth time in my life, I have a deep flutter of *why, oh, why can't this man be mine?*

"Come on!" He leads me inside to the bar. They have a little merch corner with cute custom glasses and T-shirts, a wall of bottled ciders with fun names. It's incredibly charming. We step up to the bar, where a man in plaid is hunched under the counter. Theo pounds the counter.

"What do I have to do to get some damn service around here?" he bellows. The guy stands up abruptly, a little defensively, but laughs when he clocks Theo. I do a double take: It's Demetrius, from the show.

"Buddy!" He comes around and bear-hugs Theo. "Who else would come in here acting like such a jackass!"

"I'm a diva, it's true," intones Theo. "You remember Mira? Mira, Will?"

"Sure," he says, half smiling. There's something so familiar about him, but I can't quite place it.

"What's on tap, man? I need a drink!"

Will turns back to Theo, hands us drinks menus, and proceeds to give a long, detailed explanation of each one. It's his place, it turns out. Twin Orchards, after him and his twin brother. His family has owned the land for decades, I learn, but Will is the mastermind behind the cidery.

Will pours us each a flight of the summer ciders. "Drink them in the right order. Start here. They get more complex as you go."

The cider is lovely and warms my veins in a pleasant way. It's been so long since I've been among real people. I like it. I like Will. He's not exactly warm and friendly, but there's a seriousness to him that feels grounding. His vibe is different here—the rugged farm guy. He certainly looks it, with the plaid shirt rolled up to his tattooed forearms and his stubble and gruff voice, but there's also something calming about him. I flash back to him hovered over me, his mouth so close to mine, and my blood quickens. In the city, on the rare occasion I am out at a bar or a party, I dial up my Leo rising and flirt aggressively, to make sure men see me, I guess, and so they do. I then act like an idiot, then they act like assholes, and it ends bitterly, and the cycle restarts. But here, I feel almost like me.

Will pours us each a pint of the new pear cider, then leaves us as the bar gets busier. Theo and I park ourselves at one of the firepits. There are big chairs, and I see some people with blankets but can't find one. It's a little chilly, so I inch closer to the fire. The cider has loosened me up. I'm feeling chatty.

"What is it about forearms?" I murmur, my eyes lingering on Will at the barn.

"You're staring, Belmont!"

"I'm not." I am.

"Will's the best," Theo says, feigning casualness.

I change the subject. "I ran into Kelsie . . . from high school?"

"Oh my," says Theo. He takes a long slug of cider.

"She's as vapid as ever. She calls her children 'littles.'"

"Huh."

"She married Mike Bale. Can you believe that?"

Theo looks in his drink. "Yup."

"He's gone bald," I press on. "And he got fat. Well, like, hockey dad fat. And she's—"

"Jesus, Mira, were you always so mean?" Theo says. I jolt back in my chair, stung.

"Um," I say. "Sorry. What, are you friends with them?"

"No," he says. "That's not the point."

"Like, sorry, but what exactly is the point, Theo? Can't two old friends talk shit about people who were assholes in high school?" *And probably still are,* I want to add, but it seems like Theo's threshold for my sass has been breached. I change the subject. "So, Will," I say, hoping to make amends. I rub my shoulders and move even closer to the fire.

"He's the best." Theo seems happy to move on. "He's one of my oldest friends."

"Then how do I not know him?"

"He went to the other high school."

"Cool." I'm not sure what else to say. "Does his brother work here too?"

Something strange passes over his face.

"No," he says, but before he says more, Will appears with three more pints and a blanket, which he hands to me wordlessly.

"Oh! Thanks!" I'm surprised he noticed. He's sweet.

"Finally dying down," he says, settling into the open seat next to Theo.

"Apples!" I say, apropos of absolutely nothing.

"What?" Theo looks at me sideways.

I'm staring at Will. "You smell like apples." I catch his eye, and we hold it there.

"What are you talking about?"

"I think she means from rehearsal?" Will says. I smile and shrug. "I was processing apples before I came, and I forgot to change. I often smell like apples," he says, smiling a little at me. "Occupational hazard."

"Good to know," I say, my eyes still fixed on his. Theo looks between us, clocking the energy.

"I need to . . . go to the bathroom . . . or something," he murmurs, chuckling a little. "I'll be back in five minutes. Don't get married without me." He all but bolts, and then it's just Will and me.

"What an odd man," I say lightly.

"Absolute lunatic."

"Did you know he was my first kiss?"

"Actually, I did know that." Will smirks a little, then: "I won't lie; I was a little jealous."

Interesting.

A log splits in the fire, setting off a shower of sparks. Our eyes turn to the fire, then back to each other.

"Would you want to hang out sometime?" Will asks.

"We are hanging out," I say.

"For real, I mean." He looks at me, hope on his face. "I mean, no pressure, or whatever." He takes a drink.

I have been a version of here before. I have been here too recently. I am still shaken from the aftermath of Nick. Will is nothing like him. I can see right away that we could go out, we could probably have a really lovely summer thing. I want to hang out with him. I want to very much.

"I don't think that's a good idea," I say. To his credit, his expression doesn't change. "I'd like to. I-I'd really like to. I just got out of something . . ." It sounds so lame. "I—I just think, maybe, with the show, and it's my parents' company . . . I feel like I shouldn't do anything . . ."

"Hey, it's cool." He smiles kindly. "I hope you won't feel uncomfortable or anything working together, knowing I . . ." He stops as Theo returns, plopping himself into one of the large chairs. I smile and shake my head, *No, it's all good,* but the truth is, I am realizing in a rush, that it is going to be extremely uncomfortable working with someone whose smile, whose apple scent, makes my insides flip like this.

Chapter 11

Mike Bale threw a big party every year on the last day of spring exams at his parents' cottage on Cedar Lake. It was usually reserved for athletes and hot people, but there was a small intersection with Cool Arts Kids, which we, as newly minted Drama Club Royalty, were adjacent to. We weren't invited until the grade-twelve party, and we spent a lot of time discussing our outfits. Theo went for jeans and green hoodie. I wore a royal-blue satin halter top with lace trim, as was the rage, and jeans. I put gold glitter on my eyelids and twisted my hair into a tight, spiky bun. When Theo picked me up, he clutched his heart, pretending to swoon.

"You're the most beautiful girl in the world," he said, and I believed him. I felt cool. Upon arrival, I realized that I'd gotten it half right: The girls were all in strappy, stringy handkerchief tops, but I'd overshot it with the glitter.

"Going to prom?" asked Carissa, a girl in my science class, looking me up and down.

"Oh!" I said. "Uh, yeah, maybe?"

She walked away laughing, and I quickly dipped into the bathroom, where I wiped off the eye shadow and pulled my hair out of the bun. It fell loose and wavy around my face in a way that was suddenly pretty.

Theo was waiting in the hall and handed me a Smirnoff Ice. I took a large gulp. "This tastes like candy," I said. He grinned.

"You changed your hair," he said. I shrugged. "I like it." He squeezed my hand.

We did intentional laps around the party, pretending to be looking for people we knew, or pretending to be heading somewhere, all the while taking it all in. At one point, someone handed me another drink. It turned out they relaxed me.

I had five. I think. I lost count.

Somewhere, later in my blur, Kelsie clapped her hands.

"Spin the bottle!" she announced. "Everyone sit in a circle." A few people shuffled out of the room awkwardly. Theo glanced at me and reached for my hand.

"Let's get out of here," he said, but Kelsie grabbed us both and pushed us into the circle. I giggled, too drunk to notice that Theo had gone very quiet.

We sat. It was a strange group, mostly the hockey team, a few hot nerds, and even fewer artsy kids. I did a quick scan of the group: The boys were all people I recognized but certainly never spoke to. I sat up as straight as I could. Even in my stupor, I recognized a social opportunity. If the role called for it, sure, I would kiss any of these idiots. I looked across the circle at Theo, my beautiful, handsome Theo, who was so much more appealing than any of them. I smiled at him, and he smiled back tightly. Was he mad at me, that I was so willing to kiss these other boys? I searched his face for a clue, but he was staring at the bottle. Kelsie spun first. It landed on Mike Bale, our host, the coolest guy in our grade, by conventional standards. Rumor had it they were already sleeping together.

"Fixed!" whooped a hockey player named Jake something. "Go again!" Kelsie smirked and crawled over to Mike and stuck her tongue down his throat for about five minutes, much longer than was comfortable to watch.

"I hope that's not the precedent," I said quietly to no one in particular.

"That's Mike," said a drunk girl next to me. "He's not the president. It's Canada, duh." She looked at me like I was completely stupid.

Mike spun next and got Carissa, which made Kelsie sulk, especially since he didn't exactly hold back. Carissa spun hard. The bottle did about five full rotations before slowing in front of Brittany, a girl who sat behind me in math and never stopped talking.

"Oops, I'll go again!" said Carissa, but the hockey boys were already chanting *"Kiss her! Kiss her!"* Carissa looked at Brittany, who gave a bored shrug. She crossed the circle hesitantly, leaned down, and kissed Brittany quickly on the lips. She pulled away, laughing awkwardly.

"Hey!" boomed Mike. "Too short! It has to be ten seconds!"

"Says who?" snapped Kelsie.

"New rule," he said casually and the boys high-fived. Carissa rolled her eyes. She leaned in and pressed her mouth to Brittany's closed mouth, hands on her hips, while the boys counted down from ten, whooping.

"Are you happy?" Kelsie asked Mike. She was truly pissed off by this point.

"Very!" He laughed. "Brittany, go!"

Brittany sighed but spun the bottle. The boys were fully riled up by now, their guttural grunts somehow adding momentum to the bottle. It stopped in front of Theo. I scowled, but he caught my eye from across the circle and winked at me. He jumped up and met Brittany in the middle of the circle, put one arm around her, flung the other across his neck, dipped her dramatically, and gave her a big, emphatic smack on the lips, and nine more little ones on alternating cheeks while the boys counted down. When Theo stood her back up, Brittany, who I had never seen crack a smile, was belly laughing. She hugged Theo, and everyone clapped. He glanced across the circle at me, and I joined the applause. My sweet, silly boyfriend: He knew how to put on a show. He was saving his real kisses for me. My heart surged with love.

"Nice one, Raymond," said Jake. "Your go!" Theo shrugged, emboldened by his success, probably already planning his next performance. He spun with aplomb.

It landed on Mike.

"Whoa, whoa!" Mike held up his hands. "Go again." The hockey players grunted in agreement.

"No!" Kelsie jumped up. "You made the rules." She smirked, looking around the circle for support, but all eyes were on Theo. He looked at Mike, questioning, but Mike just stared at him hard, dead-eyed.

Theo slowly made his way over, not breaking eye contact. It felt like we all leaned in to see what would happen. Theo stopped a hair away from Mike's mouth, then dipped his mouth forward.

"Ten! Nine! Eight!" Jake started to shout, but no one joined him. They were silent. They were watching what looked like a pretty real kiss. Between boys.

It lasted maybe three seconds before Mike grabbed Theo by the shoulders and pushed him.

"What the fuck, dude!" He jumped back as if Theo had bitten him. Theo fell to the ground.

Everyone was staring at Theo. He stood up and shrugged. "You made the rules, dude," he said with surprising bravado, staring evenly at Mike.

"Fucking homo." Mike said it so quietly that for a moment I thought I had misheard him. I looked at Theo and knew instantly that I had heard right. He stepped back out of the circle and left the room. We all looked at Mike.

"Beer pong!" he yelled, jumping up, and his lemmings fist punched the air in support. The circle broke up quickly, and I ran out of the room after Theo.

He was in a bedroom, sitting on the bed, head in his hands. I closed the door quietly behind me.

"That really just happened?" His voice was low and dull. I'd never heard that tone before.

"Um, I mean, yes," I said. "But everyone is really drunk, like, you know what, they will probably all forget about it by Monday."

Theo looked up at me. There were tears in his eyes. "No, Mira. They won't."

I sat next to him. I pulled him toward me. "Who cares what they say. You're with me. You have a girlfriend." He looked at me blankly. "Mira."

"Kiss me!" I said. "No one kissed me. I want you to kiss me. Everything is okay." I kissed him hard, too hard to know if he was kissing me back. I slid my hand between his legs. I'd never done that before.

"What are you doing?" He pulled back, his eyes wide.

"I want . . . I want to be with you," I said. "We don't *do* anything. I want . . ." I felt wild, emboldened by the alcohol. "I want to have sex."

Theo sighed. "You don't get it . . ."

"I do! I do!" I jumped up. "You're nervous. You respect me. You wanted to wait." All these months, these were the refrains. All this time, I had felt treasured, exalted, beyond objectification. But now I was drunk, and confused. I reached behind my neck and untied my top. It flapped down to my waist, exposing my breasts. Theo looked at them, alarmed. I leaned in to kiss him again. I grabbed his hands and placed them on my chest. He jumped back, his hands up like he was guilty.

"Mira, *stop!*" He stood up, his back against the wall, looking at me wide-eyed. "You're ruining everything!"

I pulled my hands to cover myself. "I'm your girlfriend! I—I love you!"

Theo slid down the wall. "No, you don't."

I stood up over him. "I do. I always have." This was not how this moment was supposed to go.

"I . . . You're my best friend." His voice was strained. "But we need to break up."

It felt like he had punched me in the throat. I looked at him, incredulous, but couldn't speak.

"I-I'm . . . I think I need to figure out . . . I think I'm . . ." He looked at me helplessly.

"Are you . . . gay?" I whispered, the thought barely in my head before it was out of my mouth.

He was quiet for a minute. "Maybe," he said softly. "Yeah." He looked up at me again, his magic brown eyes searching my face. "I'm sorry," he said. "I do love you too . . . just . . ."

I was drunk. I was seventeen. And I was fucking heartbroken.

"Figure that shit out on your own, Theodore Raymond," I snapped. "I'm done with you. God, I'm such an idiot!"

I stormed out of the room, nearly knocking over Kelsie and Carissa, who were pressed up against the door, listening. "I told you he was gay . . ." I heard Kelsie murmur to her friend as I brushed past, tears streaming.

The party was back in full swing. I looked around wildly. I grabbed a half-full glass that had been abandoned on an end table and chugged it. Tequila. I coughed, sputtering, but downed the rest. I charged across the room and out to the deck, where a few of the hockey boys were pouring beer down each other's throats.

"Somebody, kiss me," I demanded. They stopped and stared at me.

"What are you saying, Drama Girl?"

"I need to kiss someone. Right now." I glared at them. A couple shook their heads, laughing.

"Crazy bitch," one muttered. But a tall blond guy named Cole laughed, finished his beer, grabbed my face, and kissed me. He tasted like beer and smoke, and his tongue felt large and muscly in an unappealing way, but he went for it in a way Theo never had, his hands roaming down my body. We came up for air, and his friends whooped.

"Much obliged," I said pertly, and turned to leave.

"Hey, wait." He grabbed my hand. "That was weird. And hot. You're weird."

"And hot," I said.

"You wanna go somewhere?" he asked. I shrugged, mostly because I didn't know what he meant.

He meant we should go find an empty bedroom, and, failing that, Mike's dad's boat, which was parked in the driveway. He meant he should fumble around with my halter top tie before giving up, unzipping his fly, and pushing my head down. I never even saw my first penis before it was in my mouth. I threw up on it. He left me there.

Theo and I didn't speak for two weeks. It nearly killed me. It was a welcome relief when I came home from school one day and found a bouquet of daisies and a note.

> *Mirabel,*
> *I'm so sorry I hurt you. I'm sorry I can't love you the way*
> *you want me to. But I do love you. So, so much. Please*
> *forgive me. You're my best friend.*
> *Love, Theo*

I sniffed the daisies. He was right: They didn't smell very good. But they were still lovely. I went inside and phoned him.

"Tempest is doing *Romeo and Juliet* this summer," I blurted out before he even had a chance to speak. My parents had told me over dinner two nights before, and it had killed me not to tell Theo immediately. "I think we should audition."

Chapter 12

Seven weeks until Opening Night

I am looking forward to our first rehearsal now that Theo and I are back to good, now that I know I might actually do a decent job with Helena. I'm looking forward to working with Max and Bailey. And Will. I am looking forward to seeing Will again, even if I have decided not to go there.

This summer might be okay after all.

I am just pulling up to the theater when a text comes in from my mother:

We have a surprise for you!

What surprise? I shoot back.

You'll have to wait and see!

I sigh. I am in no mood for mischief.

I see him as soon as I enter the room. His back is to me, his wavy blond hair perfectly in place, in a linen shirt and jeans, trying to look down-to-earth, but he isn't. He is surrounded by a group of young women, his natural habitat. They are laughing at something he's saying—that is, until they see me, and they stop and look at him expectantly. One of them leans in and whispers to him, and he turns around. And there he is. Nick Fucking Nolan, the movie star. My ex-lover, ex-costar, and current mortal enemy, and for some inexplicable reason, he is in North Lake, in my rehearsal hall.

Why, why, oh, why is he here?

On set, in the TV world, being surrounded by beautiful people is normal. Here, among mere mortals, he is practically luminescent. He seems taller, more chiseled, more intensely beautiful. He looks in every way to be the dreamboat leading man. He's chatting away as though he somehow belongs here, as if his presence here is to be expected. He's charming the locals, showing what an everyman he is. He doesn't know how to breathe without the adoration of women raining down on him.

He turns in slow motion, it seems, sees me, and I catch it: I see that hair of a flicker of the real him, the real man even I only barely know. It's almost imperceptible. He covers it instantaneously with bravado, and the real him is gone, replaced with the plastic version. He tilts his head to the side, clutches one hand to his heart as if to say, *At last, here she is.* He strides toward me and opens his arms wide; everyone is watching us, everyone nervously thrilled. *What will they do? Are they friends? How is this going to go? Will there be drama? We love drama!* But no. There will be no drama. I'm a fucking professional.

Nick throws his arms around me, and I respond gingerly. I don't want to press my body against his body. He smells expensive, the same Tom Ford cologne that used to make me nearly vibrate if I caught a whiff. I bought a bottle so I could spray it on my pillow when I went to sleep without him. Now it turns my stomach. Once I stole his shirts from set. Now he's unrecognizable, which is a relief.

"Mira," he says fondly. "Here you are."

"What are you doing here, Nick?" I keep my voice flat, as though any emotion at all will betray all manner of mayhem inside me.

"Theater, darling!" He spreads his arms and turns grandly. The plethora of women titter. "Your parents didn't tell you?"

I glance at my parents. My mother's fists are clenched up to her face in excitement as she looks wildly at me for my reaction. My father avoids my glare and drops his eyes toward his script. "Tell me what?" I ask, although every cell of me is already sinking with suspicion.

"I'm here to play"—he glances at his script—"Dimitry?"

"Demetrius."

"That guy!" He laughs. I bet he hasn't even read the play.

"Why, Nick?"

"Why am I, an act-or, act-ing?" He rolls his eyes and looks conspiratorially at the woman nearest to him. She nearly chokes on her giggle.

I grab him away from his harem. "Don't fuck with me. Why are you in my town, in my parents' play, in my life at all? What about . . . *Batman*?"

His head drops. "*Lego Batman* fell through." He sighs. "Something about copyright . . ." He reaches for my hand. "I thought maybe you'd be glad to see me. I miss you. I should never have let you leave."

"I'm not," I huff, though the touch of his hand has sent a jolt straight to my cervix.

"Listen." He takes my other hand. "I'm sorry. I've been a total ass. I don't know . . . I just really miss you." He leans in, and I snatch my hands back.

"Stop it," I hiss. "No one knows about you." He smiles; everyone knows about him. "About *us*." His smile drops. He looks almost disappointed. "No one knows that we are anything but colleagues." I blink at him. "No one even knows I'm off the show yet."

"Okay, well, that explains why your parents were so easy." He smirks.

"What? How did . . . Nick, *why* are you even here?"

He puts his hands up in defense. "Can't a guy give back a little to the community and do a little Shakespeare between seasons of his international hit TV show?" I want to interject that this is my community, not his, but truthfully, these days, we have about equal claim to it. "And maybe get his girl back in the meantime?" He winks.

"But how . . ." I am interrupted by my mother clapping us all to attention. We are about to begin. "We aren't done here."

"I sure hope not," he whispers, too close to my face. My blood quickens, despite myself.

"Everybody! Take a seat!"

I stalk off to the other side of the room, where Theo has saved me a seat.

"Do tell . . ." he murmurs, not looking at me.

"He's an asshole."

"I mean, that's evident. Why is he here?"

"To woo me back, it seems."

"Back?! Girl!"

"I'll tell you later." I pause. "He's playing Demetrius, apparently."

"What about Will?" Will was supposed to play Demetrius.

"Ugh. I don't know." I glance around the room, only now realizing that Will isn't here.

Theo sighs. "Does he know?"

"The irony? Probably not." The irony being that Demetrius treats Helena like hot garbage before Puck's misdirected magic transforms his heart. That won't be happening here.

My mother makes an embarrassing, gushing speech about how lucky we are to have a real star in our show (Theo kicks me under the table), and everyone is a little confused but mostly just excited. Nick soaks it up like the synthetic sponge that he is.

At the break, I pull my parents into the small kitchen in the rehearsal hall.

"Why is Nick Nolan here?" I demand. "What's going on?"

"Well, he's going to play Demetrius, darling," my mother coos. "Aren't we so lucky?"

"What about Will?" I glare at my father, since my mother is clearly going to be useless here. My father clears his throat.

"Will, uh, well, the, uh . . . opportunity, you see . . . and Mr. Nolan, well, Nick, as it were . . . presented himself . . ." He is bumbling. My father is a lot of things, but he never doesn't know what to say.

"Presented himself, how?" I turn back to my mother. "What's he talking about? What's going on here?"

"Goodness, darling, I certainly didn't expect this kind of reaction. We thought you'd be pleased."

"Why would you think that? You know nothing about me!" My sigh is nearly a growl. "How did this happen?"

My dad clears his throat again, a second attempt at coherence. "We were contacted," he says, then, pleased with this new footing, continues, "by Nick's agent."

"Nick is between seasons of the show." My mother looks at me pointedly. "As you know." Obviously Nick has given her only a version of the story. "And he very generously offered to lend a little more, well, star power"—here, she avoids my eyes—"to our production. Free of charge, if you must know." She raises her eyebrow at me, as though I should have thought to be this benevolent. "And he brings with him some significant sponsors. And with the additional ticket sales, well, it will fund our entire next two seasons. Our production value . . ."

"Pyrotechnics!" blurts my father in an uncharacteristic display of enthusiasm. "We can do pyrotechnics!"

"Where is there a need for exploding fireballs in William Shakespeare's *A Midsummer Night's Dream*, Ross? Don't be asinine."

"We'll find a place," he says. "Maybe Oberon throws fire, or at the wedding celebration . . ."

"That's much too heavy-handed. Honestly, what next? An army tank onstage?"

"Stratford already did that," my dad says. "The Scottish play, 2009." Even in an argument, my parents won't say the name *Macbeth* inside a theater. None of us would. Old theater superstition.

"Um, hello? Excuse me, can we circle back to me here?" They both look at me surprised, I know, because they have indeed forgotten I am standing here. "What about Will? What about the person you already cast in the role?"

"Will understands," my dad says. "It's what's best for the show. We've only had the one rehearsal so far. A big Hollywood actor brings too much to our show to turn him down." They have no idea of the levels to which Nick is too much. "We will make it up to Will. He knows that. It's . . ." He softens a little. "It's not good form." He clears his throat. "I—I don't like it, I'll say that. But what are we supposed to do?"

"So, a famous person approaches you out of nowhere and randomly asks to be in a community theater Shakespeare production, and you remove an actor whom you know and trust, who is already doing well in the part, in order to put someone who is famous for playing a real estate detective in his place?" I look between them, for answers. They are, blessedly, silent. "And he's going to do it for *free*. And he's going to inject a ton of money into your production. And it has yet to occur to you both to wonder *why* this man is doing all of this?" They look at me blankly. "It never occurred to you to talk to *me* about this?"

"Oh, Miranda." My mother sighs. "I know we raised you in the theater, but not all things revolve around you. We thought it would be nice for you to have someone you know here. Someone you work with." I hope to God that Nick doesn't clarify that part. I can't handle any further humiliation.

I am at a crossroads. On one hand, I do not want my parents to know anything about my sex life, ever. Telling them exactly how well, how intimately, I know Nick would take us far past the usually very tight and tidy boundaries of our relationship. On the other hand, if I told them how this man has used me, how he got me fired . . . If I'm honest, I am not completely certain that they would be sympathetic enough to do anything. They might even blame me. I am hit by a rush of . . . what? Clarity? Suddenly I am very tired and very sad, because I have parents who don't even know me. They have no idea about the world I have come here from, about who is or isn't in my life. We have spent my whole life playing within a confined space, like the taped-off stage we rehearse on. Suddenly my disappointment in them is so palpable that I can't go on.

"He's not a good guy," I say. "He's not here for the reasons you think. And it's going to be a shit show."

They look at me like I'm the disappointment. "Well." My mother sniffs. "We certainly hope you'll be able to maintain your professional composure while he's here."

I turn and fling the door open. A couple of the fairies are in the hallway, and scatter innocently. "It's community theater," I hiss back at my parents. "Nothing about this is professional." My mother looks shocked, and I can hear her outcry as I storm away.

The thing I don't want to admit, to Nick or anyone, is that I actually fell for the guy. I know. So incredibly predictable. It's your classic secretary-and-CEO scenario, the powerful man and the underling, no promises made, no labels given, but a feeling, right? An innate understanding beyond words. We loved each other, right? It was really something, right? He wasn't the smartest man I'd met, or the most talented, or the best looking, even. He was definitely the richest, the most famous, and say what you like, but those things cast an extra sheen on everything. It was the idea that I could get underneath those things, literally and figuratively, to access a version of him that was only mine, only visible in early-morning light, in whispered con-fessions and soft gazes and tenderness that vanished the second he stepped out of his apartment, a precious bubble that was only ours. What little I had of him was mine, and it was real. And then it was denied, cast out, completely dismissed.

Needless to say, I am outraged he's here, even if he still smells like a fever dream.

Luckily the rest of the rehearsal is the first scene with Helena and Lysander: I don't actually have to deal with Nick. It's our second rehearsal with this scene, and I have that first big monologue. I hear him laughing in the back of the room. I can hear him watching. It's the first audience reaction, and I hate myself for being glad that he's watching, that he's seeing me do well. After rehearsal, I march straight up to him.

"Didn't know you could act," he says. I think he actually believes this to be a compliment, despite our working together as professional actors.

"Meet me outside," I say. His eyes light up.

"With pleasure." He beams.

Out back, behind the dumpsters, I corner him.

"Okay. So you have clearly swindled my parents," I say.

"What? No!" he says innocently. "I just really love Shakespeare."

"Name ten Shakespeare plays," I say.

"That's a trick question," he says. "He only wrote six."

"That's Jane Austen, idiot." I'm surprised he even knows that.

He laughs and leans in. Close. Too close. "You know, I didn't know how fiery you could be. Where was that girl in the city?" He steps toward me. "I like her." I push him away, holding my arm out, barring him from further invasion. I don't want him near me.

"No," I say. "You don't get to do that, not here. I can't do anything about you being here; it seems you have ingratiated yourself pretty well, especially financially. And I don't want to be the reason that two seasons of the company lose funding." I step back. "But I have some rules."

"Seriously, there's some super interesting dynamics happening here, and I have to say I'm really feeling it—"

"Stop it!" I want to shake him, punch him, but people are around, walking to their cars, already curious about what is going on here. "Why are you here, Nick? What do you want?"

"I feel bad about . . . you. I was an asshole."

"You *are* an asshole."

"I *am* an asshole. And I treated you like shit. And I got you . . ." *Fired.* I fucking knew it. "And I'm sorry." He looks up from under his long, perfect eyelashes, a look I know well, a look he knows works on me. I say nothing. I do not move. "And fuck, Mira, are you going to make me say it?"

"I'm an actual person, you know."

"I know, and I am realizing by the second what a remarkable person you are, and I'm stupid, and I'm sorry, and I miss you." He looks at me straight, for the first time all day looking at me like an actual human. "I really miss you. I want you back."

People always wonder if celebrities are actually that attractive, how much is makeup, or lighting, or editing. Nick Nolan, up close, is not an objectively perfect-looking man. Not like Theo, who looks sculpted from gold, who is so purely beautiful it's actually insane. Nick Nolan has an expensive haircut and a good colorist, making those seemingly sun-kissed streaks in his hair appear natural. He has a personal trainer and a really good dermatologist. I can neither confirm nor deny his use of Botox. Nick Nolan's eyes are 10 percent too close together, and if you isolate his features, objectively, individually, they are borderline unremarkable. Nick Nolan is five eleven, but he has the sort of perfect body that extensive training and juice cleanses can buy. But what Nick Nolan does have in spades is charisma. He has star quality. He knows what people want from him—his attention—and he can administer it so deftly that you don't even realize his effect until it is suddenly, ruthlessly, taken away.

I'm one of the lucky few who know this. But I also know how he looks when he's asleep. I know how vulnerable he really is. I know how every inch of his body feels against every inch of mine. I no longer want to know these things. I was trying to forget him, and now he's here. This is a problem.

I know unequivocally, whatever his presence might be stirring up in my body, that I cannot let him near me ever again.

I take a deep breath. It occurs to me for the first time that I have options here. "Okay," I say slowly. "This is how it's going to go. First of all, nobody is going to know about our personal history." Except I'm absolutely going to tell Theo all of it, of course. "It's pretty clear already to them that I don't like you, but I can play it that you were a diva on set, and you can prove me wrong by doing your whole schmoozy thing, and everyone can fall in love with you, and I'll be the bad guy." I raise my eyebrows to make sure he's listening.

"Okay . . ." he says. He is at least smart enough to know that telling people we were together at all means telling them I dumped him.

"I don't seem to be able to do anything about you being here. So, fine, be here. But nothing is going to happen between us. You will not get me back." I say it like I mean it. I am a good actress.

"I'll die trying," he says, doing that one smile that he knows undoes me. It threatens to, I'll admit, but I press on.

"You and I will not hang out socially. You will not flirt with me. You will not look at me unless the script tells you to. You will stop texting me. There is nothing here. If you insist on spending your summer in North Lake doing Shakespeare, I can't stop you. But"—I lean in—"I know you. You're going to get bored, and you're going to bail. It's what you do. I give you two weeks. *Thou spotted and inconstant man.*"

"Huh?"

"It's from the play, stupid." I walk away, feeling victorious.

I have, however, made two grave errors.

One, I have forgotten that under the golden retriever demeanor, Nick Nolan is a fucking pit bull.

And two, I have forgotten to consider fairy magic.

Chapter 13

I am in no mood to go home to my parents, and I am in mighty need of a drink. That's what I tell myself, but really, I just want to see Will. Nick's arrival has placed a vague panic in my gut, a sudden sense that something has been lost. I hardly know the guy, but I have this sense that the grand order of things has been tampered with. I jump in the car and head to the cidery.

I feel suddenly odd pulling up without Theo, as though I am trespassing, as though this place belongs to him. It's golden hour, light streaming through the orchard, and the place is pretty empty save for a few couples sitting outside in the big Muskoka chairs. After the angst and the chaos of the last three hours, the shock of Nick, fighting with my parents, it feels like I have slipped under the covers into a place of total peace.

I see Will before he sees me. He is coming out of the back casking room, hauling a crate of bottles, ball cap low over his forehead, in jeans and a vintage band shirt. He looks more familiar like this, somehow. I can't shake the sense that I know him from somewhere aside from the play, aside from the night here with Theo. I can't help but notice how easily he swings the crate down, his lovely lean forearms, how perfectly proportioned the distance between his eyes is. They are a sort of a dark golden brown. I like his face immensely. He is the physical opposite of Nick—taller, leaner, dark floppy hair raked back under a ball cap.

Where Nick is polished, Will is rugged. I like it. I can't help but note that he is no longer in the play . . .

He looks up and sees me, and I realize that I have been staring. "Mira."

"Oh! Hi!" I say too brightly. "I, um, I was just . . ."

"Can I get you a drink?" My blood quickens a little before I remember that offering me a drink is his job.

"Well, actually, very much yes, but I also . . . I'm glad to see you. I was hoping to see you." His face is so unreadable—this gift he has for keeping it pleasant and guarded at the same time.

"Well, let's start with a drink. What'll you have?" He leads us inside.

"Oh! Um, I . . . Well, what do you recommend? I had a flight with Theo, but I forgot all the names." I pick up a menu for something to do with my hands, scanning furiously for any name that sounds familiar. "I think I prefer the fruitier ones?" His face doesn't move. "I mean, it's all fruit, it's cider, obviously, I just mean . . ."

"I've got one for you." He gestures to the bar. "Take a seat." He leaves, heading into the back room, and I sit there awkwardly, waiting. I look around the place. It's cozy. It's cool, but it also feels warm, rustic, natural, somehow, as though it just sprang up in the middle of the orchard, which, I guess it did. Something about this place quiets my insides, and I haven't even had a drink yet.

Will returns with an unmarked bottle. "My secret stash." He smiles.

"Is it poison?" I ask. "I wouldn't blame you. Will, I am so sorry about my parents, I . . ."

He stops me by holding out a tasting glass. "Try this. Tell me what you think."

I take a tentative sniff. He is watching me carefully with that microsmile. I take a sip. It's heaven. It's fruity but also herbal and effervescent but also smoky somehow.

"What is this?" I breathe. I take another sip. I close my eyes to taste it better. When I open them, he is fully smiling.

"Right?" he says. "It's new. Well, I was making it for the cast party." He shrugs. "It's, well, maybe it's dumb . . ."

"What?"

"Well, it's like, I wanted to sort of . . . If you could bottle the play, right? Like, *A Midsummer Night's Dream* in a cider."

"It's really . . . perfect." I finish my little glass and hold it out for more. He lights up a bit at that, his guard down. He pulls a larger glass off the shelf, fills it, and hands it to me.

"So, it's like a strawberry prosecco, with mint and a little lavender, so, trying to get that feeling of summer and magic, and then the kind of grassy herbs, like the forest and also the magical flower Puck uses." I'm nodding along. "And then it's blended with this local wildflower honey, sort of a nod to the honey mead made in Elizabethan times, like to what Shakespeare might have been drinking. And . . . yeah." He looks so sweet, so proud. God, he's attractive.

"I love it," I say, and I mean it. "It's the most poetically perfect beverage I've ever had."

He laughs lightly. "I'm glad you like it," he says. His eyes linger on mine.

"I really do." I sigh. "And it's such a beautiful gift for the cast . . . Will. What my parents have done here is . . . shameful." He shakes his head to stop me. "No, it is, they are being such assholes. I knew they were all about their plays, but this is next level. Nick Nolan . . ."

He holds up a hand. "Hey. It's fine. I get it. He's a big name. It's the summer show . . . It will be good for the show, the company, the town."

"But they just dumped you." I don't get why he's so calm.

"They were very apologetic." I wince. I'm so mad at them. "And they owe me. They told me I can do any role I want in the next season. They'll make it up to me."

I sigh again. "And you believe them?" I take another sip of the magical cider. "This feels like the scene in *The Devil Wears Prada*."

"Am I Meryl Streep?" he asks with a wink.

"No, you are Stanley Tucci. My parents are Meryl." I take another big swig. "And they do *not* deserve to be Meryl."

"I haven't actually seen that movie."

"It's tremendous." My glass is empty.

"Want another?" he asks, and I do. He is leaning casually on his side of the bar, bottle dangling from his hand, and I am feeling the most myself I have since I got home, longer maybe.

"So how long have you been doing theater?" I ask. "You seem . . ." I stop myself.

"What?"

"Never mind." I look away.

"Nope, you have to say it now!"

"Well. Like, too cool to be a theater person."

"Whoa!" He laughs. "How do I respond to that?"

"Ugh, I know, sorry, I just mean . . . you just have this sort of like edgy, indie-music, outdoorsy thing going on . . ." He actually blushes, which makes me blush.

"I'm not that cool." He clears his throat and takes a sip of cider. "I started going to plays with my grandma, and it sort of became our thing." Well, shit, that's adorable. He shrugs. "Then I tried out for one and . . . it's really fun. I love the people. It's good to get out." He smiles. "You?"

"I mean . . . yeah, same. It was the most fun thing. And I was raised in it, right, so it's kind of all I ever knew."

"It's so cool you, you know, really went for it. And did it! That's really rare, right?"

I smile and shrug. "It's not all it's cracked up to be."

"It never is." He looks at me with an expression that is somehow both light and intense.

"So how did you get into the cider thing?" I ask as he fills my glass again.

"Well, my family had the land. The orchard was already there, and my brother and I opened it the year we turned thirty."

"Twins, right?"

He takes a large gulp of his cider. "Uh-huh."

"So, you run it, and your brother—"

"Died." He looks up at me, surprised. "I assumed you knew that . . ."

"Oh, God, Will, no, I am so sorry, I had no idea!" This new detail totally throws me.

"I thought Theo might have told you. It's not a secret. Everyone knows." His face has gone back to completely neutral. "People who live here."

I reach my hand out and clasp his without even thinking. "I'm so sorry," I say. I look at my hand and quickly snatch it away, but he catches it and holds it tight, just for a second, before releasing me. I don't know what to say next.

"He was hit by a drunk driver." He reads my mind. "Almost three years ago."

We sit there for a moment, both staring into our drinks. "What was his name?" I ask finally.

"Jonah. He was the best." He swallows hard. "The absolute fucking best."

"I'm so sorry," I say softly. "I'm sure everyone says this, but it must be so much worse, losing your twin . . ." He nods, that half smile. "Sorry, that was dumb, obviously . . . I never know—"

He stops me. "I appreciate that, Mira. And yeah. There is nothing worse than losing your favorite person." He leans in. "But also, and don't get me wrong, I'd give anything to undo it, to have him back. But there were two of us, and now there is one, and I don't know, I feel like I need to live for both of us, you know? And I'll be damned if I don't live fully. Like . . . wholeheartedly. You know?" He smiles, and my heart clenches, not just at his grief and his courage but also because I don't know who my favorite person is. And I couldn't tell you the last time I did anything wholeheartedly.

Will slaps his hands on the bar. "That's enough of that!" He smiles. Conversation closed.

"Thank you for telling me," I say.

"It's better when people know," he says. "Promise me one thing?"

Anything. "Yeah?"

"No pity, okay? I don't want it to change how you see me. You know, the . . . what was it? Sexy emo farm boy?"

"Wow." I laugh. "Okay, um, you added some adjectives there." He smiles for real this time and time fizzles. "I don't know what it is," I say. "There's something so familiar about you."

He raises an eyebrow. "Huh," he says. "That's very interesting."

We are interrupted by a large group arriving through the door. Will nods at them in greeting.

"I should go," I say. I pull out my wallet.

"On the house," he says.

"Oh! Thank you." I realize with disappointment that I won't see him at rehearsal. "I'll see you . . . ?" I very much need to know when that will be.

"See you around!" he says, already busy with the new customers. "Promise." I am halfway out the door when I turn back, just for a second, catching his eye as he watches me leave.

I am halfway to my car when I realize that I left my wallet on the bar. I turn back for it, but he is already jogging toward me, holding it out. I reach for it and our fingers touch. Without thinking, I reach up and kiss his cheek, too close to his mouth, and then I linger there. He doesn't move until I step back. I can't do this.

"Thanks," I say.

"Anytime," he says. "Anytime at all." He touches the tip of his ball cap ironically, and turns away, leaving the ball firmly in my court.

Chapter 14

Nick's first rehearsal is the next day. Sally assembles us, as usual, but before my dad can tell us the plan for the day, Nick stands up.

"May I say a few words?" he asks, though it is clear he is unconcerned with permission. My father sits back in his seat. "I just want to say what a pleasure it is—an honor, really—to be so welcomed into your production. I know I am in great company here, that this stage has been shared with many other famous actors, and I am excited to join in their footsteps." Theo smirks at me from across the room. I roll my eyes. "I know the process by which I came into the role is a little, uh, different than usual, but I saw the opportunity to give back, so I took it."

Took the role from someone else, I want to say, but I am trying to be on good behavior. I look around the room to see how everyone else is responding. A few people are drinking the Kool-Aid; they practically have stars in their eyes. The fairies are all sitting together in the back row, crocheting calmly, and I can tell they are tuning him out. Nick finishes his speech and looks around. I think he is hoping for applause.

My father stands up abruptly. "Act two, scene two," he barks. "Titania and Oberon. Wynne, Marcus, get into position. Lovers," my dad calls out. "Please go in the other room and review the scenes you know with Mr. Nolan. Take him through the blocking, get him up to speed." He pauses. "Mira, you lead." I catch his eye pleadingly; for a moment, I feel like a kid complaining that I have to do my chores, but he just nods staunchly at me and turns to the actors at hand.

Max, Bailey, and Nick follow me into the large dressing room. They all stare at me expectantly. "Okay, so, opening scene, Nick, you just enter along with everyone else. This is the palace of Theseus, the duke of Athens. Hermia's father has come to ask the duke to force his daughter to marry Demetrius, but she loves Lysander." I take them through the basic blocking, Demetrius's exit with the duke. "Okay, good, then Hermia and Lysander run away together. They meet Helena, me, on their way out of town and tell her their plan. Helena is jealous of their happiness because Demetrius played her and dumped her."

"Yeah, he did!" Nick chirps, before realizing the admission he's nearly made. Max and Bailey laugh a little. They seem intimidated by him. I stare at him for a long time before continuing.

"So, Helena plans to tell Demetrius, and he decides to follow them, and she follows him. So that brings us to . . ." It's too much. "Um, Demetrius and Helena alone in the forest. So, she's chasing him, and he wants nothing to do with her. So, we enter from here . . ." I lead him upstage right.

"It's a little on the nose, don't you think?" Nick whispers as we're walking.

"Shut up." I hate this man. "Okay, so you go ahead of me, and I chase you, then we end up on that bench there by this line." I point to his script. He gives me a thumbs-up. "You should be writing this down," I say.

Nick taps his head. "It's all up here. I'm a pro."

"Theater is different." It's very hard to not contort my face each time he speaks. We go back to the starting place. "Okay, go."

Nick storms onstage. *"I love thee not, therefore pursue me not!"* he bellows in a booming, exaggerated British accent. Bailey looks at me, wide-eyed. I blink at her, a quick understanding passing between us, a hint of a smile on my lips. We let him continue. *"Hence, get thee gone, and follow me no more!"* It's not even British. It's terrible. It's a caricature of what he thinks Shakespeare is. *"Do I not in plainest truth tell you, I do not, and can not love you?"* He pauses. "Pretty good, huh?" He looks around proudly.

"It's my line," I say. I don't know how to begin to comment on his performance. *"And even for that do I love you the more . . . spurn me, strike me, neglect me, lose me, only give me leave, unworthy as I am, to follow you."*

Nick stops.

"Why aren't you acting?" he asks.

"I am acting."

He pretends to think very hard. Or maybe it is hard for him. Who knows. "So, I just feel like our vibes aren't matching. Like, could you do it more . . . Shakespearean?"

"It is Shakespearean, by virtue of it *being Shakespeare.*"

"See, now that was better."

I will kill him. "Let's just get through the blocking, okay?"

We get to the part by the bench. This is the single moment I am dreading.

"Okay, so, here he sort of turns on her to call her bluff, so you are going to back me up against the bench and sort of . . . push me down on *You do impeach your modesty too much . . .*" I hate this. "He's messing with her head, teasing her, like, *You want me? I'll let you have it,* and she's like, *Give it to me.*" Nick is facing away from the others, and waggles his eyebrows at me.

"Sounds sexy," he murmurs. "Sounds . . . familiar . . ."

"Fuck off," I whisper. "Run the scene."

It's hard to feel nostalgic about your former lover when they are bellowing in a fake Shakespearean accent, so it's actually easier than predicted. Nick pushes me down, leans over me, shouting, *"To commit yourself into the hands of one who loves you not, to trust the opportunity of night and the ill counsel of a desert place."*

I reach up, pull him toward me, Helena's attempt at seduction, but I grab him by the collar and twist it as I coo my lines. *"It is not night when I do see thy face . . ."* He pulls back, coughing.

"Jesus, Mira, you're choking me."

"Shakespeare is very violent." I shrug. "Let's stop here."

Nick shakes himself off. "I should get a sword for this scene."

"You have one," I mutter. "It's just not very big."

My dad enters and asks us to show him the scene.

"With pleasure," I say.

Max, Bailey, and I play the scene as previously directed. Nick throws himself around grandly, in his big, booming, Shakes-pee-ah voice, dipping in and out of the accent. He has decided to mime a sword, despite the fact that in this scene he is fighting with a woman alone in the woods. When the scene is done, he steps forward, beaming.

"Don't worry, boss," he says, and my father flinches. "I'll help them with their accents." My father sits, stunned. I can see the blood draining from his face as he realizes that his big get for the season is not such a coup after all. He leans in and whispers to Sally.

"Nick, a word, please." She gestures to him.

"Oh, no, anything you have to say to me . . . We're all here to learn, right? Go ahead!" He looks around at us encouragingly.

"Oh!" Sally is flustered. "Um. Okay. So. The voice."

"Ye-es?" booms Nick in The Voice.

"Yeah, so, don't . . . do it?" I've never seen her so nervous. She's usually such a battle-ax.

I see him tense instantly. I've seen it a hundred times on set. Nick is a treat until you give him feedback.

"What? Sorry, I thought this was a Shakespeare play. I thought maybe you wanted to see some real acting." Beside me, Max and Bailey snort.

"As you so aptly said," my dad interjects, "we are here to learn. And while the instinct to take a fully, ahem, classical approach is . . .

a choice"—he pauses—"it can be distracting from the character's true motivations and"—he clears his throat—"the integrity of the scene."

"So, what, two sessions with my acting coach just out the window?" Nick says. "I spent five hours perfecting my accent."

My father coughs, and I nearly choke on my laugh. "Let's consider a more natural approach," he says. "Just . . . say the lines. Like . . . a person."

Theo has snuck up beside me. *There we may rehearse most obscenely and courageously!* he whispers in Nick's Shakespeare voice. *Take pains! Be perfect!* I explode laughing. Everyone turns to look at me, and I hold a hand up in apology, my body shaking with laughter. I slip out into the hallway, where I lean my head against the wall.

"That bad, huh?"

I pull my head back, surprised to see Will.

"What are you doing here?" I catch myself. He flusters me. "I mean, hi, but—"

"I'm helping with the set build," he says. The side of his mouth twitches as he tries not to laugh at me.

"Ah, lovely," I say. "That's very nice of you, considering . . ."

"How heartlessly I was cast out?" He shrugs genially. "Tell me, though." He leans in. Apples. "How is rehearsal going? Am I . . . Is it bad to ask that?"

"Not as bad as this rehearsal," I say.

"Gotcha."

There is a small pause. He is wearing a denim button-down. I like it. I like him.

"I didn't know if I'd see you again," I blurt. "When? If? Um . . ." I am really nailing this. I want him to ask me out again, but I'm worried I've blown it. He hasn't brought it up since we were at the fire with Theo.

He smiles for real this time. "Small town," he says. "You run into everyone eventually."

"Not that small," I say.

"Yeah, well . . ." There is another pause. "I guess I'll run into you again sometime."

"I guess so," I say, hoping I sound cooler and more casual than I feel.

"Good." He nods, smirking a little, and heads up the stairs to the main theater, giving me a little wave. Something about that guy makes me a mumbling, smiling idiot. It is a most unexpected sensation. Maybe even a welcome one.

And that's it. That's when I remember who Will is.

It was that night at Mike Bale's, the spin-the-bottle fiasco. I know I had gotten really drunk really fast. I don't remember much after the thing with the hockey player. I know he left me there. I don't know how much time passed before Theo found me. I was curled up in the fetal position with my shirt ridden up. Theo carried me to a car. Some guy was driving.

"Whose car is this?" I mumbled.

"This is Reed," said Theo. "He's driving us home."

"Oh. Okay."

Reed had shaggy hair that swooped across his forehead. He was nice. He was in a band. There was very loud, emotional music blaring.

"*Shhhhhh,*" I said, covering my face with my hands. So loud. He turned it down. We drove in silence. Theo and I, anyway, were out of things to say.

We dropped Theo off because his stop was first.

"You okay, Mira?" Theo asked before getting out. "He's a good guy, I promise. He'll get you home safe." I just stared at him.

"Anyone is better than you," I slurred. Theo sighed and closed the door. He fist-bumped Reed wearily as he left the car.

A few minutes into the drive, Reed said, "What was that about? I thought you guys were best friends."

"You didn't think we were . . . lovers?" I asked.

"Uh, no." He looked at me sideways.

"Well, I did." I start to cry. "I've lost the only boy I'll ever love."

He chuckled. "We're seventeen. I bet you'll be okay."

I sniffed, and he reached behind the seat and handed me a box of Kleenex. "I won't. I love him. And he barely wants to kiss me."

"I wouldn't take that personally."

"And"—I blew my nose loudly—"I kissed this stupid athlete."

"It happens."

"And he left me!"

"That was a shitty thing to do."

"It WAS! Right?" He smiled and kept driving. "Nobody likes me. Girls don't want to be my friend, and boys don't want to kiss me." I noticed where we were. "It's up there. The big house."

"Yes, they do."

"Who do what?"

"Boys want to kiss you." He pulled over in front of my house.

"Name one."

"I would." His eyes were on the road as he put the car in park.

I undid my seat belt and pulled him toward me and kissed him.

He pulled away. "What are you doing?"

"You said you would kiss me!"

"I didn't mean now. I meant in theory."

I slumped back in my seat. I started to cry again. "Nobody wants me!"

"Hey," he said, wiping my face with his sleeve. "*Shhh.* I'm sorry. I can't kiss you now."

"Why? Are you gay too?" I snapped. He sat back. There was a long, heavy pause. I hung my head. "I'm sorry. That was so mean."

"It was." He took back the Kleenex. He was quiet for a moment. "I can't kiss you because you're drunk."

"I've kissed three boys tonight, and none of them like me. I'm weird and ugly."

He turned to me, a soft look on his face. "I think you're cool. And beautiful," he said softly. "And I promise you, if you ever want to, I will kiss you for real."

"Oh." I wiped my nose on my sleeve. "Thank you." I opened the door. "Thank you for the ride." He nodded.

I stumbled up the steps to my house and felt around for my key. My parents were out. When I finally got the door open, I turned around—he was still there. He waved and pulled away.

I woke up the next morning so heartbroken over Theo, so humiliated over the athlete, I forgot all about the sweet guy who drove me home.

It's the little wave he gives me across the room that triggers the memory.

"Hey, wait!" I call to him. He turns on the stairs. "I know you!"

"Um, yeah?" That smirk again.

"No, I felt like I remembered you, and I didn't, but now I do."

"Yeah, we met once."

"You knew Theo. Why did I never see you again?"

"I went to another high school. We were childhood friends."

"You drove me home."

"From that party, yeah." He looks at me, surprised. "You seriously didn't remember?"

"I remember that night. Very well," I say. "That was a big night."

"It sure was."

"And I was so embarrassed . . ." He comes down a few steps back toward me. "But then I never saw you again. But wait—your name wasn't Will, it was . . ."

"Reed."

"Yeah!"

"Will Reed." He watches my face as all the parts click into place.

"Okay, wow." I feel oddly flustered. "So, um. Hello."

"Hello." He's standing right in front of me now.

"I'm sorry I forgot you," I say.

He laughs a little. "Don't let it happen again."

"I probably won't, now."

"Probably? Rude." The half smile is full again, and I feel like I'd do anything to keep it there.

"Hey." Am I saying this? "If memory serves . . ."

"I mean, so far it hasn't . . ."

"Right, so, correct me if I'm wrong . . ."

"Happily."

"Didn't you promise to kiss me?" He raises an eyebrow. I think we are both a little impressed by my bravado. I think we both know that I just have to say the word. He opens his mouth, but just then the teenage ASM runs after me and hands me a note.

The Fey Have Summoned You!
Tea at Barb's, 4 o'clock.
Bring cookies.

I read it and look up in surprise.

"Like, today?"

She nods. "I think so?"

"Who is Barb?" I ask. "Where does she live? This is a very incomplete invitation." I glance back at Will. The moment has vanished.

"Barb is Cobweb," Will says, as though this is common knowledge. He chuckles to himself.

"Cobweb the fairy?" I ask. The ASM nods. She turns over the invitation and points: Barb's address.

It is very presumptuous of this Barb that I am available to be summoned at a moment's notice and that I will indeed bring cookies. But I am amused and intrigued. Also available.

"I'll be there." The teenager nods and scurries away. When I look up from the note card, Will is halfway back up the stairs.

"Offer still stands!" he calls down, laughing as he walks away.

Chapter 15

Barb's house is a sweet century cottage with a white picket gate and a cobblestone path toward a wall of ivy, in the center of which is a coral-pink door. I twist the old-fashioned doorbell. A person, Barb, I assume, appears at the door. I recognize her from rehearsals, a trim, perky woman in her early seventies with a halo of wily white curls.

"I have been summoned," I say. She looks me up and down, as though reconsidering the summons. I hold out the white bakery box. She takes it and peers inside.

"Well, what's this, dear?" She holds up a small pink cube covered in sugar sprinkles.

"Fairy bites," I say, a little proud. Her face breaks open into a smile.

"Oh, well done, girl," she says.

"I also brought this," I say, holding up a bottle of floral pink gin. "In case it's that kind of tea party." She cackles and grabs it from me.

"It most certainly is." She waves me inside.

We pass quickly through a hallway filled with a framed collage of vintage photos and art prints into the kitchen, which is pale yellow, bright, and warm. Flowers and vases of greenery spill off every surface. She grabs a tray of glasses and hands them to me. "Bring those out to the garden," she says. "I'll fix some punch with your gin."

I step out the back door, expecting a patio, or at least a backyard. Instead, I find a wild spray of flowers with a small stone path that leads to an armored gate with climbing vines. I hear voices, so I step through and am shocked to find myself in a wonderland—long winding paths and sinewy trees, little benches along the way, and here in the middle, under a giant old apple tree, a table full of fairies.

"Is this what I think it is?" I look around, amazed. "This is my secret garden! I came here with Theo when we were kids!" It is. It's amazing. I had no idea.

"You came!" A tiny woman with pink hair and a Scottish accent bounces up and hugs me. "I'm Glory." She is five hundred years old, tiny, and wearing an actual tiara. "Sit down." She pushes me into a chair with surprising force. "Say hello," she instructs the others, gesturing around.

"I'm Peg," says a long-haired woman wearing a caftan. She's smoking—yup, a joint. "Resident witch."

"Oh!" I try to sound less surprised. "Excellent."

Peg holds out the joint. "Want some?"

"Oh! No, no thanks." She instantly withdraws, offended. "Weed just doesn't agree with me . . . I tend to overreact to it." Peg sniffs. I have clearly failed somehow.

"I'm Ron," says a giant man with a very long gray beard.

"We're lovers," says Peg. "But it's casual."

Ron nods solemnly.

"Wow, okay, good . . . boundaries," I say. I've been here five minutes, and this is the most sex, drugs, and rock and roll I've experienced in years. And I work in television.

"They've been casual for twelve years," says Barb, returning with a pitcher of punch, which looks like mostly a lot of ice cubes and flowers.

"We were married for thirty-five years before that, but it wasn't working out," says Ron, downing his teacup and holding it out for Barb to fill with punch. She fills all the teacups, clearly forgetting the glasses I just brought out. I take a sip. I choke.

"Whoa, this is . . ." Straight gin.

Barb beams. "My special recipe," she says. "Gin and ice and flowers for decoration." Oh, wow. She sits down and passes the plate of the fairy bites around. "The girl brought these. They are for fairies."

"They are fairy bites," I clarify. "They're just from the bakery." They nod in approval, mouths full. I take another sip of, well, gin. It's not exactly Will's cider. I can still taste it. The thought warms me. "So, do you own this garden, Barb?"

"Some of it," she says. "Glory lives on the other side. We opened our backyards up years ago. There was this big unclaimed green space between them, and over the years it's become a community project."

"How lovely," I say. "It's amazing to see it again."

"So, Miranda Belmont," says Barb, all business. "We have brought you here, into our inner sanctum."

"Circle!" says Glory.

"Coven," says Peg.

"We have brought you here under false pretenses."

"Well, for starters," I say, "this isn't tea." I hold up my cup of gin. They laugh.

"I have to say," says Barb, "I didn't think you'd be this friendly. You're such a cold fish in rehearsal." That stings, but it's fair.

"It's complicated," I start to say, but they all nod as though this is sufficient explanation.

"As I was saying"—Barb takes the reins back—"we brought you here because we need your help."

"Okay?" I'm intrigued.

"The play is doomed," blurts Glory.

"Oh!" I say. "I know there's been some weird stuff, but . . ."

"No," says Peg. "That Nick Nolan is nothing but trouble. He's bringing bad energy."

I burst out laughing, but looking around the table, I realize that's not the vibe.

"Um," I say. "What? Nick is stupid, but he's, you know, harmless." Unless you date him.

"There are no signs yet," admits Glory. "But Ron heard him whistling."

"So?"

They look at me, stricken. "Backstage," whispers Glory. "That's bad luck."

"And I saw him walk under a ladder yesterday to get around the set painting," says Barb.

"Bad luck," says Glory.

"And when someone warned him, he just laughed." Peg sets down her teacup and sighs. "I . . . We are concerned that he's a liability."

"I . . . Listen, Nick's a TV guy, he doesn't know all the superstitions. I'm sure he didn't mean any of that." Defending Nick hurts my brain, but it seems like the thing to do.

"That's the problem. He doesn't know and he doesn't take it seriously," says Peg. "What's next? Unplugging the ghost light? Saying '*Macbeth*' in the theater?" Even I never say "*Macbeth*" in the theater.

"And this thing with poor Will, kicking him out like that," Peg adds. "Taking a role from a loyal, talented member of our community."

They all start to talk over each other.

"Will is such a good boy."

"The dearest boy—"

"And so handsome."

"Mira, do you think he's handsome?"

"He's single, you know."

"Hush, Glory!"

"Well, he is!"

"And what your parents have done—"

"That weasel from the television, he can't even act!"

"To say nothing of your mother carrying on with—"

"Hush, Glory!"

"It's disappointing, is what it is." Ron frowns. They nod in agreement.

"Wait, what about my mother?" I ask.

"Never mind."

I let it go, for now.

"Naturally we're very worried," says Glory earnestly.

I look at their faces. They look serious as death. Again, I need to resist the urge to laugh at them. "And you all believe in this?" I ask.

"Oh, dearie," Barb chastens me. "You can't mess around with theater." The others nod sagely.

"Well, okay. Be that as it may. And I have to be honest, respectfully, I don't have a ton of experience believing in this stuff." Though, come to think of it, it would explain the last month of my life. "What exactly are you hoping I can do for you?"

Glory claps her hands. "Yes! Good! We need your help."

"We just ask that you keep an eye on things for us. You're friends with Nick, right? Could you talk to him?"

I don't know how to answer. "We work together, yes," I say. "We aren't friends exactly. I can try." It's a lie. I can barely talk to Nick about the scenes we're doing, let alone school him in theater superstitions.

"Just try to keep a lid on him, if you can," says Peg. "How well, exactly, do you know him?"

I sit back. "Um, well enough," I demur. "But sure, I can try."

"Good," says Peg. Glory claps, and Barb and Ron high-five. Quite the crew indeed. "Thank you. I'm glad that it's settled."

"Fairy bite?" offers Barb. I take one. It tastes like cherries and almonds.

"So, Ron," I say. "Which fairy do you play?"

"Peaseblossom," says Ron, with zero irony.

"Have some more punch, dearie!" Glory fills my glass without waiting for an answer.

They are lunatics. I think I'm in love.

Chapter 16

Six weeks until Opening Night

Theo has a crush on Max, which means we are meeting Max and Bailey at the lake on our day off under the guise of cast bonding, or something. I assumed meeting at the lake meant the main beach along the waterfront, or even one of the smaller neighborhood beaches, but he picks me up and we drive down one of the long cottage roads out of town to a small dirt parking lot where Max and Bailey are waiting for us. And Will.

"You didn't tell me Will was coming," I murmur. He waves as we pull in, our eyes catching briefly through the window.

"Didn't I?" says Theo. "I thought you guys got along." He's being overly cheerful and not quite looking at me.

"We do," I say. "Sure we do." He smiles to himself. "Jeez, Theo, what?"

"Nothing," he says innocently as we get out. "Can't I just surround myself with beautiful men?"

"Sure you can," I say. "As long as they're just for you."

"How dare you insinuate otherwise," he says with a wink. I know then exactly what he's up to.

We greet the others, hugs and high fives, even though most of us saw each other yesterday at rehearsal. Bailey hugs Will, and I wonder if I should. I stand there awkwardly and give him a little wave. He laughs and gives me a quick squeeze. He smells of sunscreen and clean laundry.

"Let's go! It's just a short hike from here!" says Bailey, as if this is good news.

"Hike? I thought we were going to the beach?" I look down at my flip-flops.

"No," says Theo. "I said we were going swimming." He gives me his most charming smile and hands me a small cooler. "That's the booze, Mirabel, don't drop it." I nearly stagger under the weight. I look around for a chivalrous man to offer to carry it for me, but they are all heading up the path with their own gear.

It is a short hike, but it is steep and awkward, and I'm wearing the wrong shoes. Max takes pity on me and hoists the cooler up over a particularly ragged set of rocks. The rest of them practically skip up with me sweating and swearing behind them. The last stretch is nearly all rock, no path at all, and I look around helplessly for a way around it when a hand reaches down. I look up. Will.

"I've got you." He smiles and hoists me up easily. When I stumble to the top and look around, I see why we're here. It's not the big lake at all, but a small lake nearby, shimmering in the sunlight, surrounded by trees and high rocks, including the wide sloping one we are on, which pools out at the water's edge into a sort of smooth rock beach. There is no one here but us.

"Oh, wow."

"Indeed!" says Theo, removing his shirt with conspicuous aplomb, and yes, I catch Max noticing. I smile to myself until I see Theo run toward the edge of the rock and leap off, and then I scream.

"What the fuck!" I shriek, running toward the edge. "Theodore Raymond, if you drown yourself, I will kill you!"

Will comes up beside me, laughing. "He's fine." He pats my arm. Sure enough, Theo comes up, sputtering, laughing. Will applauds, whooping. He's loose here. I like it.

"Isn't it, like, terribly dangerous?" I ask.

"We've been coming here since we were kids," Will says. "Obviously I do not support my friends just leaping from anywhere." He looks at me. "You gonna try it?"

"Oh, no. No, thank you. Absolutely not."

"Didn't you grow up here?" asks Bailey, peering over the edge. "Aren't you used to doing things like this?"

"I was more of an indoor cat," I say primly.

I step away from the edge and make my way down to the water to set up my towel. Next to me, Will peels off his shirt, revealing his full sleeves of tattoos and a few scattered across his (oh, wow) surprisingly toned torso, and one by itself, over his heart. I feel caught somehow with his naked chest in front of me, my eyes roaming. "I like that one." I point to the jagged line over his heart.

"Oh, yeah! It was my first one." A heartbeat.

"Isn't it a little on the nose, though, to get your heartbeat on your heart?" I say, trying to sound coy.

"It's not mine," he says vaguely, then seems to reconsider. "This is Jonah's."

"Oh." God, that's sweet. "Oh, wow. And he . . . ?"

"Yeah, he had mine." He smiles, a sliver of sadness way back in his eyes.

"That's so lovely." What a wonder, that there used to be two of him. What a loss.

"Yeah." He shrugs.

"Yeah." What else do I say? "I'm sorry."

"Don't worry about it." He smiles in that practiced way of people who have lost someone.

Without thinking, I reach out and trace the line tentatively with my finger. He looks surprised but doesn't move. His skin is satin smooth. We stand there staring at each other. We are interrupted by a loud shriek and a splash as Bailey leaps off the cliff. I jump back as if my hand is on fire. We turn to watch her resurface, and the moment is broken.

We have all cobbled a picnic together, and I find the small cooler I hauled to be full of ice-cold cider from Will. He hands me a dripping can and our fingers touch. "This one is my take on a margarita. I think you'll like it." He smiles, some little something now sparked between us, a tether I want to pull toward me. He throws Theo a can as I crack mine open. It shocks my throat in that perfect bubbly summer way, and he's right, I love it. I seem to love everything this guy gives me.

We lie in the sun, the others taking turns jumping off the rocks. We open more cider and gulp it greedily in the heat. Max passes a joint around; I refuse again. The last thing we need is me on an acid trip from a single puff. Theo has brought a small nylon pouch that opens up into a hammock, which he sets up between the trees for a nap. Bailey has brought a book, and Max has brought his script. I only brought one swimsuit from the city, a basic, scooped navy tank with a plunging back. Bailey is in a baby-blue crocheted bikini. I wish I were wearing something cuter.

I am hot, the sun is bright, and I feel my skin burning. I reach into my bag for sunscreen, and without a word, Will holds out his hand. The half smile. I hand it to him and slowly turn my back toward him.

"Thanks," I say as casually as I can muster.

"Sure." He places his hands on my back gently, rubbing the lotion in, carefully avoiding getting too close to the edges of my suit.

"It's okay," I say. "You can . . ." He clears his throat, pausing for a moment before he moves his fingers under the edges of my suit. Suddenly I am aware of exactly how plunging it is. The last man who touched me was Nick. We don't speak. When he is finished, he pats my face with finality, as if to break whatever tension is brewing.

"All done!"

"Thanks," I say. "Do you . . . Should I . . . ?"

"Nah, I'm good," he says. I can't see his eyes behind his sunglasses. I wish I could.

I lie face down on my towel, and he lies next to me. I see my face reflected in his lenses. I wonder if he likes me. As if reading my mind, he takes the glasses off and looks at me.

"Hey," he says. He smiles at me.

"Hey." My heart is racing.

"I'm glad we're hanging out." He pauses. "Finally."

"Yeah, me too!" I say too brightly. He makes me nervous. I swallow hard. "Totally." My body is buzzing—the heat, the cider, him. I glance over at Max and Bailey, reading on their chairs. I look back at Will. He has rolled onto his back, one arm slung lazily under his head.

"Tell me about your tattoos," I say. He laughs. "I know that sounds like a pickup line or something."

"Are you trying to pick me up, Mirabel?"

"Hey." I point right in his face. "Only one person gets to call me that."

"Yeah, yeah, I know. I was trying it out."

"Mirabel has to be earned."

"Yeah." He looks at me closely. "Yeah, I know she does."

"Hey," I say. "You're not in the play anymore."

He smiles slowly. "I am not."

"That's interesting."

"Sure is."

I'm a tiny bit tipsy, and the sun is too bright, and there is a half-naked man on a beach towel next to me who promised to kiss me when we were seventeen. I have the slow-burning sense that I may be in trouble here. I have half a vision of rolling over, pulling him toward me, tipping my mouth to his, slipping my tongue across his . . . I glance over quickly, in case my mind somehow projected my thoughts above me, in case I am as transparent as I feel. Will is still on his back, eyes covered, a small smile on his lips.

I need to cool off. I sit up, then stand up, then walk toward the edge of the rock, a lower spot than where Theo jumped, and slip into the water. It's a delicious jolt after the heat. I swim out as far away from him as I can, the sun obscuring the horizon. When I turn around, Will is sitting up, watching me, and suddenly, it's inevitable: I swim slowly back to shore, watching him as he stands. The rocks where we sat are smooth and flat, jutting out to a small point. Off to one side is a small alcove obscured by a cluster of bushes at the water's edge. I tilt my head in that direction, a question. An invitation. Will walks slowly into the water. Our eyes don't leave each other. He slips around the rock point into the alcove, out of sight of the others, waist deep and waiting for me. My heart is racing, the heat, the cider, and then a near explosion when I arrive and he pulls me into him. We collide, our mouths meet, his hands are in my hair, lake water running down our faces, my hands running over his body. I have wanted to kiss him for so long. I am helpless and hungry, pulling him in closer. I push my knee between his legs and feel him hard against me. His hands rake my rib cage, sliding down my ass. We are drowning in each other. We pull back, and he looks at me, almost alarmed, then kisses me again more deeply, more tenderly, so beautifully that I can't stand it. I push him away. He stumbles back in the water, and we stare at each other, chests heaving, breathless.

"I can't," I say. "I'm sorry."

"I'm sorry," he says. "I thought . . . It seemed like you . . ."

"No, I did, I do, I'm . . . ugh." I push my wet hair off my face. "I . . . I don't know. I can't. I'm sorry." Whatever I am feeling right now feels completely dangerous. I've never felt anything like it. It's terrifying.

He steps back, his face hurt, confused. "Okay." He rubs his face. "I—I just can't tell what you want from me, Mira."

I may spend the rest of my life regretting it, but for now, all I can do is shrug and sigh and swim away.

Chapter 17

Five and a half weeks until Opening Night

Sometimes I wonder if I really have a passion for theater, or if it's just habit. I was raised in rehearsals, watching my parents' work. I did my homework backstage and was brought up by theater people. I don't mean my parents; their general attitude to me was similar to that of a structural column onstage that can't be moved so must be worked around. I think they had a child because it seemed like a thing people should do, except that they didn't know what a child even was. I was outsourced to kindly costume ladies who taught me how to do simple mending, or patient stage managers who let me sit beside them, coloring, or later, when I could read, following the scripts for line prompts. On summer break, they never sent me to camp or day care.

"There's no better education than the theater!" my mother announced.

"But it's summer," I'd whine. "I already was educated all year!"

"That sentence structure suggests otherwise," my father would pipe in and then return to his script.

Summer, at least, had musicals, with the high school kids who I thought were so cool. I would follow the choreographer around and stand in the back of the dance studio, and by the end of the summer, they always moved me to the front for the other kids to watch. It wasn't that I was an especially good dancer—I lacked everything that makes a dancer watchable in terms of fire and grace—but I had a meticulous memory for detail. I could see that dance, not just my own body following movements, but I could envision it as if from above. I knew innately how all the bodies needed to move in space. I could see the big picture. I guess Jess, the choreographer, commented on it to my parents because at dinner one day they asked me if I wanted to take dance classes.

"I had hoped your tastes ran more classical, but I suppose a background in musical theater never hurt anyone," my father said with the bland disappointment of a former college football player with a passionate badminton player for a child.

"I don't want to," I said. "Thank you." It was so rare that my parents took real interest in me, I didn't want to take it for granted.

"Ballet is classical," my mother said.

"I like helping Jess. But I don't think dance is actually my thing."

"You're an actor," my mother said, apropos of nothing, since so far, I had only done two very mediocre school plays. "You need to focus on your craft."

I was eight.

Rehearsals have entered full swing. Nick continues to be an idiot, but many people are still completely charmed by him. I keep thinking about Will, wishing it were him instead, grateful that it isn't too. Whatever Will is, he is best kept at a distance. Whatever that was between us is too big, too much for me to possibly deal with. I can't let another man ruin me. I have a job to do here. I need to focus.

Nick has dialed down the Shakespeare voice, still doesn't understand the difference between upstage and downstage, and whispers things backstage that he hopes will win me back. I pretend that his voice in my ear doesn't send my whole body into an old shiver of pleasure. But aside from that, we are all finding our groove.

The whole time we were together, Nick would introduce me as his "date," which was sometimes funny if we were at a work event where everyone knew me already. It was acceptable in public for a while, but then we were closing in on four months, five months, and I was spending several nights a week at his condo. We were more and more in each other's lives, and it grated on me. The whole time we were together, he insisted that he wasn't cut out for anything serious, that he could never fully commit, which was fine with me, because like all women, I believed that this wouldn't apply to me, that I would break the cycle.

I knew the rules, and I caught feelings anyway. Tale as old as time.

It wasn't totally my fault. We would be lying in the bath together, veins thick with my favorite wine that he'd brought, and he would wash my hair so gently, kiss my temples, and say, "Dammit, Mira, maybe we could really be something? I can half see it, you and me, in LA, tearing up the town, going to galas . . . getting out of fucking Toronto and just really going for it."

He didn't say these things to me so much as near me, within earshot, but I drank them up. They were just further confirmation that I would be the one to break through.

To what end, though? I knew deep down that he was an idiot, that he never remembered people's names even though he'd worked with them for three years. He never ever had oat milk for my coffee at his place because he drank his black, even though I spent several mornings a week there. I knew that he was talented in the way that is entertaining. He was grandiose, cocky in a way that was appealing on-screen. People love a despicable lead. But I also knew that he gave zero thought to what he was doing, that as soon as someone called "cut," he had no reverence for the work. He had done it, so it was good. Whereas I would play a take over and over in my head, re-blocking it, rewriting scenes in my head that I knew were half-assed, because they had been written on a napkin twenty minutes before we shot them. Nick, in all capacities, was blissfully unbothered. And when the next chance came for him to go to LA, he didn't actually want me there.

Which is why I am surprised that he is actually doing this play. I thought he would bail. I thought he would be a caricature of himself and bumble off into the sunset after the first two weeks. He's not particularly good. I'll give him this: He has found his genre, as my father would say, which is that he plays the role like he's in an action movie, stomping around and pushing Lysander and being sexually threatening to Helena. And sure, that's all there in the script. He is just completely without nuance or depth. I'm surprised that he seems to genuinely want me; he is trying to be sweet to me, opening doors and offering to run lines with me. As if I need his help. There is still a physical pull to him, but it's funny: Being here, in a different place with different people around us, I am somehow blessedly immune to him. I know what a disaster he is for me. Funny, that he and Will are both so different, yet both so differently dangerous.

Nick has taken to doing little speeches before rehearsal, which infuriates my father but seems to have a rallying effect on the rest of the cast and crew. It's as close to a football coach as possible, with some name-droppy anecdotes about Hollywood, life as a TV star, all the stuff that the locals eat up. At rehearsal he is never alone; he is always swarmed by fans, who are now daring to consider themselves friends with him, and I know that this is his investment, so people will say, *Nick Nolan was just the best guy, so down-to-earth, so funny, so jacked, so handsome.* That is the oxygen Nick Nolan survives on. This is why the man has no need of real relationships. His superficial ones give him so much. He has also made a regular joke out of whistling backstage, because it gets such a rise out of everyone.

He takes it all a step further in today's opening remarks. "Folks, you have made me feel so welcome here, and I'm just loving being a part of your community. We have all been working really hard on this show, and I'm really proud of us."

Someone starts to clap in the back. "Yeah! Yeah, that's it, that's right!" A few more join in, and suddenly he has the frenetic energy of a youth pastor.

He pulses his hands: *Calm down*. "So I was thinking you all might like to join me at my cottage for a little social gathering this weekend, some beers, barbecue, campfire." He is pandering so hard. Beers? The man only drinks red wine over sixty dollars as a personal rule. "All are welcome, bring your sweetheart." Jesus, he is fully invested in this down-home local-boy thing. "I've got everything else covered. Hope to see you there!" He pauses dramatically. "Oh, and friends, it's a *costume* party! Theme is Shakes-peah!" Now there is wild applause, a few people looking at each other wild-eyed that they have a personal invitation to enter the big star's domain. He bows dramatically, catching my eye. I look away. "Okay, now let's get onstage and give it a hundred and ten percent!" He fist-pumps and the group cheers and disperses.

"Oh, hello, I did want to discuss some of the merging themes in act two," my father calls out, but the team is loose and ready to play.

The fairies don't so much call me over as draw me to them with their eyes.

"Morning, ladies," I say. "Ron."

"Oh, Ronnie's one of us girls," says Glory, and Ron smiles pleasantly.

"So, obviously I am not attending Nick's soiree," I say.

"Ohhhhh, no, you have to!" says Glory. "We need you to!"

"You're all invited," I say. "You go!"

"Oh, we are, dear. We're going to light up!" Glory beams.

"Do you mean light up, like, a joint?"

"No, she means get lit," says Peg.

"We will make a cameo," says Barb. "People like it when old people party." This is true.

"But we need you on the inside," says Peg. "To keep a lid on him."

"Yeah, guys, I just, I see how this is a really fun opportunity for . . ."

"The 'locals'?" says Barb.

"Ha! Well, yes?"

"And you are royalty in this scenario?" Peg has a tightness in her voice that I don't love.

"I'm just a regular gal who has been forced to socialize with Nick Nolan enough to fill a dozen lifetimes, and a night off wouldn't kill me." They don't need to know how much of that socializing was conducted in the nude.

"Unless it does," whispers Glory. "He's trouble." She raises her eyebrows in what I think she thinks is an ominous way.

"You're our eyes and ears on the floor," Ron says, even though we are all on the same floor.

"We'll see you there." Barb pats my arm, a confirmation, and I wonder why I have let a band of septuagenarians bully me.

I make my way backstage for rehearsal. I slip behind the curtain leg upstage right, in place for my entrance, and notice my parents off to the side, out of sight from the audience. They are whisper-fighting. Mom has her hands on her hips, Dad is pointing at her, furious. I can't tell what they are saying. I have rarely seen them like this; they often bicker but never fight. She throws her hands up and storms off to her entrance spot. I watch my father: He stands there for a long moment, shoulders slumped. He rubs his face wearily, sighs heavily, then bolsters himself and makes his way across the stage and into the audience, calling, "Places!"

Chapter 18

Five weeks until Opening Night

After theater school, I didn't see Theo for years. I was twenty-six and living in the city. I managed to get an agent a year after our program ended, my ill-fated showcase audition still haunting me, and he was sending me to every audition in the city. No theater stuff, but I was still young enough to feel that it was on the horizon. I was a serious actor; eventually, people would see. The problem was, my agent only sent me out for TV spots, barely a step above extra work. I went out for a lot of commercials and saw a lot of the same people out for the same stuff I was. There was a sort of collective humbling: I saw a girl who won awards for her one-woman *Antigone* at the Fringe Festival the prior summer enthusiastically trying to sell dog food, and I couldn't judge. I just tried to sell it more enthusiastically than her. I wasn't getting much, nobody was, and there was the dream of theater: The rejection still felt aspirational, rather than the soul-sucking drudgery that was to come a few years later. Theo, meanwhile, was a rising star. He seemed to be making his way through all Toronto's independent theaters, to be always working. He invited me to everything, but I never went. His success only reminded me of my failure.

I ran into him just once, at the opening night party of an indie theater play a classmate of ours was in. I had been moving in the Toronto theater scene haunted by the fact that I knew, one day, we would run into each other. And here, it finally happened. I saw him across the room. My heart leaped and my stomach sank. His eyes lit up when he saw me, and he rushed over and threw his arms around me.

"Mirabel! I'm so happy to see you! I always sort of hope I'll find you at one of these things!" He was warm, open, bubbling over. It had been four years. I was two drinks in.

"Oh, hey, yeah, good to see you," I said, gingerly returning his hug.

"So, what are you up to? How's life? How's work?" He was like a puppy.

"Yeah, pretty good, pretty busy. Auditioning a lot. I booked a commercial for Tide." If he knew that was two years ago, he didn't say so.

"So cool, good for you! Yeah, auditioning sucks, but that's the gig, huh?"

"Totally," I said. "What about you?" I asked, hoping like hell that he too was barely scraping by.

"Uh, yeah, good," he said. A shy smile crept across his face. "I, uh, it's not out yet, but I actually just got a gig."

"Oh, cool." My heart sank. "A commercial?"

He looked at his shoes, and when he looked up, his eyes were shining. "Stratford."

I swallowed hard. "Stratford?" The Stratford Festival was our shared dream. In tenth grade, we had gone with our English class to see *Man of La Mancha*. We held hands as we watched it, our hearts pounding. Theater! Real theater! Real actors! The whole ride home, we planned our escape from North Lake. We would go there together. We would live there for the season. We would get married and be the Great Canadian Theater Power Couple. I kept that last one to myself, but it was no less part of the plan. "Stratford," I said again, trying to sound normal.

"Yeah," he said. "They signed me on for two seasons."

"That's amazing," I said too loudly, taking a big swig of my drink, spilling it a little. "So, what roles did they give you to start with?"

"Well. Um. Romeo, actually." He looked at me carefully, catching on that I might not be as happy for him as he hoped.

"Romeo." I almost whispered it. The thought of him doing Romeo again, without me, made me want to throw up. I took another drink. "Good for you."

"I'm sorry," he said.

"No, I'm happy for you." My voice was tight, and he was wise enough to let it go.

"Listen, do you want to go get a drink or something?" he asked finally. "I think a few of the cast are going out . . ."

"Oh." I pretended to look around me for some phantom acquaintance to excuse me. "I'm actually heading to a party after this."

"Oh!" he said. "That sounds cool."

"It's, uh, this guy I'm seeing. I'm not sure it's cool if I bring someone." Disappointment flickered ever so briefly, but he recovered quickly. Ever the actor.

"Oh, no, totally, actually, I think my friends are heading out too."

"Totally, cool, well, great to see you!" I hugged him quickly and turned away before he could say, *What about coffee or brunch, or see a play sometime?* There was no other party. There certainly was no other guy. I wanted to make him jealous, if not romantically, then at least I wanted to appear in demand, busy and important. But I wasn't. The truth was I couldn't stand to be near him. Everything about him made me feel like shit: his success, his talent, the ease with which he had just slipped into actor life. I was still taking shifts as a cater-waiter to pay rent. We were supposed to have succeeded together, but here I was, a total failure. And worst of all, against all reason, I was still marred: He didn't, would never, love me. I knew how foolish it was, how pathetic, that my best romantic relationship to date had been with a gay man. But still, no one seemed to live up to him.

I walked out alone and threw up in a garbage can in the alley next to the theater. I wiped my mouth and stalked off down the street. I heard his footsteps before I heard him.

"Mirabel!" I kept walking. "Mirabel, wait!" I sighed and stopped. I didn't turn around.

He came around to face me. "What are you doing?"

"I'm leaving. I'm going home."

"You said you were going to a party."

"I lied, okay?" I snapped. "There is no party."

"You just don't want to talk to me." His voice was soft. I didn't answer. "You've barely talked to me since school. You don't come to my shows. And I tell you my dream is coming true, and you literally run out of the building." I stared straight ahead, not looking at him. "Are you really that, I don't know, selfish? Are you really so immature that you can't be happy for me?"

"I guess I am," I said flatly.

"Well, fuck that!" he said. "Fuck this, and fuck you!" He started to walk away, reconsidered, and spun back to me. "You are one of the best actors I know. Okay, yes, you have had a couple of setbacks, and what? You just give up? That's fine if it's working for you, Miranda, but you still need to be happy for me." Miranda. He'd never called me that before. It felt like a slap. It felt like losing him.

"No, I don't." I could feel our whole history splitting apart in slow motion, and it was all my fault.

"You do. It's always been you and me, and you just ditched me, and now you're acting like my success is some, like, personal attack on you. And that's bullshit." I'd never seen him so angry. "I earned this. I'm allowed to be successful, and it's not my fault you're not, but a good friend wouldn't do whatever the hell this is."

"We aren't friends," I said. "We haven't been friends for years." I watched his face crumple. I stepped aside, around him, my heart thrumming resolutely as I walked away.

In the morning I called my agent.

"Please stop sending me out for these TV things," I said. "I'm a theater actor. I want to do theater."

He was quiet. Too quiet. "I've been trying," he said. "The showcase . . . I think it kind of sank you." There was a long pause. "I'm sorry, Mira, but I don't think it's going to happen. Not here in Toronto anyway."

"Oh," I said, my eyes filling fast. I could only squeak the one word out.

"I'm sorry." He was kind. "But there's this new pilot that just came through. A real estate thing. I actually just sent you the sides."

That show, of course, was *Listings*.

I hate costume parties as a rule, which surprises people. "But you're an actor!" I just don't enjoy looking like an idiot unless I'm being paid for it.

But this is a theater people party, and I'm part of an ensemble and trying to shrug off the "semi-famous-director's daughter" notoriety, so I allow Theo to outfit me from the Tempest costume warehouse. He has decided we should come as a pair. I used to love it here when I was a kid. Some kids have dress-up boxes; I had an entire storage unit. Even now, it has a certain magic. Theo and I move up and down the racks, pulling out crazy costumes, adding pieces to each other's outfits. By the time we reach the Shakespeare racks, I am wearing a fedora and a feather boa, and Theo is wearing a satin cape and a tutu. He pulls out a sword.

"Should we give this to Nick?"

"Ha!" I say. "No. He'll think it's a romantic gesture." I start to sift through the racks. We have done a Shakespeare every year at Tempest, so it's quite the collection. "Please let me be Lady Macbeth!" I beg. "Or we could be the twins from *Twelfth Night*?" Theo stares down at me from his great height and pats my head.

"Yes, Mirabel, we would absolutely pass for twins." He pulls out a garment bag. "No, my darling. We are kicking it old school." He is holding up my Juliet costume. "One night only, baby."

"No, Theo! Romeo and Juliet is so basic!"

"Most of the literary world would disagree," he says, pulling out a second bag. "And anyway, it's our show. Do you think I will fit into my old tights?"

"This is . . . ugh." I hold up the bag and rummage through it. "I'm not wearing a corset to a social event." I feel my chest. What little boobs I had in my teens have shrunk to nothing thanks to barre class. "Not that I need to." In the bag are the three velvet and brocade dresses I wore in the show, one still bloodstained from my dagger scene, but there is one more item at the bottom. "Oh, hey!" I pull it out, a long cream satin slip dress with cross back straps and a delicate vintage lace bodice with a ribbon tie. "The bedroom scene!" This was made by hand for me; it was the first garment that I ever felt really beautiful in.

Theo's face lights up, and he pulls out the white muslin tunic and leggings he had worn.

"Theme is postcoital R&J?"

"Yes!"

I add a thin gold headband and a long, dainty strand of pearls, like in the famous Waterhouse painting of Juliet. Theo emerges from behind a clothes rack in his costume.

"What do you think?" he says. "Not bad, huh?" He looks like a painting himself. Where once stood a very beautiful, tall, skinny boy is now a grown man with a personal trainer and chest hair.

"What a dreamboat," I say. "You're absolutely sure you're gay?" He does a twirl and winks at me. "Oh, yup, okay, there it is."

"So," he says. "You kissed Will, huh?"

"He told you?"

"No. He would never." That's a relief. "I, uh, saw. I got up to get a drink, and the cooler was down by the rocks . . ."

"Ah. Shit."

"So, what's going on?"

"Nothing." I smooth the fabric of my dress.

"Mira . . ."

I face away from him, but he catches my eye in the mirror. "I dated my last costar, and it fucked up my whole life."

"Will's not your costar."

"Yeah, but he's around the play. He's always at the theater doing set stuff, and I just feel like it's a bad idea."

Theo comes around and gently lays his head on top of mine like the sweet, giant puppy he is. "And what's the real reason?"

I shrug him off me. "Nothing."

"Mira."

"Ugh, fine, the real reason is he gave me very big feelings, okay? Like, scary big. And I am not accustomed to big, scary feelings and I'm a coward and I'm only here for the summer. I don't need anything complicated."

"Well," he says. "Good for you. Sounds perfectly uncomplicated."

Theo picks me up again a few hours later. Waiting on my front porch dressed as Sexy Juliet, I feel like Drew Barrymore in *Never Been Kissed*. Or *Ever After*. Or both. I feel dreamy and nervous. I do not want to attend anything with Nick ever, but also . . . I feel pretty, for once. I have my sweet friend with me, and the fairies are counting on me to be their spy.

Chapter 19

There is a lot swirling in me as we pull up to Nick's cottage. We arrive two hours later than the invitation said, just to be cool. He said bring nothing, so I have brought an expensive bottle of wine that I know he hates as a sort of an elegant flex. He throws open the door.

"Well, hey there!" He is booming before he sees us, his greeting for all his new besties, but when he notices it's us, he drops the act. He is dressed as Hamlet with a skull in his hand, a neon straw sticking out of it.

"Oh, hey. Jesus, Mira, you look amazing." He looks between us. "Oh, oh, I know this, you're, um, the ones who die."

"Way to narrow it down," I say, but Theo is friendlier.

"Yeah, Romeo and Juliet! Mira and I did this play the summer before college."

Nick narrows his eyes. "Well. That's adorable," he says. "You wore a couples costume to my party."

"We did." I place a hand on Theo's chest. "Theo and I have a lot of history." Nick looks at Theo, scowling for a moment, sizing up his competition.

"I'm the skull dude!" He holds out the skull. "Vodka tonic?"

"Who's your friend, Nick?" I ask, gesturing to the skull, which any theater person will tell you is Yorick the clown.

"Uh . . . Doug?" He laughs like this is a very clever name for a skull full of vodka.

Theo laughs awkwardly. A group of people arrive behind us, and Theo and I slip inside while Nick does his host routine.

Tempest puts up the visiting actors for the summer, but the accommodations are modest. Nick opted to rent out his own place. It's a spectacular cottage: five bedrooms, a built-in hot tub off a long wraparound deck facing the lake. It's set back from the road and surrounded by woods. I heard him mention trails nearby. It's beautiful but flashy, too much. It's very Nick.

Theo and I make our way into the kitchen. The fairies are gathered around the punch bowl, dressed as the Weird Sisters from *Macbeth*. Even Ron.

"Oh, look, the star-cross'd lovers!" cries Glory.

"Glory gets it," I say. "Have you seen Nick's costume? He doesn't know who Hamlet is."

"Philistine," snarls Peg, and for once I agree with her.

"Want some of our special brew, dearies?" warbles Barb.

"How special?" I don't trust them. "I know how you roll, Barb."

"Extra gin."

"Then yes, please." She hands me a cup.

"Barb, why is there a gummy worm in this?"

"We wanted something that resembled rats' tails, for authenticity . . ."

"Ah. Of course."

"And I made brownies!" Glory holds out a plate. "They're vegan." The brownies look a little iffy, but I take one to be polite and take a small bite.

"Oh, Glory, these are actually . . . these are really good!" I realize I haven't eaten all day.

"Have another!" I do. "The secret is a whole bottle of vanilla."

"Oh, wow, okay. So"—I lean in—"what's the scoop. Are you lit, Barb?" I'm already feeling a little revived by a couple of brownies and Barb's punch. Maybe it will be a good night after all.

"I'm not lit," Barb says. "I decided to play it cool. I don't want to arouse suspicion."

"Oh, yes, four seniors dressed as witches circling a punch bowl with gummy rat tails is a super casual look," I say.

"Sassy!" says Ron. He looks perpetually amused.

"Okay, top me up, I'm going to do a turn around the room," I say. Barb adds extra worms to my glass, pats my ass, and sends me off into the party.

It is always a good idea to arrive two hours late to a party: People are in full swing and are usually already tipsy, so they don't notice if you are socially awkward. This is my thesis, anyway. There are a lot of people dressed as fairies, a predictable, easy costume, but all the glitter adds a certain sense of occasion. Some people are dressed just vaguely Elizabethan. The lighting guy is wearing the same *South Park* shirt he always wears. I mingle a bit, making small talk. At least costume parties give you something to talk about. Theo has already been absorbed by the room, and I am without an ally. I glance back at the fairies, who are conspicuously staring right at me. Glory gives a very overt thumbs-up.

I make my way around the room, clocking my mother in the corner with Arthur, her hand on his knee, heads bent together. They look like naughty children, whispering and giggling. Weird. I don't love the look of it. I pass by the open patio door and spot Theo and Max leaning against the edge of the deck, looking very flirty indeed. I smile. I'm glad to see Theo happy. My dad is in another corner with two of the mechanicals, earnestly discussing which words Shakespeare added to the English language. I stand there for a long time, listening to them. Words, words . . . words. For some reason, my brain feels . . . slow.

I've only had the one drink, but it's hitting me hard. I don't realize that I'm dizzy until someone catches my arm.

"Hey there." It's Will. My heart leaps.

"What are you doing here?" He looks . . . good. He's wearing jeans and a white button-down and a vest with aviators and . . . a Shakespeare wig. "Oh. Ha! I get it. Will is . . . Will." Somehow even with a skullet, he looks . . . shiny.

"I mean, I'm still part of the show," he says. "I was, you know, invited." I look at him blankly. "Set builders are people too."

"You just keep . . . being places." I'm feeling a little fuzzy.

"That's the thing about people." He looks at me closely. "You good? You look a little . . ."

"I'm really hungry," I say suddenly. "I need food." I turn and leave for the kitchen, and he follows me. I haven't seen him since the lake, the kiss . . . I don't know how to be.

The fairies are still gathered in the kitchen.

"Oh, hey, have you met my fairies?" They chuckle and Barb winks at Will. Cheeky. "Fairies, have you met my . . . cider man?" They look at each other, amused by something. I don't know what. I find a baked goat cheese and tuck in. "This is amazing. Who made this? I need the recipe. Oh, no. I need to learn to cook."

Peg and Barb exchange a glance. "Oh, hell!" cries Glory. "Shit balls. Now I've done it."

"What?" I ask, but I'm not really listening. I'm pretty busy eating, and she seems very far away on the other side of the counter.

"Um," says Glory, "the brownies."

"What about the brownies?" asks Will.

"Glory uses a whole bottle of vanilla," says Barb.

"Okay? I mean, that's a little heavy-handed but . . . so?" Will keeps looking at me. Will likes me. I probably like him. I'm not allowed to like him.

Peg exhales heavily. "I gave Glory a bottle of my weed oil."

"For my knees," says Glory mournfully.

"As well as a bottle of my homemade vanilla extract."

"We like to soak the bean pods in bourbon," says Ron. "Gives a really rich flavor." Peg looks at him sharply, and Ron sits back.

"And it would seem, well . . ."

"I mixed them up," says Glory. "I lost my glasses, and I didn't see the labels."

"Mizzed what up?" I call over.

"Ah," says Will. "So these are *special* brownies."

"They really are!" I say, finishing off my third one. "I need the recipe of this too. Guys, should I be a cook?"

"Who gave you that?" Glory bats the last bite out of my hand. Rude.

"I found it on the plate."

Glory covers her face with her hands. Now she has no face. Weird.

"Okay, okay," says Will. "So, Glory, nothing wrong with weed brownies. I'm quite a fan. But let's either label these or remove them?" He looks around. "Have a lot of people . . ."

"I made a double batch. These are all that's left," says Glory, waving her hands fretfully at the nearly empty plate. "Oh, now I've done it! Oh, Glory, you stupid, stupid . . ."

"Okay, okay," says Barb. Glory has started to weep. "Let's get Glory home, okay?"

"How much did you use?" Will asks.

"All of it! About a cup?" Glory looks at Peg, who nods.

"Whoa," says Will. "I'm surprised they taste okay."

"Well, we use bourbon for the weed oil also," says Ron. "Kind of caramelizes—"

"For fuck's sake, Ron!" Peg smacks his arm.

"Well, we do." He is unfazed. He helps himself to a brownie.

"Will, how sober are you?" asks Barb.

"Not too bad."

"Okay, try to stay that way? See if you can get Mira out of here?" she asks. He nods. "Good boy."

"I'm going home to see if I can get a ritual going to undo this," huffs Peg.

"You think you're going to manifest the THC out of this poor girl's bloodstream?" Barb shakes her head.

"What's THC?" asks Glory. "That wasn't in the recipe!"

"What girl?" I ask. "What happened to her?"

Will chuckles. "Somebody accidentally brought weed brownies to this party. And she ate . . . three of them?"

My eyes grow wide. Very wide. "That's terrible! I hope she's okay! I never touch marijuana; for some reason, it makes me go completely blotto." "Blotto" is such a weird word. "Blotto. Bllllot. *Ohhhhhhh*." I laugh. Everyone is looking at me. "Glory, why are you crying?" I give her a hug. "Oh, Glory, your sweater is so soft." I stroke it. It's like she's wearing a kitten. "Are you my little kitten?" Glory starts crying harder, and Barb leads her away.

Will puts his hands on my shoulders. I like his hands. I like it when they're on my body. "I'm going to help Barb carry her cauldron out. Stay here, okay? I'll be right back."

"You're touching me," I say. I feel nice and tingly.

He pulls his hands back quickly. "Sorry!"

"I liked it. Do it again."

He shakes his head with a little smile and points firmly at the stool next to me. "Sit."

"I am your spaniel!" I shout. "It's from the play," I whisper to the person next to me, but it turns out there's no one there.

I wait for Will for so long. Really, really long. Hours, probably. He doesn't come back. "I'm going to find him," I tell the fairies, but they are gone now too. Where did they go? There are people everywhere. They are laughing. Everyone is having so much fun! I love them all. I should talk to them more. "I love your costume," I say as I pass people. I stroke their arms. So beautiful.

I find the door and step outside. It's a magical night. There are stars and they are so bright. Why am I out here? I have to find someone. I look around. The lake is lovely, but there is no one in the lake. There's a path. I will follow it. I'm in the woods now. It is dark, but I can see the water on the other side of the trees and the moon on the water is so bright and so beautiful. I look around. I forget why I'm here. I forget where I am. I walk for a long time. Everything is sort of shimmery and lovely.

"Ohhhhh," I breathe. I touch the branches as I pass through them. They tickle. I laugh. "Hello!" I say to no one, but the sound feels nice in my mouth. "Hello! *Helllllllllloooo."*

"Oh, hello." It is a voice. It is a man. I know him. He's very nice. He looks very beautiful.

"It's you," I say. I step toward him. It's the Shakespeare man.

"What are you doing out here?" He laughs.

"Looking for you?" I think? Someone . . . "But you found me!" I giggle.

"You're having a good time?" he asks.

"I'm having a beautiful time!" I spread my arms wide over my head and I twirl. He catches me in his arms. "Oh, hi," I say, surprised. "I remember when you were touching me before," I say. "That was lovely."

"Yeah?" he says. He pulls me closer. He kisses me softly on the lips. Oh. It's not my favorite. "Mira."

I feel all spinny. "I want to spin!" I break free and start to twirl. He laughs and catches me, and we fall to the ground. He pulls me close again.

"I like you like this," he says. "You're delightful."

"It's because I'm so re-laxed," I murmur as he nuzzles me. He kisses me again. He moves his hands on my body and up my dress, the satin slippery on my skin. I push him away, but he laughs and kisses me again, shoving his tongue in my mouth.

"No," I murmur. I'm not supposed to be here.

"I missed you, babe," he says. "I want you so bad."

"But I'm right here," I say. I feel confused. He has so many hands. "No . . . no, thank you, sir . . ." I don't know how to stop him. "I don't like it." There are hands everywhere. Then there are hands coming out of the air, and—

"What the fuck, dude!" There is another man! Or is it two of the same man? I wonder if maybe I'm drunk. One of the men pulls one of the men off my body and throws him to the ground. "She's off her tree, she's blotto."

"Blotto!" I say. "I forgot I love that word!" I spread my arms overhead. "I'm in the trees!"

The kissing man is standing up and pushing the new man. I know them. They are Will. Are they both Will? I like Will.

"I found her out here alone."

"You sure took advantage."

"Back off, man. We're together."

"Mira, are you together?"

I look between them. I look so closely. Oh, no. Nick is here. I do not like Nick. "I do not like Nick," I say, but I am not sure if my sounds are coming out of my face. I shake my head. I feel very tired. I look at them again. One of them is bad. One of them is good. I let the good one take my hand.

"Let's get you out of here." We start to walk away, but the bad one grabs the good one and hits his face with a loud smack.

He stumbles back. Now he is bleeding. I don't like this. I watch the good one hit the bad one back, and I start to run. They are fighting and I'm scared now, so I run along the path. The branches aren't tickly, they are scratchy, I fall down, and now my arm is bleeding. I get up and I run and I run. I see light ahead. Am I dying? I keep running toward the light. I am not dead, it is a cottage, there is a beautiful moon over the lake. I need to wash my arm, there is blood running down my arm. I walk into the moon, it is the lake, my dress floats around me. I am an angel in the watery moonlight. I am night magic. I turn around slowly. My arms are clean, the water is lovely. I am a mermaid! I am a tired water fairy. I will rest in the water. I will just float for a minute, I will . . .

I feel arms around me, pulling me up. "Jesus, Mira!"

"I'm sleeping." I'm all mumbly. "I'm the Lady of Shalott in the watery webs."

"You're going to drown yourself." It is the good one.

"I am Juliet," I say. "Not Ophelia."

"You're high and drowning, and you're still schooling me on Shakespeare." He laughs a little. He pulls me up and his hair falls off. Now he looks even nicer.

"Your hair fell off," I mutter. He throws it toward the shore.

"It's a wig. Not my real hair." He pulls me to standing.

"Oh, yes." I put my hands up to his head. "Your real hair is lovely." I twist it in my fingers. "I like your . . . head . . . and your face . . . and your body . . ."

"Okay, lady, let's get you out of here."

"You promised to kiss me," I say, leaning in and falling against him.

"I did kiss you."

"I know! I loved it. We should do it again."

"Not tonight, my friend."

"Oh." I sigh. "Another time."

"We'll see."

"I want to," I murmur. "Promise you will."

"Uh. You said we shouldn't . . ."

"Promise!"

"I promise to discuss it when you're sober."

"I'm so tired." I slump forward. He scoops me up in his arms and carries me. "Oh," I say. "Romeo."

"I'm Will," he says. "Not Romeo."

"No, where is my Romeo?"

"*Wherefore . . . art thou Romeo?*" He sounds like he's talking to a child. I'm not a child.

"I came with Romeo. I lost him." Will smiles. He has a lovely mouth. I reach out a finger to touch it.

"Oh." He gently pushes my finger aside. "Theo, he's inside."

"You're very strong." I lay my head against his chest. "I like it." I close my eyes.

"Okay. Go to sleep."

"I like you."

"Okay. Thank you."
"Don't you like me?"
"At this moment?"
"Yeah." I reach up and touch his face. It feels so nice. It feels familiar.
"I guess I do."

Chapter 20

I wake up with a raging headache in a strange bed with a man's arm flopped over my shoulders. Oh, God. What have I done? *Who* have I done?

I glance over, but his head is under a pillow. Whoever he is, he has an incredible body. I frantically run the evening through my mind. I was talking to the fairies. There was something about brownies . . . Did I kiss someone? Was it Will? I hope so. I hope not. Did I punch someone? My arm hurts. I look down and see a long strip of bandage, carefully applied. What happened to me? My hair is clumped. Did I get wet? I try to peel the mystery arm off me, but that wakes it up. A head emerges.

"What angel wakes me from my flowery bed?" Theo. What a relief. Wait . . . Did we?

"You're a vigorous lover, Mirabel." He yawns. "Best I never had." He sees my stricken face. "Oh, honey!" He pats my head. "Hi. Nothing happened. No thanks to you. I had a thing maybe going with Max . . ."

"Oh, I'm sorry."

"It's okay. I'll get him next time. I like him," he whispers.

"I know," I say, but I'm distracted. "Where am I? Why are we sleeping together?" I pat my body. My dress is gone. I look under the covers. I am wearing a Twin Orchards T-shirt and a pair of men's sweatpants.

"We are at Will's," says Theo. "He brought you home. We didn't think you should be unattended."

"What did I do? Oh, God." A dozen blackout city nights of my youth flash before me. "I feel like I only had a drink and a half?"

"You also had some unfortunately seasoned brownies, courtesy of Glory and her apparent dealers, Ron and Peg." Theo laughs. "Theater kids! Love it." A memory is starting to dawn. "And then I guess the brownies made you pretty snacky, so you had another."

"I don't smoke weed!" I say. "I'm allergic to it or something. It puts me on, like . . ."

"An acid trip?" Theo laughs. "Yeah, I mean, we were worried, and I'm glad you're safe, but it was pretty amazing to behold."

"So, Will saw all this?"

Theo nods. I think he's enjoying this. I throw the covers over my head and scream into the pillow.

"She lives." Will's voice from the doorway. Ugh. I have fantasized about a morning after with him, but this isn't it. Our eyes meet. I can tell he has thought about it too. Although in both of our visions, I was ideally dewy and impossibly lovely, not this swamp-thing vibe I am currently giving. He hands me a huge mug of coffee with oat milk and cinnamon. I look at him, surprised. "I listen." He smiles. "Theo brought you coffee to rehearsal last week?"

"Oh. Yes. Thank you." I sit up, and Theo puts a pillow behind my head. Will hands him a coffee too and sits on the edge of the bed.

"Well, Mirabel," says Theo. "Three brownies will get you two gorgeous men in bed with you."

"And a coffee." I salute them with my mug. I take a gulp of coffee. "Oh, God, this is perfect." Will looks pleased. "Okay, okay, tell me how I humiliated myself. Don't hold back."

They look at each other. "Okay," says Theo. "So the fun stuff is that while you were the most-developed brownie situation of the evening, there was all kinds of chaos. A lot of people really let their hair down. Suffice to say, rehearsal is going to be a collective walk of shame."

"So I'm not the only one."

"You're a key player." I hang my head. "But honestly, most people don't even know."

"You guys didn't have brownies?" I ask.

"I'm gluten-free." Theo shrugs.

"And I'm not a total lightweight." Will grins. "I had one, but I can handle my weed."

"Okay, and the . . . less fun stuff?" Theo looks at Will. He nods at Theo.

"Jesus, guys, what happened?"

"Okay," Theo says. "Well, your brownies kicked in, and you decided to go on a little field trip into the forest. You wanted to play *Midsummer Night's Dream*."

"Don't be cute, just tell me."

"Okay, well, Will saw you were gone and went to find you. And he found you with . . ."

"Nick," says Will. "And you guys were, well, he was . . ." He looks at me closely. "You don't remember?"

"What?"

"You really don't remember?"

"No, what?"

"Well, you were kissing, and he was getting pretty out of hand."

"Nick did that?" My insides are burning.

"Yes," says Theo darkly. "Can I kill him? Pretty please."

I shake my head. "I'll deal with him. Fuck." I sigh heavily. "I remember kissing someone," I say. "I, well, I thought it was you," I say to Will.

He surprises me by blushing furiously. "No, it was Nick." His eyes darken. "I pulled him off you. I hope . . . I hope that's okay? I wasn't . . . You were pretty far gone, and it seemed like you didn't know what was happening, so I wasn't sure if you, you know, consented. He told me you guys are together."

"No." I sigh. "We are . . . no longer together." Will does not look surprised.

"Good." Our eyes meet ever so briefly.

"I told him," says Theo. "It felt relevant."

"Fair," I say, but I wish he didn't know. "I dumped him. *Methought I was enamour'd of an ass.*" I shrug.

Theo laughs. "Nice one."

I look at Will. "So then what happened?"

"I pulled him off you and he punched me. And we fought. And you ran away again."

"You went for a swim," says Theo. "Lady of Shalott cosplay?"

"That's what she told me!" says Will. "How do you know that?"

I give a wry laugh. "He knows me. And then?"

"Will came running out of the woods and pulled you out of the water and carried you like a goddamn Harlequin heartthrob"—Will cuts him off with a sharp look—"and he found me and we decided to bring you here rather than giving your parents any more ammunition than they already live with, and . . ."

"Where's my dress?"

"Don't worry. I undressed you, and I didn't look," says Theo.

"You could have looked."

"Nope. Not interested." He pats my hand.

Instinctively I look at Will, who is watching me. "Thank you. Honestly. I'm so embarrassed. Both of you, you took such good care of me . . ."

I take in this room: It's warm and bright, this perfect cup of coffee in my hands, these two lovely guys who protected me and defended my honor and tucked me into bed. It occurs to me, in a sudden rush, that I don't think I have ever felt so cared for in my whole life. I have never felt so loved. Tears fill my eyes, surprising me.

"Oh, hey," says Theo. "You're okay." He pulls me in. "I've got you." I let him hold me.

"Whose room is this?" I ask weepily. "It's cozy."

Will clears his throat. "Uh, mine."

"I'm in your bed?"

"What a waste, huh?" says Theo, and I swat him. Something new passes over Will's face. He shakes his head slightly at Theo.

"How about some breakfast?" asks Will.

"Do you have any more of those brownies?" I ask. They laugh, and I feel warm all over. I never want to leave this room.

Chapter 21

I arrive back home to find Nick sitting on my parents' front steps. A small crowd has gathered across the street, watching him, and he is skillfully looking both crestfallen and gamely photogenic. He is holding a bouquet of flowers and has two cups of coffee. He holds one out to me as I approach.

"Peace offering?" He tries a charming smile. I scowl back.

"What do you want?" I grab the coffee, though. I take a sip. Black. I want to throw it at him, but people are watching.

"I want to apologize," he says. I say nothing. "Can I come in?"

"Nope." I gesture to the front porch chairs. "You can sit," I say. I stare at the group across the street until they get the message and casually disperse. Nick gives a big neighborly wave, then turns back to me. Always the showman.

"I hate myself for what happened. I don't know what to say." He holds up his hands. "I . . ."

"No. Stop. You don't get to talk."

He steps back, dropping his head.

"You followed me into the woods, you saw I was incapacitated, and you completely took advantage. There is a version of this that could go very, very badly for you. You know that, right?"

"You know how I feel about you. I would never want to hurt you. I . . ." He puts his head in his hands. "I feel like I could try to explain all day, and there would be nothing else really to say other than I was not myself . . . I was under an influence I didn't plan on. Those brownies . . . I had one also. SO trippy. I was also doing shots with the crew, trying to get in with the guys. You know." I know. Nick Nolan's fatal flaw is that he can't stand people not loving him. "I know how it looked, Mira. I would have punched any guy who touched you." He looks up at me, his macho face on.

"Yeah, you did that too. What the fuck, Nick? Will was coming to help me! To . . . protect me from you!"

He sighs. "I'm sorry. Okay? I was fucked up. I fucked up. What else am I supposed to say?"

I have a feeling that was his big finish. It's not an unfamiliar sensation.

I say nothing.

"So, what do you think?" He sits back. Yup. He thinks he's nailed it.

"Yeah, really good job, Nick," I say. "You did it. You apologized to a person."

He laughs. "See? What am I supposed to do without you?"

"That is absolutely none of my business," I say.

"When are you going to stop punishing me?"

I look at him in disbelief. "Dude, I never started. I'm not punishing you."

"You are, you're breaking me!"

"No." I lean forward and point very close to his face. "I broke up with you. End of story."

"Maybe I'll just leave the play," he says.

"Do what you've gotta do," I say. I'm half hoping he *will* leave, play be damned. But I know him. He won't. His face proves it: I've called his bluff.

"It would just be pretty bad press if I did," he says, a slight sulk in his voice. "A lot of people would be disappointed." He straightens up. "I'm staying."

"Fine," I say. "Whatever."

"No one can say that I walk out on my commitments," he says. "I'm not leaving. I'm going to be great. It will be the best show ever, and then it will never be as good again because I won't be here," he says, as if now he's really got me, as if I'll stop him.

"Well, I guess I'll see you at rehearsal, then." I smile at him. He storms down the porch steps in a big huff. "Hey, Nick." He turns around hopefully. "I take my coffee with oat milk and cinnamon."

"What? No! That's not true!" He sounds like a toddler. "You take it like I do!"

"No," I say. "You just never bothered to get it right."

"Jesus, woman. Why am I even trying?"

When he's gone, I lay my head back against the chair. I am very tired. I seem to have an excess of men in my life at the moment, all waiting in the wings. Nick with his empty threats and ego. Theo, whose friendship is my saving grace these days. And Will, who is so guarded, but who will run into the woods after me and beat up any man who messes with me.

Will, who remembered how I take my coffee after one conversation, when Nick didn't after five months. Will, whose kiss still burns in me.

At rehearsal, Glory throws her arms around me. "Oh, my dear girl, I'm so sorry, I'm such an ass. I've been worried sick!"

"We hear you've had quite the night," says Peg.

"We do make pretty sturdy stuff." Ron puffs his chest. "The secret is . . ."

"Bourbon, yes, we know, Ron," says Barb.

"So, did anything happen after we left the party?" asks Glory.

"Glory, I don't remember the party," I say. "It is a complete blackout in my memory."

"We heard some things," says Peg. I stare at her.

"You know, I'm actually not interested in what you heard," I say. "I know the brownies were a mistake."

"It's well-known lore that you shouldn't take food or drink from fairies," says Ron, and we all turn to look at him.

"You aren't fairies, Ron! You're amateur actors!" I snap, and they all look at me. They look . . . hurt. Disappointed. Glory gasps. Peg stares at me, eyes blazing. She storms off. Glory, panicked, follows her. Ron leaves and goes to sit in his usual chair. Barb stays.

"We are all a little on edge at the moment," she says. "Glory and Peg, they feel things very deeply."

"No shit," I say. "Listen, I didn't mean to be rude, but . . ."

"No, we put you in a sticky situation. Then we drugged you. Albeit, accidentally, but you're right."

"Yeah, well, thanks for saying that."

She looks at me straight on. "It's all going to work out," she says.

"What do you mean? Which thing?"

"All of it," she says simply. "The play. The heart." She arches an eyebrow.

"What do you know about my heart?"

She casts her gaze casually around the room, landing on Theo, laughing in the corner with Max, then Nick, who is, alarmingly, in an intense conversation with my father, then lingering on Will, who is lifting a riser with another stagehand. Then back at me. It seems Barb knows plenty about my heart.

"I'm telling you," she says, "all will be well." She pats my arm.

I'm not sure what she knows, or what exactly she is saying. I look back at Will and find him looking at me. He holds my gaze, gives his twitch of a smile. I start to walk toward him. I'm not sure why, I am simply pulled, I would just like to be next to him, but my mission is diverted by my father and, it would seem, my ex.

"Miranda, come here, please." They look serious.

"Hey," I say. "What's up?"

"Miranda, I've been having a chat with Nick here."

"Oh? Should I be worried?" A joke, but a geyser of truth underneath it. I am suddenly afraid my dad knows everything, that my secret of Nick is out, that the events of the other night are now public domain. I catch Nick's eye as I approach, and he smiles slightly and shakes his head: *No, you don't need to worry.* What, then?

"I was looking over our first scene in the woods," Nick says. For once he sounds borderline professional. "And I feel . . . I just wonder if the vibe is a little . . . predatory." He is talking about when he pushes me down and hovers over me. *"But I shall do thee mischief in the woods."* He is talking about the version we played the other night at the party, in the forest. Doing that scene with Will felt thrilling, but Nick is right: It's different now, with him.

"So, I was just discussing it with your dad, the possibility of exploring some other . . . uh, staging."

"On the one hand, as I told Nick, it's quite uncommon for a director to change blocking at this stage." This isn't totally true: My dad is throwing his weight around, and I get it. The scene itself looks good. There is tension, it is working. Why would we change it? "And I suppose I assume that if you were uncomfortable with it, you could have come to me directly?" He looks at me hard. I look at Nick, who shrugs apologetically.

"This isn't my idea," I say to my dad. "It seems like Nick is suddenly a feminist and is just expressing concern about my comfort." *Because he feels guilty about doing me mischief in the woods.* Nick looks at the floor.

My father looks between us. "Is there something I don't know here?" He looks especially hard at me, and while I wish that I had a paternal relationship where I could say, *This man is my ex-lover, has a past history of treating me like shit, he got me fired as revenge for dumping him, and took advantage of my drug-addled state,* I say nothing.

"It's my fault." Nick's head is down. "I'd prefer not to go into details, and I am telling you this in the strictest confidence." My father nods. "But . . ." He pauses here, glances at me. "I have behaved badly in the past toward Miranda, and I don't feel that it's fair for her to have to reenact it."

My father sits back, clearly shocked. "Is this true?" he asks me.

I shrug. I nod. I look at Nick, who is looking at his hands. I am floored.

My dad is quiet for a long time, thinking. "Would it be appropriate," he asks finally, "if I entrust the two of you to come up with something that you both feel comfortable with? And we will review it together?" Nick and I look at each other and nod slowly. "Very well," he says. "Nick, leave." Nick steals another glance at me. Suddenly I don't know him at all. I get up to leave. "Miranda, stay."

I sit. My father leans toward me.

"Are these events that he mentioned related to his presence here?"

"Yes."

He looks closely at me. "Has his being here caused you harm?" I hesitate.

"Not too much." I smile a little.

"Ah," he says. There is a long pause while he thinks. "Does he need to leave?" He looks at me intently. For the second time in five minutes, I'm floored. "You're an actor in my company. But you're also my daughter." This is as close to a declaration of love as I've ever had from my father.

I think about it. Nick leaving would end a lot of my problems. At this point in the production, it would also create a lot for many other people. And his actions, just now, have confused me completely.

"No," I say. "I appreciate that." *I love you too?* "Re-blocking the scene would be fine," I say.

"And we will drop the kiss at the end," he says. "No need for that." I nod, grateful. "It has just occurred to me," he says, "that perhaps we don't, in fact, know each other all that well." I say nothing. "You've behaved like a true professional," my dad says. Then, because we both know that's not enough: "You're a lovely Helena." He takes my hand and kisses it briefly. "I knew you would be." He stands up abruptly, his display of affection clearly too much for him. "Back to work," he says gruffly.

I remain where I am, a little stunned.

Theo passes by me and leans down. "What was all that?" he asks.

"Nothing," I say. Then: "Everything."

Chapter 22

July
Four and a half weeks until Opening Night

A few days go by without seeing Will, and I'm surprised: I feel it. I think I miss him. I keep hoping I'll run into him. The stagehands are starting to think I'm interested in carpentry because I keep strolling by the set build, hoping to find him there. I keep thinking about Nick's party, Nick's inexcusable behavior, but more importantly, how kind Will was. How gentle and tender and good he was to me. How that is all he has been since I've known him, even in high school. It's not just me; it's how he is to everyone. Nick has been on good behavior, but his motives are always right under the surface.

I don't even have Will's number. I could ask Theo, but it would thrill him too much, and anyway, I'm not even sure what I need it for. Just . . . contact. Access. I have a day off rehearsal while my dad focuses on the mechanicals' scenes, so I drive out to the cidery.

The main sign says CLOSED when I arrive. I pause in the driveway, unsure if I should proceed. My plan was to casually cruise by to purchase some cider. It never occurred to me that he might be closed. I idle there a moment but am interrupted by a cloud of dust coming toward me: Will's truck with a canoe strapped to the top. He slams on the brakes when he sees me. He looks confused.

"Hey!" I call out. "Sorry, I, uh . . ." He gets out of the truck and stares at me. "I was going to buy some, um, cider?"

"Sorry, I'm closed." He gestures to the sign. He seems different today, more guarded. I was hoping he'd be happier to see me. "I'd open up for you, but I'm just heading out . . ."

"Yeah! Yes, of course, no worries, it was just, I was just passing by and . . ." I'm rambling.

"I'm glad to see you," he says. He gives a tiny smile, but there's something blank behind it.

"You are? Okay, good, I'm sorry to be weird, just showing up, I just . . ."

"You just needed some cider." His smile grows a bit.

"I did," I say, gaining ground. "Like, really badly."

"Here I was hoping you had just come to see me."

"Oh! I mean, it's great you're here, but you're going, so, I mean, I . . . I can fill my, uh, cider needs elsewhere."

"You'll never get it as good as mine." He smiles, and my insides liquefy. "Sorry," he says. "The joke was right there."

"Totally," I say. "Anyway, I won't keep you. You clearly have some seafaring adventure to deal with." I glance at the canoe.

"I was just going for a paddle."

"I figured." There is a small pause. "Okay, well, let me just turn my car around, and I'll be on my . . ."

"Do you wanna come?" The words tumble out as if in spite of himself.

I glance again at the canoe, then at him. I can't figure out his face, some strange blend of hope and sadness. "I don't know how to do . . . canoe."

"Oh, I can show you. Easy."

My plan for a cute casual drive-by is so long gone. I'm flustered. But I have waited for days to see him, and now I'm being offered an exclusive audience. "Yeah. Okay."

I move my car and hop in his truck. I'm suddenly shy. His energy is strange. He's not super chatty to begin with, but today he is oddly silent. He turns on some music, a sad, quiet acoustic song, and we drive.

We arrive at another little lake outside of town, at an empty boat launch on a long, narrow stretch of water. Will tosses me a couple of paddles and a backpack, releasing the canoe straps and hoisting the canoe onto his shoulders and over his head effortlessly. It's the most attractive thing I think I've ever seen. He leads us to the water and swings the canoe down.

"Wow," I say, impressed. He shrugs, but I can tell he's pleased.

"Okay, hop in," he says, pushing the canoe halfway into the water. I make my way around and sit in the middle, facing him.

"What are you doing?" he asks.

"I don't know, this is my first canoe."

He shakes his head. "No way did you grow up here."

"I was inside a dark theater, learning Shakespeare. I didn't have time for paddling around in little boats." He throws his head back, a laugh bursting out of him, and it feels like a victory.

"Oh my God," he says. "Okay. Go to the front. Face the front."

Once I have awkwardly shuffled forward and Will is in, and we have pushed off from shore, everything awkward becomes smooth. The lake is silent. It's lovely.

"Grab your paddle."

"Oh, no, that's okay!" I call back. "Thank you, I'm fine. You go ahead."

"This isn't a Central Park rowboat," he says.

"Okay, so?"

"So pick up your paddle, Belmont." I sigh and do as I'm told. "One hand on top, one halfway down." I slap the water uselessly. "We're not icing a cake; you need to pull the water."

"You're very bossy." I hear him grumble behind me. I try to pull the water like he said, but my paddle keeps going sideways. "I'm no good at this." I huff. "I don't know why people like this."

"It's usually very relaxing," Will says.

"It's hard."

"Yeah, well, sometimes life is hard, Miranda." His voice is clipped. "Fine, you know what, just throw the paddle behind you. I'll paddle." He starts working harder. He has already given up on me. He's annoyed. I don't blame him.

"No," I say, a little stung. "I'll do it." He doesn't reply. I start again, making a better effort.

"Move your hand down the shaft. Grip it harder." In a lighter moment, I would flirt here, but I just nod and adjust my grip. "Good, now try to keep it close to the canoe, plunge it deeper." Jesus, he's killing me. "Yeah, that's better. That's good."

We get enough of a rhythm going that it starts to feel purposeful. I'm stronger than I realized, and once I get the feel of it, we move across the lake at a decent pace. It's warm but cloudy, giving the day a sort of hazy feeling. We can hear kids at a cottage across the lake, but as we move into the narrower end of the lake, the cottages give way to huge cliffs on either side of us. There is virtually no shoreline, just water and rock. It's stark. It's humbling.

Will sees me looking around. "This is a dangerous stretch of water," he says. "There was this terrible tragedy years and years ago where a Boy Scout group got caught in a storm out here and had nowhere to land."

"That's terrifying. What happened?"

"Well, they all drowned," he says.

"Oh. That's awful."

"Yeah."

We don't talk for a while. Something about the rhythm, the sound of the water, the way my arms burn in a good way all lulls me into a quiet I haven't felt in a long time. It's active and passive. Meditative. It's not the most picturesque day, and something is up with Will—I feel it coming off him in waves—but still, it feels good out here. Finally, the narrow stretch opens up to a small bay, at the end of which is a rocky peninsula with a scattering of trees. Will guides us in and pulls up alongside the edge of the rock. We hop out, lifting the canoe onto the shore, and stagger onto the rocks, our legs like jelly after the paddle.

We sit on the warm rocks, and Will pulls out a couple of beer cans.

"No cider?" I ask. It's surprisingly generic beer for a brewmaster. "I haven't had one of these since high school."

"Not today," he says. He cracks his open and takes a long slug. He swallows hard. I open mine and take a sip. It tastes thin and metallic. I set it down on the rocks.

"This is nice," I say, even though it isn't, not really. The air feels heavy. Will feels heavy. The beer isn't good, and I'm sitting on a patch of lichen in shorts and my legs itch.

"It's our birthday," Will says quietly.

"Oh my God!" I say. "Happy . . ." I look at him and catch his eye. Of course. *Our* birthday. I don't know what else to say. "I'm sorry." It feels so limp.

He sighs heavily and downs the rest of his beer. I hand him mine, which he takes gratefully. We sit in silence for a while before Will finally speaks.

"We started doing a birthday canoe trip when we were in high school. Just the two of us. We'd paddle out to an island somewhere and camp. People always wanted to make a big deal out of our birthday. Our parents were great, they did these big parties, but as we got older, we just wanted something for just us. And it was just always the best time." He stares out at the lake. "This was my first paddle without him." I glance over at him, surprised. "The first few years, I just couldn't bring myself to, you know? I just couldn't do it alone."

"And you got a terrible substitute," I say. "I'm so sorry, Will."

"No," he turns to me, eyes wet. "I'm really glad you're here. I was just sitting in my driveway with the canoe on the truck, and I couldn't bring myself to leave. And then there you were."

"Well," I say softly, "I'm honored. Even though I suck."

"You were actually doing pretty well toward the end there."

"That's generous." I pick at the lichen on the rock. "Would you . . . could you tell me about Jonah?" I am so aware of him beside me, his shirt damp with sweat, his shoulders slumped, the stubble on his cheeks. I'm aware of the weight of him.

He thinks for a moment. "When you're a twin, people love to categorize you, like, this is the nice one or the mean one or the smart one or whatever. I think a lot of twins really want to be, like, individualized like that? But in a lot of ways, we were really similar. We liked the same stuff. We had the same values. We had really similar goals. The cidery was his idea. So, it wasn't like we were polar opposites at all. But he was the better one." I open my mouth to interject. "No, but he was. He had an edge on me; he was funnier and cooler and kinder. He was like this future version of myself, myself if I could just be a little better, walking around next to me." He sighs. "And he's gone. And I'm just me. And I don't have him there, two steps ahead of me, showing me how to be." He blinks rapidly and takes another deep swig of beer, and I know what he's doing, he's trying not to cry. I gently pull his arm down. I take the beer and set it aside. I take his hand. He looks at me surprised, then looks away, letting out a heartbreaking, ragged exhale, and the tears fall, silently running down his face and his neck onto his T-shirt. We say nothing, just sit there facing out while he lets the wave of grief pass over him.

The clouds start to clear after a while, and the sun comes out. Will stands, peels off his shirt and shoes, and goes to the water's edge. He looks around cautiously at the rocks before jumping into the water, surfacing, then swimming out. I didn't bring a swimsuit. I strip down to my bra and underwear, which thankfully are passable. He catches me undressing out of the corner of his eye and turns away until I am in the water. I swim out to him. He leans back, starfish limbs, and floats on his back, belly up. I do the same. The sky has cleared, and the few clouds left drift past us. Our hands bump in the water, and he clasps mine, and we float there for a long time, the sky above us, holding each other up.

After we have paddled back, after we have driven back, making light, easy chat about bands he likes, concerts we've been to, we pull up in his long driveway in front of my car. We get out, and he pulls me into a long hug.

"Thank you," he says into my hair. "I'm glad you were there."

I resist the urge to make another thin joke about my poor paddling skills. "Me too," I say. "Happy birthday." I lean up and kiss his cheek quickly, then turn away, waving as I jump into my car.

Oh, there is something there. But today isn't the day to find out what.

Chapter 23

Four weeks until Opening Night

We open in a month, which means we need to crack down on publicity. The shows usually do well between strong community support and summer visitors, many of whom make the trip to Tempest every summer. Still, my mother is leaning hard into her additional role as producer and hands everyone a stack of posters to put up over the weekend. I look around awkwardly, watching the pile of posters shrink, relieved when the last one is picked up.

"Sorry." I shrug. "They're all gone."

My mother laughs. "You thought you'd get out of it! Don't worry." She hands me a shopping bag filled to the brim with mini posters. "These are for you!" I look at her in disbelief. "It's tradition. The guest actors always hand these out." She nods toward Nick, who holds up an identical bag and gives us an enthusiastic thumbs-up. "You can pass them out at the farmers' market on Saturday."

I sigh. "Together?"

"Yes, Miranda! Together!" Her voice is singsongy, which I know is one step before fully clipped. "It's exciting for the community to see our visiting actors. It's a wonderful opportunity for you to reconnect with people." My mother is famous for offering "wonderful opportunities," which are almost exclusively things I do not want to do.

"Lovely."

"Wear something nice!" she calls after me as I start off. "You're representing the theater! And the family!" I hold up a hand in acknowledgment, grimacing.

The farmers' market is a long row of stalls along the path by the lake, the same place I ran into Kelsie. I look for her now, as though the waterfront itself could conjure her. There is a sea of blond mothers with strollers, so I remain on alert. Nick is late. I don't want to do this with him, but even worse is the idea of approaching strangers alone, so I sip a lovely iced lavender coffee thing from a stall near the parking lot and wait. The whole town is out, it seems; it's a gorgeous, sunny Saturday in July in a lakeside town. This is the place to be. When I used to think of North Lake, it was from the perspective of a much younger person: I wanted to get out of here. There was nothing for me except working in my parents' theater, nothing else this small town could offer me, so I left. Over the years, a skewed narrative crept in that this town was outdated and simplistic, boarded over in my mind. But the scene before me is vibrant. The booths are cool, and the kind of "wholesome, homespun" thing considered cool in the city is just organic here. There are people everywhere. A local folk singer is performing in the small bandstand in the park, and her voice floats in and out of the sounds of voices and activity. There's a drag artist doing story time in the gazebo, storyteller and captive audience alike decked out in matching tiaras and fairy wings. Way off down the park, I see an outdoor seniors' yoga class. I'm surprised by how much exists here, how much is happening. How much seems to have changed.

Where is Nick? If he bails on this, I'll kill him. I can think of nothing worse than stopping people to advertise our play by myself. I imagine people pushing past me while I feebly call out, *Shakespeare! Anyone? Come see some . . . theater?* I check my phone yet again.

"Hey!" Nick trots toward me, golden and eager. He looks expectantly at my coffee. "Didn't get one for me?"

"Nope." I tilt my head. "The stall is back that way . . ."

"I brought you a coffee last time!" He pouts excessively for a grown man.

"The coffee you brought when you showed up at my house after your very bad behavior?" I don't even bother reminding him that he has yet to ever get my coffee order correct.

"No worries. I just had a protein shake, so . . ."

"I bet you did." I take one final gratuitous drag of my drink and toss it in the garbage. "Okay, let's get this over with." I pull out a handful of flyers. "I guess we just . . . talk to people?" I say, but Nick has already headed down the path and removed his sunglasses, revealing his identity, and thus is swarmed.

"And this here is Miranda Belmont!" he says, pulling me into the fray when I arrive. "Hometown hero!" I cringe at the phrase but am surprised by the beaming smiles.

"It's so nice to have you back, dear!" a woman says to me. "I watch your show every week! The town is very proud of you!"

"Oh! Wow, um, thanks. Please, uh, come to our show!" She takes three flyers.

Nick and I make our way slowly down the path, handing out flyers, stopping for a chat with almost every person. It's weird. People are obviously excited to see Nick. Before *Listings*, he had done a few action movies, a Netflix zombie miniseries. He's legit famous. I'm just from here. Or so I thought. People keep saying things to me.

"I've been following your career since you got that Tide commercial! The town is so proud of you!"

"You went to high school with my daughter Tracy! Do you remember Tracy?" I do not. "She was so jealous of you!" Poor Tracy.

"I saw you and Theodore in that high school *Peter Pan*. I was his piano teacher! And even then, I could see there were budding stars onstage!" That one warms me quite a bit.

People ask for photographs, autographs. At first, I step aside, assuming they mean with Nick, but they pull me in, as though I am an equal draw. In the city, sometimes people notice me. I get the occasional free coffee at my local café, where one barista is a big fan of the show, but I am certainly not exciting enough to count as famous. But here, I seem to have a celebrity status that I didn't realize. My parents have shown such disdain for my show that I kind of assumed that it was mildly embarrassing to my entire home-town, but it turns out people watch it. It's important for me to remember that not everyone is like my father, who reads the Greek theater canon every year just to "keep sharp." Some people, lots of people, it turns out, enjoy salacious, murder-y, real estate prime-time dramas. I just hadn't had occasion to meet them until now. My time in North Lake, I am realizing, has been so insular: the theater, the cidery, the lake . . . I haven't been out much among the people. I might have done this sooner if I'd known I was famous. Or not. I don't know. It feels strange. A fun planet to visit, but who really wants to live there?

Nick Nolan does, of course. He's a pro at this. I know this is his favorite thing—the attention, the adoration, an abundance of people to worship him. He's good at it: He leans in, he asks them questions, he holds their babies, he smiles, laughs widely at their pedestrian jokes. He is relaxed, but with an underlying mania that I know, for him, is adrenaline. I'm more easily overwhelmed, but the attention grows on me. People want to talk to me. People want to see our play. Lots of people have already bought tickets! People think I'm great on *Listings*! Except, of course, I'm not on it anymore.

"I think your character should be bigger!" says one man. "You should tell the producers to give you more lines. You should post on the community Facebook group, see if they would start a petition. We love a petition!" I feel Nick watching me out of the corner of his eye. I'm grateful that he doesn't correct these compliments.

We stop for a break and a lemonade from a small booth run by little girls in unicorn headbands.

"Do you ladies have a permit?" Nick crosses his arms and glowers, and they giggle. He hands them a twenty, and their jaws drop and they give us each a sticky high five. I leave some flyers on their table.

"I'm sorry about the show," Nick says when we are seated on a bench, away from the crowd. "It must be tough with everyone making such a big deal about it." For a moment, I am confused, then realize he means *Listings*. Already, *Midsummer*'s has replaced "the show" in my mind.

"Oh. Yeah, well, it's nice that people watched it anyway." What else am I supposed to say?

"I was thinking." Nick turns to me. "I should talk to Jay. We should get you back. I was angry . . . I was being an asshole." He looks at me, and I nod. "But I can talk to the team . . . You and I are good, right? We could work together? I could see if we could, yeah, you know, sweeten your role . . ."

I'm surprised that his words spark nothing in me. A little validation, maybe, but my heart doesn't leap at the thought of returning or a bigger role. I shrug. "We'll see," I say. "Let's just get through the play." The truth is, I don't know if I could work with him again. The truth is, I don't know that I'd go back if given the choice.

"I'll make a call," says Nick.

"Sure," I say. Might as well see what my options are. I stand. "Let's finish these flyers." I'm having a surprisingly nice day. I don't need to talk about the past, or the future. Today, for once, I'm happy where I am.

We make our way farther down the path. The farmers' market is winding down, and most of the people who want photos and auto-graphs have seen us already. Some wave as we pass by them again, like we are old friends now. I take in a few of the booths: There's a witchy-looking young woman with whimsical earrings selling essen-tial oil blends. There's a booth with artisanal cheese (I pick some up for my parents), and another with wooden birdhouses painted in cheerful colors. Between the booths and Nick and the flyers, I don't even notice Will until we are almost face-to-face. I look up and see the Twin Orchards logo above me.

"Hey!" I do a double take. "Wait, you have a booth?" I can feel my face light up. Do we hug? I want to. "I'm so happy to see you!" I burst out. I'm not being very cool. Ugh. I look around the spread before me, his whole line of summer ciders. It's impressive.

His smile is thin. "Yeah, Jenny's sick, I had to cover." I rack my brain for Jenny, instantly jealous, before I remember his bartender Mark, whose lovely wife is also an employee. There's a coldness to Will . . . why? I search his face, but the answer comes sidling up beside me.

"Hey, man," Nick says, raising his hand for a fist bump, which Will doesn't return. I push Nick's arm down.

"I think you two have had enough fisticuffs for one summer," I say. Will doesn't smile. "Nick, the yoga class just let out. You should go see if they want some flyers." He narrows his eyes at Will, looking between us, but one of the yogis has caught his eye and is waving him over.

"You coming?"

"In a minute," I say. "I want to talk to Will." Nick snorts lightly but shrugs and saunters off. "We're doing flyers," I say lamely, offering him one. He doesn't take it. He looks down at his table, straightening some bottles. "Will. What?" It's been, what, four days since our paddle? It felt like we had gotten closer. It felt like something was really brewing between us. Now I'm not sure. "Are you upset with me or something?"

He looks up, eyes flashing. "I'm pretty surprised to see you with that guy. Considering last time we were all together, I was pulling him off you." There's something else in his face that I can't place. Disdain, maybe? I open my mouth to defend myself. "It's fine, I have no claim on who you hang out with."

"This"—I gesture around the market—"is my mother. She made me do this. With him." I try to catch his eye, but he's avoidant. "I have no desire at all to hang out with Nick Nolan. My parents don't know anything about . . . anything. It was easier to just do this." Will shrugs, but I can see him relax a bit. "Anyway. It turns out that I have a lot of fans in North Lake. Can you believe it?"

"I believe it." He still doesn't smile.

"We are just supposed to be handing out flyers, but we ended up doing all these autographs and, like, people wanted pictures. It was really weird but also kind of nice?" I smile at him hopefully, trying to find whatever thread pulled us together just days ago.

"That's nice, Mira. You deserve that." He smiles a tight half smile that means nothing.

I try again. "Do you want my autograph?" I all but bat my eyelashes, hoping he'll laugh.

But he looks at me, he locks in, and there he is. "No, Mira, I don't want your damn autograph."

"What? Jeez, I was joking." I feel stung.

He leans in. "I don't need an autograph to know that I met you. I don't care about all that stuff. I don't care that you're kind of famous."

"You don't." I have felt genuinely famous for all of an hour, and Will is rapidly pulling the wind from my sails.

"I'm sort of surprised that you do," he says. "I don't really believe in autographs. It's a weird thing to want from someone." I drop my eyes to the cider on the table. I straighten a bottle that he missed. I don't know what to say. I swallow hard, chastened.

"You seem mad at me."

He shakes his head a little in disbelief. "I mean, Mira, it's just a lot of mixed signals. I don't know what you want from me."

"That's fair." I don't know what else to say.

"Hey." He reaches across the table and catches my wrist very gently, finally looking right at me. "It's just, I don't want anything from you if it belongs to everyone else. I don't want anything from you but . . ."

"But what?" booms Nick, beside me suddenly. He slings his arm around my shoulders, which I shrug off and, in doing so, also shrug Will off.

"Nothing. Go away," I say, and Nick laughs, not moving, and whatever spell that was is broken. "I think I'm done for the day," I say to Nick.

"Go team!" He tries to high-five me, but I duck away. He still doesn't leave.

"I'll see you around?" I ask Will. He smiles. He nods. Nick stiffens. I can see Nick won't leave until I do, and I'm not in the mood for another showdown between them. I wonder what Will was going to say? "Okay, well, Nick, thanks, see you at rehearsal. Will . . ." I'm not sure what else to say, so I wave lamely and set off in the opposite direction from both of them.

Chapter 24

Three weeks until Opening Night

We have two weeks of rehearsal left before tech week, and finally we've hit our stride. *A Midsummer Night's Dream* is a three-ring circus: You have the fairies, the lovers, and the mechanicals, each mostly in their own world with some overlaps. It's starting to come together, not just in concrete ways with set building and decoration and costume fittings, but also, the scenes are getting tighter. People know their lines, mostly, and we are moving past the messy middle toward something that resembles a real play.

I haven't been in a play since theater school, not really. I had forgotten the sense of community, that magic of things coming together, inching toward a common goal. On set, we were so compartmentalized; there were members of the cast I only met at wrap parties. Nick, for example: Our scene schedules never overlapped. I made my contribution and left. Here, there is a swell of togetherness; all these parts need to come together at once for it to work. The stakes are higher. There is no fixing it in post. That's the magic of it.

I've started sticking around after my own rehearsal slot to watch the others. My mother, whatever she is offstage, is luminous as Titania, graceful and beguiling. Arthur, who plays Bottom, the human who Puck affixes a donkey's head to, placing her under a love spell, is incredibly funny. Together, they are very charming. A little too charming. I almost can't look at the scene with Arthur spread out in my mother's fairy bower, her stroking his face and nuzzling him. My parents rarely show physical affection, so it is strange to watch her enact it with someone else.

While I doubted it at first, the choice to have older fairies is genius. Instead of sexy and flirty, they are sage and grumpy, taking zero shit from Bottom as he makes ridiculous demands of them. They move a little more slowly, but there is a dignity to it. Even Ron as the fairy Peaseblossom is somehow delightful.

Nick has been better too. He actually came to me with ideas for our scene to re-block it—weak ideas, but I appreciated the effort. We have made it a little lighter, downplaying the sinister elements, playing up the cat-and-mouse-ness of it all. It's not the most cerebral take on it, but it's entertaining, and it's easier to keep it superficial. Nick isn't a natural comedian (the guy has made a career of intense brooding), but he fully commits and has full confidence. It's a frustrating quality in real life, but it makes for engaging theater.

We are rehearsing the big fight scene in act 2. Puck has mistakenly given a love potion to Lysander instead of to Demetrius, then amends it by giving it to Demetrius also, so both men are suddenly in love with Helena. Both no longer love Hermia, Helena believes they are tricking her, and Hermia is angry and confused. The men fight with each other, Helena fights with everyone, and Hermia has a meltdown. It's a complicated scene with a lot of blocking, dynamics changing between characters every thirty seconds, and it's long—one of the most complicated scenes in the show. My father has booked us extra time to work on it. We have been at it for over two hours, and we are tired and sore but happy. For once, it all feels alchemic: It's so fast, it's Helena against everyone, which is fun to play. There is no time to fixate on Nick or what he's doing. We are, the four of us, all in flow. Bailey and I throw ourselves toward each other, claws out. At the last second, the guys have to grab us and pull us apart, then spin us around, away from each other. It is chaos. It's really fun. On our last run, Nick spins too hard, and we fall to the ground, laughing. He lands on top of me. I am still laughing before I catch his eye and see that his face has turned deadly serious. Our faces are inches apart.

"You okay?" he asks. His breath is heavy.

"Yeah," I say. He doesn't move. The weight of him, his face looking down at me . . . For just a flash, it is all right there. Everything we were, everything that for a moment was so good. "I can't breathe," I say, and gently roll him off me.

He jumps up and offers his hand, pulling me up, and there it is again, that undeniable thing that I have kept at bay. I feel a pang—is it guilt? Regret? There is still a part of me that misses him. I hate that.

I step back and circle my finger in the air. "Let's go again." We set up the scene, and this time, I am careful not to fall.

We have a break between scenes. I am up in the balcony watching the mechanicals rehearse, laughing a bit to myself. The light and sound booth guys are outside on a smoke break. It's a rare moment alone when I hear the creak of the stairs. I turn and see Nick coming up.

"Hey. Can I sit?" He gestures to my row. I nod and he sits, leaving a seat between us. "That was some fall," he says.

I glance over at him. He is staring straight ahead. "Yeah," I say. "You're not hurt, are you?"

"Nah," he says. "You?"

"No."

We watch as Arthur, as Bottom, flies around the stage, instructing the other characters. Bottom is the true diva of the show, with his inflated ego and demands of those around him. As far as Bottom knows, it's his show.

"That's me." Nick chuckles. He points to the stage. "The donkey guy. That's what I did to this show."

"Well . . . maybe a little." It's the most self-aware thing I think he's ever said.

"That guy Arthur, he's the real deal, huh? He's a good actor."

"He is," I say. "Though he hasn't had a ton of success with it. He's never really had his break. I think that's why coming here every summer means so much to him."

"We should get him on *Listings*," Nick says, and I know he can, and maybe even will, make that happen.

"He'd probably really appreciate that."

We are quiet for a moment. Nick turns to me. "I feel like maybe you hate me less these days."

"Maybe slightly less." I am feeling generous. "You're doing a good job," I say. "Once you dropped the accent."

"Was it that bad?"

"Oh, yeah."

He laughs a little. "You might not realize this, but I've never actually had any formal acting training."

"No, I know. I knew that."

He looks at me, surprised. "I'm famous," he reflects.

"Uh, yeah."

"But I'm not sure I'm talented." I say nothing. "I'm incredibly handsome, though, so, you know . . ." He turns to me again with that megawatt smile. That movie-star smile. The smile that got me in the first place.

"Okay, yes, I know."

We watch the scene quietly together. Nick laughs out loud when Bottom tries to kiss his lover through the hole in the "wall." "And to think," I say. "You could have been doing *Lego Batman*. And here you are doing Shakespeare." I smile at him. He is quiet.

"Yeah," he says after a while. "So, *Lego Batman* wasn't canceled," he says, looking straight ahead. "I left."

"Wow, what? Nick!"

He shrugs. "I kept thinking about that thing you said. About doing something creatively interesting." I am shocked into silence. "I keep doing things for the money, you know? Like, I guess because of how I grew up, and now I have more money than I could ever need. I bought my mom a nice house. She's good. I started this whole acting thing for her, really, and, like, when is it enough, you know? And you left, and I realized I was choosing this thing, this job, over real life. Over you." Now he looks at me.

"You gave it up for me?"

"Well." He shifts in his seat. "Not really. I gave it up for me. Like, I kind of felt like, what's the point of all of this, if I'm throwing people away, you know? Like, who does that make me?" I watch him quietly. I've never met this version of him before. "But I realized that losing you . . . not having you . . . wasn't good."

"Those are some big thoughts."

He turns all the way around now, facing me. "Is there no chance, Miranda Belmont?"

"Chance of what?" I ask, but I know.

"Of us. I fucked up." He swallows hard. "And there's lots I didn't say to you. I lied to you."

"About what?"

"I had real feelings for you." It's still so little, so late. "I was falling for you." His voice is as soft and as earnest as I've ever heard it. "I kept it casual because I was scared . . . You're so amazing. So talented, so smart, Mira, I can barely keep up with you, and you scared the shit out of me." It's the most naked I've ever seen him. I think he really means it.

The fact of us turned real, and he dismantled it the second it did. I felt it too. He hurt me. "You acted like we were nothing. You forced my hand. How was I supposed to stay?"

"I'm sorry," he whispers. "I'm so sorry. I'm a shit. I know." He grabs my hand. "I will make it up to you. Let me show you, let me prove it to you . . ."

I take my hand back. "I appreciate the apology, Nick. I really do. And I'll admit, your commitment to trying to win me back is, well, it's surprising. But . . ."

Nick slumps back in his seat. "I won't stop trying."

I face him full on. "You will," I say. "You don't love me."

"Hey, hey, I never said I loved you . . ."

I laugh to myself. "Wow. See? There you go." I look at him closely. There's a determined set to his eyes that I've seen before. *"Ohhhhh."* I get it. I saw this look in the months leading up to the Emmys. "You want to win." It's so incredibly simple. It's that I dared to reject him. "You don't want me."

He sighs. "No one says no to me." He sounds defeated, like he genuinely can't believe it.

"And how is that serving you?" I ask gently. He looks at me hopefully. "It's not going to happen, Nick."

"I missed you."

"I'm right here."

"Yeah, but . . ."

"We can be friends," I say firmly. "Nothing more." We both know I'm saying it because it's a thing to say, and that when this show wraps up, we will likely not speak again. "Let's just get through this thing, okay? Like . . . peacefully?"

He nods. "Yeah," he says. "Yeah, okay."

We ended because there were real feelings, and he couldn't handle it. It occurs to me that I am doing the same thing with Will. What I feel toward him is so wildly unknowable, I've shut it down before even giving him a chance to tell me what his feelings are. Nick's ship has sailed, but it's not too late with Will. Maybe in trying to protect myself, I am hurting him. I dare to wonder where things might go between us if I am brave enough to let them.

Chapter 25

Two weeks until Opening Night

"A few of us are going for karaoke," Max announces after rehearsal. "You have to come." I glance over at Theo, who gives an enthusiastic thumbs-up. Karaoke is generally against my personal belief system. This is where I would normally tap out, but I'm in a good mood, the evening is young, and we don't have rehearsal tomorrow. I am finding at every turn that the more I engage with people here, the better it goes.

"I'm not singing," I say, even though I will, and it will be awesome. They will just have to work for it.

"Amazing," says Max.

I arrive at the pub to find a small group, Theo and Max, Bailey, a few of the mechanicals. Nick. Will. They are sitting at opposite ends of the table, a free seat next to each of them. I go to pass by Nick, but he beckons me to sit down. I glance at Will, catch a hopefulness in his face, but Nick pulls me down next to him.

"Is it okay that I'm here?" whispers Nick.

There is already a buzz among the other locals in the bar that Nick Nolan is here, and I know he will put on a show for them later. Nick loves karaoke. That should tell you everything you need to know about him.

"Sure," I say. "Who am I to stop you." It's my fault for suggesting we be friends.

"Yeah, but . . ." He looks nervous, a tiny crack in his veneer that seems to have stayed there since our talk in the balcony. "I just want you to be, you know, comfortable. I don't have to stay."

I'm inclined to snap back with some quick jab, but he looks sincere, for once, and for once, I am feeling generous toward him.

"Stay," I say. "It's just a drink."

"Karaoke is never just a drink." He grins. I smile back at him. It feels foreign but also kind of a relief.

Out among humans, Nick almost passes for a regular person. I have only seen him in performance mode for so long, I've forgotten the version of him that can be genuinely funny. He doesn't have a lot of interesting thoughts, but he is a great pretend listener, so he makes the people around him feel interesting and tended to. Pitchers of beer and platters of apps appear for the table. He winks at me, and I know he has just told some server to "keep 'em coming," that he will pick up the tab, that this will render him heroic to the group and still be less than he spends on wine in a week.

The only thing worse than karaoke is public karaoke. You should at least have the decency to rent a small room in a karaoke bar where you can enact the strange contortions of your ego in relative privacy. I have been dragged to many of these, the perils of being young in the city. I finally stopped accepting invitations to birthday parties if they were held at a karaoke bar. It's always the same girl who just wants everyone to cry while she sings a power ballad. Usually Celine Dion. Usually off-key. For people who can actually sing, it's intolerable.

Karaoke in a pub with the general public and either a jaded or hyped-up host, waiting for your turn to be called, is just torture. There are amusing moments, sure: Max and one of the mechanicals doing an extremely dramatic rendition of "Tribute" by Tenacious D. I glance at Theo to laugh at them, but he is starry-eyed, watching Max pretend to be a demon. I make a note to self to get an update there. Some local guy in a trucker's hat with a giant beard sings a tuneless, earnest "Faithfully" by Journey.

Under the table, Nick gently knocks his knee with mine. I knock back aggressively, and he bangs his knee on the table.

"Ouch." He looks at me, injured. "What?"

"This is not a moment we're having."

"What moment?"

"We are not going to bond and reunite at karaoke." I look at him pointedly. "Friends!"

He pretends not to hear me and grabs the sticky black binder with the song list. "You know in the movies where the hero woos the heroine with the perfect song?" he says in general to the table. This time, I smack his knee under the table. He's going to give us away. This doesn't stop him. I have a feeling I've been swindled. Whatever middle ground I thought we'd found back in the balcony seems, like everything else, an act. "Let's see . . . 'Sorry,' Justin Bieber? Oh! 'If I Could Turn Back Time.'"

"I love Cher," says Theo. "Sounds like a naughty hero." He winks at Nick.

Nick nods. "Unfortunately, in this movie, yes. I could do 'Everytime.' Britney. Classic."

"It's actually a very sad song," says Bailey. "Poor Britney." Every woman at the table nods.

"How about 'Apologize' by OneRepublic," I say. "Or 'Take a Bow' by Rihanna."

Nick laughs. "Maybe the heroine should sing those."

"Maybe the heroine should sing every Taylor Swift song. Like, ever."

Nick settles on "Take On Me" because people like it, and above all, Nick needs to be liked. He has a surprisingly good voice, and he really sells it with some solid '80s dance moves. People love to see a celebrity acting like an idiot. It's significantly preferable to his singing me subliminal messages about our relationship with Cher as the vehicle.

Theo sings "Life on Mars?," a reminder to us all that there is no one cooler than Theo. Maybe only Bowie.

Bailey sings "Part of Your World." Unsurprisingly, she has a perfect Disney princess belt. I'm happy for her.

Nick pushes the binder down the table toward Will.

"I don't sing," says Will. He is drinking whiskey, I think specifically so he doesn't have to drink beer that Nick bought. I hope that's the case anyway. He shoves the binder back to Nick.

"C'mon, man." Nick pushes back. "It's karaoke." Will glares at him and takes another sip.

"Mira hasn't sung either," pipes up Max.

"Wow, thank you." I throw a nacho chip at him.

"Oh!" says Nick. "How about a duet?"

"Jesus, Nick, no." I catch Will's eye. I can feel some weird setup happening here, and I don't like it. Will stands up, whispers to the karaoke host, and jumps onstage.

Will has chosen "The Wreck of the Edmund Fitzgerald," a classic, but a classic that is seven minutes long, an epic about turmoil on the high seas. It's the straight man's version of "All Too Well." Will was right: He does not sing. It's more of a melodic-ish shouting. Artistically, it's not a great moment for music, but he is loud to make up for it, and around minute four, the whole bar is pounding their tables and singing along with him. He grows bolder and louder, and by minute six, he is just staring directly at Nick, screaming at him about a shipwreck.

I do not understand men.

He finishes with a big note, and the entire bar screams their approval. Three old men rush over to shake his hand and buy him another whiskey. Will looks at me, triumphant, and not a little drunk. He raises his glass to me, and the crowd goes wild.

"Wow," says Nick. "I—I don't understand why that was cool?"

"Don't underestimate the power of Gordon Lightfoot in a small-town bar," I say. I get up and go over to Will.

"That was really weird," I say. "And oddly . . . awesome?"

"I don't like that guy," he says, his voice gruff like the weary old sailor that he apparently is now.

"You really showed him," I say. I sit down. "Whiskey, huh?"

"I'm not drinking that guy's beer." He seems to be in a very salty mood.

"Why are you mad?" I ask. "You just achieved peak karaoke success."

"I don't sing," he says again. "It was either Lightfoot or that jackass was going to make us sing 'A Whole New World' or some shit." This is a new version of Will. He's a little unhinged. I don't hate it.

"You're not wrong, unfortunately." Nick would have done that. "So . . . you're mad that you did something you didn't want to do?" I glance over. "Because, dude, you won. Look at him. You stole *all* the thunder."

"Good," he says. He swills his drink. It occurs to me only now that I don't think I've seen him drunk. A cider here or there, but this whiskeyed Will is an interesting new find. A new song starts up: three drunk middle-aged women, singing "All by Myself" very loudly. Interesting choice for a trio.

"I'm pissed, okay? This guy just shows up and steals my summer." Ah. There it is. "I was going to do this play, and it would have been this cool role, with you. And you're so . . ." I look up at him in surprise, but he is staring into his drink. "And you guys have this . . . whatever, history, and I wanna be respectful, right? But I like you. There's something here. We both know it. What are we doing?"

"You terrify me," I whisper, but the bar is loud.

"I can't hear you." He leans in. I shake my head *never mind*. Our heads are close. "Hey," he says. He looks up at me now, totally disarmed, and without thinking, I take his hand. It is warm and calloused. I know Will is drunk and having a moment he might not remember tomorrow, but I feel suddenly thrilled.

"Hey," I say. The women onstage scream the big note, except they're all singing different notes, and not in a good way. I have to lean in so he can hear me. "Nick is nothing. It's shitty for both of us that he just showed up."

"Yeah." He laughs bitterly.

"And I like you too." His eyes lock on mine. For a minute, I think he's going to kiss me. I want very much to kiss him, I realize with sudden clarity, but not in this shitty bar at a table where Nick Nolan is also sitting and, I realize, glaring at us. I sit back.

"That's good news," says Will. We are just sitting there, holding hands, staring at each other, when I hear my name.

"Mira! Our song!" Theo drags me up onstage. "I saw that," he whispers as he hands me a mic.

To be clear, Theo and I do not have a song. He has selected "Complicated" by Avril Lavigne, which is close enough. We used to drive around and sing it on repeat, blaring it out the windows. It's not what I would have picked, but it's fun, and Theo and I put on a show. Our table hoots and claps, and I catch both Nick and Will staring at me like I'm candy. When we're done, Max grabs Theo and kisses him, which makes me happy for so many reasons.

I come off the stage and head back to Will, but Nick grabs my hand.

"I need to talk to you."

I pull my hand away. "You're drunk."

"Just five minutes."

"Not when you're like this." Will has clocked us and is watching closely.

"Is there some other guy?" he asks. "You're with someone else?" He stares openly at Will.

"What?" As though that's the only reason I wouldn't want to be with him.

"I see him looking at you." His tone has hardened so completely that I almost laugh. "He punches like a little bitch. Steal my girl . . ." he mutters under his breath.

"What? No." Will looks at me? "I'm not your girl."

"I don't like that guy," Nick slurs. "I don't like him talking to you."

I laugh in his face. I'm angry. "You have no say in who I talk to."

"I do." Nick's voice is getting louder, masked only by "Hollaback Girl" sung by an extremely large man in coveralls. "I did all this for you. I came here and I'm doing this stupid play in this stupid town, and I think I get to say who my girlfriend holds hands with." He's never called me his "girlfriend" before.

"I dumped you, remember?" I shout back over the music, not noticing that the song has ended. "I'm not your girlfriend anymore!"

You can all but hear the record scratch.

The room is silent. Nick looks around, smiling, then back at me.

"Looks like they all know now," he says. "Secret's out. Your move, Belmont." He smirks at me and walks away.

I don't realize that Nick has left the bar until the server appears beside me with the bill. "The, uh, famous dude said to put it all on one tab?" She looks around, but we both know he has gone.

I sigh and hand over my credit card.

Chapter 26

Twelve days until Opening Night

We don't have rehearsal for two days, but it takes no time for the news to spread among the cast. It is to be expected that everyone involved with the show would find out about the scene at the bar. It's big news in a small town. It almost sounds glamorous, sleeping with the TV star. I am dreading facing everyone tomorrow.

I have so many texts from Nick:

Mira. Call me.

We need to talk.

Babe, I'm so sorry. I don't care about anything but us.

Mira for fucks sake.

You know I could shut this whole show down, right? I just have to say the word.

I don't even like Shakespeare.

I GAVE UP LEGO BATMAN FOR YOU!!!

Really, you're just going to ignore me?

You are done in this business, do you hear me?

I sit for a long time. It's clear that being friends with Nick isn't going to be an option. I also know there is only one way he is going to leave me alone.
You were right, I type. There is someone else.
His reply:

I fucking knew it.

I'm done with this. I'm outta here.

I'm not sure exactly what he means, but I have a feeling I'm about to find out.

When I walk into rehearsal the next day, everyone is staring at me. There are whispers. I'm not sure what to say. I certainly didn't invite my personal drama to follow me and join the show. He did that all on his own.

Nick is surprisingly quiet. He completely ignores me except when our characters are interacting. At break, he makes a show of hitting on Bailey. She is sitting on a chair, eating an apple, and he keeps leaning in, whispering to her, smirking. At first, she rolls her eyes (a trigger for him, I've learned from experience), and when he finally leans in and snakes his arm around her shoulder, she jumps up.

"What the fuck, Nick?" It's audible enough that the room turns to look at her.

"Bitch," I hear him hiss. "You should be so lucky."

I've seen it a hundred times, even when we were together, I am loath to admit. Most girls lap it up, most girls are all too happy to have attention from the big star. I catch Bailey's eye and nod at her. I get it. I hate that he did that. I'll talk to her later.

We are running the scene where both Demetrius and Lysander are under Puck's love spell and are fighting over me. It's a fun scene—Max is so funny in it, falling all over me, but Nick just isn't getting it. I hear my father clear his throat from the back of the room.

"Uh, yes, good energy, folks . . . Mr. Nolan, a quick word, if you please?" Usually he bellows notes at us but tries to err on the right side of Nick's ego.

"I've said it a thousand times, Ross, you're welcome to share any notes you have for me with everyone."

"Ah, I see, yes, all right." My father rubs his face. "It's just . . . lacking urgency."

Nick stares at him blankly. "It's no good?"

"It has . . . elements of good," he says. "It just . . ."

"Spit it out, man," snaps Nick.

I see a flash in my father's eyes that I know means trouble. "It's a love scene."

"No, it's a fight scene," Nick says, as though it's obvious.

"Between Lysander and Demetrius, yes, but really, each is performing a love scene with Helena, or trying to, but your anger seems to extend toward Helena . . ."

"Well, yes, okay? I'm mad at her."

"At Helena?"

"At your daughter," Nick snaps. "Okay? I've had it with her head games and mixed signals and bullshit, okay?" Everyone looks at me. I look down at my script.

"I say," says my father. "That is between you and . . ."

"No." I stand up. I've had enough. "It's not. There's nothing between us." A few people look confused. "Yes, we dated, okay? And I broke up with him." There is a general hushed murmuring, both at the revelation and, I suppose, the fact that he was the one who got dumped. "And then Nick showed up here—followed me here—and he won't drop this thing. And I can't, okay? I can't do it anymore." I turn to Nick. "Either stop being an asshole or, I don't know, just fuck off!"

Nick does a slow clap from across the stage. He walks slowly toward me. "That might have been your best performance ever," he says, smirking. He walks up the steps slowly. "Which isn't saying much."

"Honestly, just leave me alone."

"No, Miranda, I'm actually committed to this show. I'm here because I want to be. We can't say the same for you, can we?"

"What are you talking about?"

"Have you been honest, Miranda? Does everyone know why you're here?"

"Yes, okay, fine, you got me kicked off my show!" I burst out. "Yes, this is the only work I have right now! Are you happy?" My eyes go right to my parents. Sure enough, my mother's eyes are wide. My father is shaking his head, shocked.

"You hear that, everyone? She's only here because she's desperate!" He grins wolfishly.

"Why are you doing this?" I feel Theo's eyes on me. This is news to him too. "What are you trying to achieve here? I lost the show, so what? I'll find something else."

He leans in close. "I only have to say the word, and you'd be blacklisted. You'd never work again!"

I lean in closer so only he can hear. "And I only have to say the word, and the whole world would know what you did to me at your party."

He steps back. "You're such a bitch." He snorts. "I never did ask the execs about getting you back, by the way. I had a feeling you'd fuck me over again . . ."

"I don't care. I just don't," I say, and something in him crumples. "This conversation is over. Enough." He looks at me, dumbfounded. His scowl turns into something nearly violent.

"You know what? This is bullshit. Fuck this." He moves to leave but turns back, pointing at my dad. "I'm out of here. And you know what? I hate Shakespeare. I hate theater! It's stupid . . . Left is right and up is down . . . All the weird rules, the superstitions." He takes on a pretentious, mocking voice. "Don't whistle in the theater! Don't wish anyone good luck, and whatever you do, don't say '*Macbeth*' in the theater." There is a collective gasp of horror. "Oh my God, what? *Macbeth!*" They gasp again. He raises his arms dramatically, spookily, moving toward them. *"Macbeth, Macbeth. Mac—"*

It almost happens in slow motion. The ghost light cord. Nick's foot, his frantic expression as he falls forward off the stage. The sickening crack of his landing. His scream.

If the show wasn't already doomed, it sure as shit is now.

Chapter 27

Ten days until Opening Night

Of course it was filmed. One of the high school kids in the lighting booth got the whole thing. It's viral before Nick gets back from the ER.

He has, in an almost delicious bit of irony, broken both legs. He will be in recovery for months. My mind goes straight to the show—*Listings*, not *Midsummer's*. He's done with us, and I think, having seen his true colors, everyone is pretty done with him. No, it's *Listings* I am thinking of: Shooting was supposed to start up in mid-September. They will have to write around it; he'll be out for months. They'll need to do something drastic, and fast. Not my problem.

Or, not my problem until Jay, the showrunner, calls me.

"Mira! How you doing? Up there doing Shakespeare, yeah?" I am quiet. Last time this asshat spoke to me, it was to unceremoniously fire me. "So you heard about Nick, right?" I say nothing. "Oh, shit, duh, of course, you were there! Ha! My brain. Okay, so listen, we have a proposition that might work really well for all of us. This thing with you and Nick has caught a lot of heat—naughty, naughty! But yeah, we ran some numbers, and we think audiences might actually really like us to run with this." He pauses. "Are you still there?"

"Yes."

"So what we're thinking, we bring you back, move you to the lead spot . . ."

"I thought my character moved to LA."

"That's just it—you came back!" He delivers this as though it should be good news. "And, I dunno, Nick can be in a coma or something, and until he's out, it's up to you to save the agency. And then when he gets out, you become partners." I can practically see his jazz hands over the phone.

"Jay," I say. "You saw the video, right?"

"Oh, yeah!" he says. "Pretty rough!"

"Okay, great, so, does that seem like a working relationship that should continue?" Now he is quiet. "And, given the fact that the last time we spoke, you were firing me because that person asked you to, do you think I would ever work with you again?"

There is a long pause. Then Jay says a number.

"Per season? Give me a break."

"No. Per episode."

Ah. Now that's a big number.

"Let me think about it," I say. There's nothing to think about. It's the most money I've ever made in my life. It would be a lead, first on the call sheet for a prime-time show. It would be the fame and success. Everything I've always wanted.

Of course I'm not fucking taking it.

Before the ambulance had even pulled away, my dad was on the phone to Will, who has now been rightfully reinstated in his role as Demetrius. The show opens in ten days. Now, on top of the usual chaos of tech week, figuring out set and costumes and actually using the finally finished set, we are, at the eleventh hour, bringing in a new actor. We are supposed to do our first stumble-through tomorrow. Sally has drafted up a new rehearsal schedule with as many extra hours as possible. Luckily, all the sponsors who signed on when Nick was in the show had already handed over the money. None of them have asked for the money back; it would be a bad look, and

I think maybe they are relieved to not actually be affiliated with Nick now, given how things have turned out.

On top of the extra rehearsals, my father has enlisted me to get Will back up to speed and has scheduled us a private rehearsal, giving me the keys to the theater. Max and Bailey will join us in a few hours when Max gets off work, but we have the whole morning to run the blocking and lines before they arrive.

I arrive half an hour early to open up the theater. I've never actually been here alone. It's incredibly still. Without people and words and sounds and lights, it's just a building, empty and quiet and dark. I make my way up to the theater. The stairs creak under my feet. I feel my way through the dark and flick on the lights at the top of the stairs. I pull the heavy soundproof doors and step in. The room feels thick with the energy of the past week. The last time I was here was total chaos: my world imploding, Nick's meltdown, his fall. As the paramedics were wheeling him out, I heard a lot of rumblings from the cast and crew as they left.

"He had it coming."

"You don't mess around with the Scottish play."

"It's irresponsible, is what it is."

"It's disrespectful."

As I watched the entire cast and crew descend into panic, from screams and cries when Nick's femur split through his skin to a heavy, somber silence as people gathered their things, no idea what would happen to the show, I felt many things, but mostly guilt. True, I did not ask Nick to follow me from the city and lie to my parents and steal Will's role and get the entire town excited about the big celebrity, but none of it would have happened if not for me. I caught a number of sideways looks on my way out, and it was very clear that my feelings of responsibility were shared. I knew how it looked: The director's daughter gets the role handed to her, and all she brings in is chaos. And now the show is ruined.

And somewhere deep below all that, my own deep resentment, because Nick has tainted this whole thing for me. Because without his presence and interference and drama, this show was the most fun I'd had in a long time. It was the first time in forever that I was loving acting. I was falling back in love with it, even with my hometown a little. Even with myself.

I make my way onstage. Will isn't due for another fifteen minutes. I do a little warm-up, some stretching, vocal runs. I haven't done this stuff since theater school, loosened myself, opened myself up. An inordinate amount of time in theater school is spent learning how to find your breath, land in your body, become present. It's been years since I actually put these skills into practice. The nature of my role on *Listings* was such that the more tightly wound I was, the better. I didn't realize that it had become my default setting.

I run through my monologues. The big one is that first one at the top of the play. I have been playing it comically: big and pouty and quirky. But alone onstage, when it's just me, it lands differently. I run through it, and it hits me how, under the snark and haughtiness, Helena is deeply sad. I am sad. I am maybe a little broken in the same way she is: We do not completely believe we are deserving of real love. I have had relationships. I have had a lot of sex. I've often mistaken sex for something more. I shake it off and go again: *"Things base and vile, holding no quantity, love can transpose to form and dignity. Love looks not with the eyes but with the mind, and therefore is winged cupid painted blind."*

It hits me that I am thirty-four and have never really been in love, not for real, not with someone good and attainable who could see me back. Helena is the supporting actress longing to be the leading lady. Helena, I suddenly realize, my dad's words solidifying in my mind, is not in a comedy. A comedy is happening all around her, but she's in a drama, a tragedy, even. Helena thinks she's Juliet, or could be but for all the obstacles and fairy magic and general fuckery all around her. Her resolve never changes. She loves Demetrius. She wants him. She never falters. It occurs to me that all I ever do is falter. It occurs to me that I'm not ever sure who I am.

I run it again, this time quieter. Even sadder. But I have unlocked something in this comic monologue, a deep longing in Helena, and in myself, that she has led me to. I let it all out into the dark, my voice bouncing around the empty room. My heart is racing, and I am surprised to feel tears pricking my eyes. I am alone here, and it all hits me. I lie down on the stage and close my eyes. I try to find my breath. It's been so much. Too much. I lie there for a long time. I'm so exhausted by this whole summer.

"Are you okay?" Will is standing over me.

"Shit!" I jump up, wiping my eyes. "I didn't hear you come in." I feel exposed.

"I came up from backstage," he says. He has two coffees and hands me one.

"Oh, thanks." I feel caught somehow. I wish he had come in when I was killing my monologue, not during this lying-on-the-floor part. We stand there awkwardly. I haven't seen him since the night at the pub.

"We're very glad to have you back," I say. I take a sip. Oat milk and cinnamon. We stand there looking at each other. "This is good coffee. Thank you." I wonder if he remembers the part at the pub where we said we liked each other.

"So, um, how, um, drunk were you? The other night," I ask, looking intently at my coffee cup.

"Not that drunk," he says. "Just enough to get interesting." He is watching me watch my coffee cup.

"It certainly was," I say. I look up and he holds my gaze. It feels like something hot that I shouldn't touch. I look away.

"Not as interesting as the show Nick put on here." Will glances at the edge of the stage and cringes.

"Did you see the video?"

"Would you hate me if I told you I watched it a few times?"

"Karma's a real bitch!" I say.

"But he's okay?"

"Yeah, he'll be okay." I don't know what makes me say it. "They asked me to come back to the show. To replace him. And then be colead when he returns. They offered me all the money," I say. I haven't told my parents this yet, or even Theo.

"Huh," he says. "Are you . . . ?"

"I'm thinking about it." I don't know why I lie here. To impress him? To establish some flimsy barrier between us? I knew *Listings* was over (I thought it was, anyway), but it never occurred to me that it could come back. The idea of returning feels so wrong.

"Well," he says. "You deserve success. If you want it." He clears his throat.

I'm reminded again of my realization about Helena, how like me she is, how she holds herself in such low esteem—literally a dog on the ground—that she will take any scrap of Demetrius's attention. It was so incredible to me that Nick would want me, that I was within his notice. It never occurred to me to consider what I wanted from him.

Now here is this lovely man, who is good and kind and generous and uncomplicated. The only chaos between us is all my doing. I like him. I feel like if I let us tip into each other again, it could be more, it could be everything. I'm not sure what to do with that.

"So," I say. "This damn play." I pull out my script and pencil.

"Yes." He does the same.

"I'm really glad to have you back," I say again. "We all are. Everyone."

"Not just you." He smiles.

"Nope. Barely me at all, really." I smile.

Our eyes lock again. I am thinking about that moment at the bar, our hands laced together, that sense that any second now one of us would lean in. The feeling is here now. My heart is racing. We face each other, not moving. Then he reaches toward me and slips a strand of hair behind my ear, as comfortably and casually as if he does it every day. His fingers linger in the space under my ear where my jaw meets my throat, feeling out the hollow there, feeling out my eyes as he steps toward me.

I want to kiss him. I want to run my hands through his hair and feel his arms around me, I want heat to build, I want our tongues to find each other, I want to fall to the ground, I want everything, all of it, and a version of me would go for it too, if I let her. But I am tingling with my new self, my new realization that I want to be seen, and here is someone who might really see me. I have a chance to see myself.

I catch his hand. Then I give it back to him, pressing my hand and his to his chest. I can feel his heart.

"You're not wrong," I say. "There is . . . something here." He knows. He nods. "My . . . romantic life has caused this production enough chaos." That casual phrase, "love life," suddenly feels so potent. "I'm just here for the summer, and it's half over, and I feel like . . . I can't risk it." I am clinging to this narrative like it's a lifeboat.

"So you keep saying. You're the one holding my hand."

"Maybe that's where we leave it for now?" I say.

"But you like me back?" That half smile. He's killing me.

"I like you back."

"So, what are we supposed to do with that?" he asks. "We keep almost happening . . ."

"I don't know."

"So, we just . . . hold hands until further notice?"

"I feel like that's the smart move."

"Okay." He doesn't move.

"Okay."

The truth is that I've never let a production get in the way of a hookup. I have freely hooked up with castmates before—everyone does, I think. It's not a big deal. You keep it professional on set, and whatever happens between you off set is your business. But that was before Nick. That got messy, emotional. People got hurt. The more I get to know Will, the more I know that this wouldn't be just for the summer. This would be so real. I have never done real. I am afraid to hurt him.

I release his hand and step back.

"Ooof," I say. "Emotions."

He laughs hoarsely. "Yeah."

"So, okay, um, Shakespeare play. Where are you at with the lines? I know we have, like, no time . . ."

"I know them."

"What? How?"

"Well, I had learned a lot of them before . . ."

"Before you were rudely ousted."

He laughs. "Yeah. And I just reviewed a lot this weekend."

"So, you're telling me you just happen to remember a whole role in iambic pentameter because you have a good memory."

He shifts uncomfortably. "Yes?"

I narrow my eyes. "If I didn't know better, I'd say you knew you'd be coming back."

He laughs awkwardly.

"Just a good memory, I guess," he says. I stare at him. "What? I didn't push him off the stage. Much as I would have liked to." I still say nothing.

"Is there something you're not telling me?"

"I . . . Yes . . . No, sort of? It's stupid, okay?"

I put my script down. "Tell me."

He sighs. "It's . . . it just sounds weird, is all." I wait. "Ugh. Okay. My grandmother told me I should just keep a handle on the lines."

"Your grandmother." I shake my head. "What does your grandmother have to do with it?"

He gives me a funny look. "Barb is my grandmother. You didn't know that?"

"Barb, the fairy?!"

He chuckles. "Among other things, yes, Barb the fairy."

"So why did she tell you that? That you needed to know your lines?" I gasp. "Is Barb psychic or something?" I wouldn't put it past those witches.

"No, no," he says. "I mean, maybe she likes to think so? No, it was because she was worried about Nick."

I gasp again. "Wait, was Nick's accident some voodoo shit? I am seriously afraid of Peg . . ."

"No, God, I hope not. They are just a bunch of weird old ladies."

"And Ron."

"And Ron. My grandma, she was worried he was going to screw it up . . ."

"Which he did."

"Well, sure, and we have lunch every week, and she made me run lines with her." He shrugs. "It's lame, I know."

"Okay," I say. "So, you know your lines. I have to say, that's a huge relief. That's . . . Honestly, the rest of it is easy. Thank you," I say. I still want to kiss him, this man who has lunch every week with his weird, witchy grandmother, who has let her bully him into knowing his lines, who is now essentially saving the show. Who I get to spend the next three weeks chasing through an enchanted forest.

"So, it's just the blocking, then," I say. "Let's get started."

Chapter 28

For all the ways adding Nick into our production was tedious and frustrating, adding Will back in is easy. It's as if he never left. He listens, he takes notes, and he does, indeed, know his lines. Max and Bailey join us later in the day, and in a few hours, we have run our scenes to the point that Max says, "In one day, we got better than a month with Nick."

"He's not wrong," adds Bailey. I smile to myself, saying nothing.

We have an hour before the rest of the cast arrives for evening rehearsal. The four of us order Thai food and sit around the dressing room, noodles dangling from our mouths, laughing, that collegial feeling when everyone is on the same page, everyone has a shared goal, and it's coming together. For the first time since the read-through, I feel like I'm part of a cast.

Max and Bailey have lots of questions about life as an actor. They have just finished theater school, and they both want to move to the city, find agents, do the whole thing.

"Is it weird being back here?" asks Bailey. "You're used to a much more professional environment."

I think back to those years on set. I think of drinking with Nisha in her dressing room after shooting, how much our friendship revolved around gossip and show drama and success. I would have said we were close friends, and yet in the absence of our shared mission, the show, what is there between us? I think of hours on set, waiting alone in my trailer in uncomfortable shoes. I remember getting a small monologue one episode, working hard, nailing it, and having it cut in post.

I wouldn't have said it two months ago, but it's true now. "This is more fun," I say. "There's less pressure, less money involved. That makes people behave better." I pause. "Except my own parents, of course." I tilt my head in Will's direction.

"*Ohhhhhhhh!*" Max snaps his fingers.

I glance at Will. He winks at me.

"So, what are you going to do?" asks Bailey. "Now that you don't have a job." Max shoots her a sharp look. "What? Sorry, is that rude?" Max nods at her slowly.

"It's okay." I laugh. "It's kind of the burning question."

I help myself to another spring roll. I'm hungrier in North Lake. It's funny: It hasn't even occurred to me that I wouldn't return. My life is there, my work . . . but what work? What life? I have the condo, a few friends, but no one who has reached out or checked in, in my absence, aside from a single text from Nisha about the video of Nick's fall. No work to return to. I picture myself driving around the city in one-way traffic downtown, finding parking, running up concrete stairs to yet another audition. Those long hallways filled with other women who fit your exact description. Women who are increasingly younger and thinner. Hours of prep for an audition that is over in five minutes, and you know within the first minute that you're not right for it. Callbacks. Waiting. Rejection, rejection, rejection.

But the thrill, the relief, and the validation when you do book something. And anyway, what else is there? My reality has been so finite, my goals so clear: Get out of North Lake. Get an agent. Be an actor. I even became a pretty successful actor, by any standards. Not the most creatively fulfilling work, but I was able to buy real estate in Toronto. I was able to pay for health insurance and occasional fancy spa days. I had a life that looked enviable to all the Kelsies of the world. I proved everything I wanted to.

But do I want to go back?

"I don't know," I say. "I'm not sure what my next steps are." I'm not announcing to everyone that I have the chance to go back to *Listings*.

"Well, what do you want?" asks Max. I look at him, surprised.

"I actually have no idea." I try to imagine life here, but every element feels amorphous: I have the show, but it will be over soon. Theo and I are back to good, but he doesn't live here. My parents and I are getting along, but that's not worth staying for in the grand scheme of things. Across the room, Will stares thoughtfully into his box of pad see ew, avoiding my eyes. Could he give me a reason to stay? The mere idea almost makes me choke on my noodles.

"Our acting prof just retired," says Bailey. "I know they haven't replaced her." She and Max look at me expectantly.

"I dunno. I'm not sure I could teach."

"You've been teaching us all summer," says Max. "You keep having to take over the scenes and explain it to new people . . . You've definitely been our leader." I look over again at Will. He smiles but says nothing. "You've been a great teacher."

"That's more directing," says Bailey. "Maybe you should try directing? Ooh, you could work with your parents! Maybe you could take over the theater?"

"Okay," I say, overwhelmed. "That's . . . a lot of options. Thank you." Conversation over.

Max gets the hint and changes the subject. "Hey, what's everyone's dream role?" Bailey launches into a prepared speech on why she would be an amazing Glinda, and I'm off the hook. For now.

An hour later, we are all assembled in the theater for our first stumble-through.

"Okay, people," says Sally. "First of all, big thanks to Will for saving the day . . ." There is an uproar of applause. "And to Mira for working with him today to get him up to speed." There is another polite smattering of applause, though decidedly less enthusiastic. "So today we are running the show start to finish, no tech, no interruptions unless totally essential. This is our first time running through the show. It's going to be messy, but we open in ten days, we are behind schedule, and we need to focus and do our best. Only person allowed to call for lines is Will." She looks pointedly at a few people, and a few people look pointedly at me. "Okay, places!"

It goes better than expected. My mother as Titania and Marcus as Oberon are powerful and commanding; they set the tone and everyone follows. Theo is their lanky, unpredictable child, full of mischief. It's my first time seeing the scenes yet with the rude mechanicals, the local peasants putting on a play for the big wedding scene at the end. It's ridiculous, a play within a play, especially when the ending feels like it should be when the lovers all make peace and land in their true loves. But no, there is so much more chaos. It really is a three-ring circus. They are such a mixed group: Age and gender were of no consequence when casting them. They are just the funniest people in the cast. There is one actor who plays the hole in the Wall in their "play," a stern, unflinching, very old man named Ted, and I can't take my eyes off him, he is so ridiculously dignified. He plays Wall like it's King Lear. I have this feeling of missing out, like all this time I didn't notice the show coming together around me, I was so fixated on my own corner of it. To be fair, considering the levels of drama in the lovers' ring, you can't blame me.

On break, I catch my parents arguing again in the stairwell.

"Ross, we are *not* using pyro in this production—"

"There's plenty of money, and you are not the production designer—"

"I am the producer. I am not approving this misuse of company—"

"Misuse? Yes, let's discuss misuse, my dear, let's discuss the ways you have taken advantage yet again of my—"

"Places!" calls Sally.

My mother shakes her head and steps back. "For God's sake, Roscoe, can you blame me?" she hisses. She turns and starts up the stairs, and I slip away before she sees me, before she realizes I heard whatever that was.

Our scenes with Will go well: not perfect, he misses a couple of cues, but not bad for his first day. I am so much more comfortable with him than with Nick. It felt so wrong, so uncomfortable, pretending to throw myself at Nick, pretending to love him madly. Ironic, since we had been actual lovers. With Will, I can actually act, except it's not all acting, pretending to want him.

Overall, the rehearsal is a bit of a shit show, people forgetting lines and props and entrances, a whole scene happening before anyone realizes there was supposed to be a scene before it, but it's also the most fun I've had with the show yet. It's happy chaos, and people are rallying to support Will. They are glad he's back, and I can tell he's happy too.

My final scene is a simple one. Once the lovers wake up from their dream and return to the duke's palace, we are basically done except for the wedding feast, where we watch the mechanicals' play. It's about fifteen minutes where we just sit there. We are blocked all together, a trio of newlyweds. We didn't do this scene much in rehearsal, so it didn't occur to me that we would have to sit together now. Just holding hands onstage.

I look up at him, smiling stupidly, and he looks back at me, beaming, his face open and lit up in a way I have never seen. Usually, I'm lucky if I can get a half smile. He laughs out loud, this joyful bark, another sound I've rarely heard, and then I remember that we're acting, he's acting. He's watching the weird play at our fake wedding. I feel chastened, silly for thinking for a moment that that's how he would look at me if he were in love with me. But then he squeezes my hand, holds it tight for a long time, and I wonder if I might be onto something after all.

Chapter 29

Theo and I walk home together after rehearsal.

"I think it went pretty well." I'm relieved.

"Yeah, all things considered," he says. "Will did well." He looks at me sideways. "So did you. It was like your whole performance just lit up."

"Oh!" I feign surprise, but I know he's right. Even in a messy stumble-through, I felt different. "Well, thanks. And yes, thank goodness for Will."

"So, what's going on there?" he asks.

"I don't know what you mean." But I do.

"Mirabel."

"Theodore."

"You like him." He stops and faces me.

"I like him!"

Theo laughs. "Oh, wow," he says. "Well, this is fun. So, what's happening?"

"Um, nothing," I say. "We have held hands with intense eye contact three times, he has punched my ex-boyfriend once, and I have slept in his bed with a gay man once." I pause. "What's the catch?"

"With Will?"

"Yeah. There's always something. What is it?"

Theo laughs. "There's nothing. Mirabel, he's the best guy. The best, most solid guy I know. He just has one huge flaw that I will never be okay with."

"What?" I ask, alarmed. Of course there's something. I should have known.

"Well, he's into women."

"Ha! I can live with that."

"I cannot." He laughs. We keep walking. "But seriously, not my business. I will just say, he's been through it. Losing Jonah nearly broke him; he wasn't himself for a long time after. And now he's back to good. He's not someone for a quick rebound or whatever. Don't hurt him."

"Yeah." My smile is gone. "I know, Theo."

"I'm just saying, what can really happen? You're leaving after the show, right?"

"Well, for starters, I don't love the implication that I would hurt him." I give him a chance to take it back, but he doesn't. I change the subject. "The show asked me to come back." I say it for effect. I don't know why I keep telling people when I know I won't do it. Maybe because I have so little else going on, it feels good to sound in demand. "As a lead. Tons more money." This would be enticing to most people, but not Theo.

"Mira," he says. "You are an artist. You're really gifted." I look at him, surprised. "No, really, you're so good in this show, and I see how you are working with the others, what you can bring out in them. *Listings* . . . It . . ."

"It sucks, I know."

"It really does." He looks at me pointedly. "It's fine if you want fame and a paycheck, but I've seen so much change in you just since you arrived. I know you see this as just a summer gig, a dumb community theater show."

"No," I say quietly. "I did, for sure, initially. But . . . no." As I'm saying it, I realize how true this is.

"Well, good, because there's something happening to you." He looks at me sideways. "Something good." I smile to myself. "Something more than a flirtation with a gorgeous man who slays your dragons and pours you cider."

I nod slowly. "Yeah," I say. "Maybe." There is a wall of fog in my mind. I can't even begin to factor the possibility of Will into this.

"Maybe it's as simple as you're just rediscovering theater?" he asks. "Like, you weren't happy in TV, were you?"

"Theater just didn't happen for me," I say. "As a career. I don't want to be on that shitty TV show, but I want to work."

"I mean artistically," Theo continues, "as an artist."

It's been so long since I've thought of myself as an artist, but of course he's right. "Yeah," I say. "No."

"There's nothing wrong with that," says Theo. "If it's working for you."

"Yeah, we can't all have two leads a season at Stratford!" I say. I'm still jealous of him. I always have been.

He looks at me sideways. "Sounds like you might need to unpack that," he says.

"Yeah," I say. "Maybe I do." I change the subject. "What about you and Max?"

He accepts the olive branch. "Max is a dream." He pretends to swoon. "He's an absolute dream. I'm probably going to marry him."

"Wait, what? Theo! You're joking!"

"I mean, sort of. But also, it's really good. He's amazing." I've never seen him so lit up. "I'm moving to New York, after Mom . . . I mean, I'm here as long as she is. And then, yeah, I'm going to see if I can get into Broadway, and Max is going to come."

"Wow, Theo. That's amazing!"

"When you know, you know."

I keep thinking about that after we part ways. I keep walking, past my house, down the street, and up past the church toward the secret garden, the fairies' garden. I slip in the hidden entrance in the hedge, and I am back in high school, back to the girl who loved theater more than anything. I am starting to recognize her again in myself. It feels good. There is a new bench under the apple tree, a new flagstone path that someone laid by hand. The garden feels fuller, not overgrown so much as bursting. It's lovely. I stand there for a moment, longing to be sixteen again, to kiss a boy while apple blossoms fall around us, to live in the bliss of the unknown. That feels like a lifetime ago.

It never occurred to me for a minute when I signed on to do this play that it was anything but temporary. I came here so reluctantly. And what, a play, a guy, a couple of pub nights, and I'm just . . . back? I think of Theo: He won't stay forever. He's here for his mom, and he will come and go, I know. He'll always come back here. He has family here. He has roots, friends, siblings. Theo always liked it here. I never did. I try to picture myself living with my parents; the thought makes me laugh out loud. Even if I were as far across town as I could be, what? Would we have dinner together? Would I be in their shows? I'll admit that they put on good ones. But that's not a career, it's not a living. My parents have money that allows them to do this, and sure, it will be mine one day. I have money from the show, I have my condo. I think of that job at the college theater program. Am I even qualified? Would I even like teaching young people how to act? The question lands gently in me. I let it sit there. Yeah. Maybe I would. Who knows. I turn around and head back home.

I arrive in front of my parents' house. It's golden hour. It's the prettiest street in town, lush Victorians and wild cottage gardens. It feels alive and brimming with realness. Something else I've been missing. Could I live here, now, as me? Is there a life for me here?

Chapter 30

Three days until Opening Night

The next few days are a blur of costume fittings and running the show with sound and lights. Our cue-to-cue, where we run the show start to finish, perfecting every light and sound cue, takes eight hours. It's a lot of sitting around and waiting, which means a lot of sitting quietly in the back of the theater, covertly staring at Will and chastely holding hands with my whole mysterious future. Cue-to-cue is the time where the designers get to do their thing, and the actors kind of just move around like props. It's the most boring rehearsal, but it does the magical thing of bringing the show to life with all the design elements. Finally, we meet our enchanted forest: tiny twinkling lights everywhere and gauzy vines and greenery wrapped around every beam, draping down.

The set is simple, a series of platforms plus a balcony where Puck lounges and sprinkles magic down on us, and the background is an intricate collage of marbled, painted trees layered on top of one another, lights filtering between each layer. A local artist made it. When my dad described it to me, it sounded like a kid's art project, but onstage, I see how huge it is, the depth it gives the stage, a vast wood you could indeed get lost in. The fairies match the stage, all in shades of green, long glittering sleeves and lush crowns of ferns and pine cones. It's not your usual pastels and gossamer wings. They almost resemble the witches in *Macbeth*, their hair gray and wild, but they are the light version. They almost look like branches of the trees that broke off, and under the lights, the effect is lovely.

These final rehearsals are charged with anticipation, of both our looming opening night and my increasing attraction to Will, which is becoming harder to ignore. Helena wraps herself around Demetrius, and I feel the broadness of Will's chest, his heart beating under his shirt. Demetrius turns on Helena, throws her down, hovering over her, and I watch his eyes flash with a heat I've never seen in him. I feel his weight on me, I feel how right that would be. Helena grabs his arm, and I feel his forearms flinch. Helena presses herself against him, and I can smell apples and cedar and sweat. It's a cathartic and confusing simulation of love.

I get to touch him and hold him and chase him, and it's safe, it's all sanctioned. It's just pretend, but I know, we both know, that this is stirring so much beneath the surface. There is also the question of the kiss at the end: It's not written in, but it's implied. I did it with Nick before we decided to cut it, and no one has mentioned it, but we both know we could. No one would question it. I get the sense from Will that this ball is in my court, as the codirector of our scenes, as the actor who has been through different versions of it, and as the woman who decided we should just hold hands. It's laughably similar to my first kiss, the play with Theo, practicing in the secret garden. It feels that way too: the butterflies, the wondering, the will we, won't we.

The worst part is the end. The wedding. Just sitting there together.

I can chase him and grab him and fawn over him, and feel completely in control, even with everything brimming beneath the surface between us. Acting and all that. But sitting here, like this, just about undoes me. He is watching the "play" in front of us, my hand in his. Every so often, we look at each other and smile. Every now and then, he rubs the side of my hand with his thumb, as if to say, *Hey. I'm here.* I am afraid to move. I am onstage, in character; there is a play going on around us, but all I am aware of is him. I just want him to tuck my hair behind my ear again. I want him to walk into the room where I'm sleeping and bring me coffee again. And I want to kiss him. So much.

"Are you free after this?" I whisper, even though there is a scene going on around us. "We need to talk." He looks at me, a question on his face, but reads my eyes. He gets it.

"Come to the cidery?" His smile is hopeful.

"Okay."

We get through the rehearsal. We get through our fake wedding, holding hands as professionally as possible. Afterward there is an hour of notes. I sit far away from him, my heart racing every time I think about seeing him later. I want him. But what do I want?

We are finally dismissed. I hang up my costume, race home, shower, scrub off all my stage makeup. I put on a simple light-blue linen sundress with a smocked bodice and plain skirt. I don't put on any makeup. I let my hair air-dry. Somehow, I need to come to him bare.

The cidery is closed; driving in after hours feels illicit somehow. *It's just to talk,* I tell myself. *We just need to talk.*

I'm not sure if I'm supposed to go to his house or the taproom. I stand there for a second, looking around. The string lights flicker on, and Will comes around the building, in jeans and a Saves the Day T-shirt. His hair is damp too.

"Hi!"

"Hi." I'm nervous.

"So," he says.

"So."

"You want a drink?" he asks, nodding toward the taproom. I stand still where I am.

"No," I say.

"Do you want to sit out here? I could make a fire." Of course he can just whip up a fire.

"No," I say, some stronghold in me weakening.

He takes a step closer to me. "Okay," he says. "Tell me what you want." He reaches for my hand, but I instinctively step back.

"I—I don't know. I want you," I say, and his face breaks open. "I mean, look, obviously there is something here. And it's . . . very difficult, not doing anything about it. I like you." His face is soft, unguarded. "I like you in a way that feels familiar and unfamiliar. Like, really big and incredibly simple." He nods, listening. "I feel like I already nearly ruined the play."

"That wasn't your fault," he says firmly. "That guy . . ."

"I know," I say. "But it was my fault, in a way, that I was involved with someone so toxic, someone who was so shitty to me."

"Mira," he says, stepping toward me. I stop him.

"Let me try to say this," I say. He nods. "It's not about the play. Not really."

"I know." He smiles.

"I guess it's that . . . I don't want to hurt you."

"Why would you hurt me?"

"Because I'm a mess! I don't know who I am or what I want. I don't have a plan. I know we already kissed; I know it was me who shut it down . . . and started it. I know we could have hooked up weeks ago. We could sleep together now, tonight, and probably have amazing sex." His eyes light up just slightly, but he lets me talk. "And have this messy, chaotic showmance, and then I would leave."

"And you don't want that."

"I don't know what I want! I feel like that would be a waste."

"Of what?"

"Of you," I say. "Of us." I take a breath. "Of whatever else this could be." I've been avoiding eye contact this whole time, but my eyes finally land on his, and lock in. "And that is so much scarier." I take a breath. "I don't live here, Will."

"You could."

"I don't know if that's actually true." There is a long beat. I am running out of excuses.

"You don't want to get hurt either," he says quietly.

"I haven't really ever let anyone close enough to really hurt me," I say. Not since Theo. Which is to say, not ever. Sure, Nick pissed me off and bruised my ego. But it was a surface wound compared to what might be here. "And I don't know why, I don't know what it is, but you . . ." I sigh. "You scare the living shit out of me."

"I don't make you feel safe?" He looks confused.

"No," I say. I almost can't get the words out. "You might be the safest place I've ever been."

He steps toward me and wraps his arms around me, solid and sure. I drop my head onto his shoulder. Tears are suddenly spilling out of my eyes onto his shirt. I raise my head to wipe them, but he uses his collar and draws me back in.

"I feel so stupid," I say when I finally pull away. "I'm acting like this is some big thing, and maybe I'm making it out to be way more than it is, maybe—"

"No," he says. "You're not."

"I'm not?"

"No," he says, his voice thick.

"I don't know what to do," I say. I've never felt so vulnerable offstage. "I don't know how to do this, how to be—"

"Hey." He stops me, dropping his lips on my temple, as if he's already done it a thousand times. I pull back again.

"But what if I leave? Or what if it's great and then you realize I'm an asshole?"

"I already know you're an asshole." He smiles.

"But you still like me."

"I do. So much." He hooks his finger under the belt of my dress, gently pulling me back in.

"How do we know we won't obliterate each other?"

He laughs. "Oh, sweetheart." I like that. "There's the rub. That's the thesis of every love story."

Something sparks in me. Hope. "You think this could be a love story?"

He reaches for me again, and I let him. "I think it already is." He searches my face, and I'm finally smiling back at him. He pulls me in all the way, carefully takes my face in his hands, and kisses me.

I have kissed an above-average number of people, both on and off set. I have had kisses that were perfectly staged to make audiences swoon. I have kissed movie stars.

Nothing, and no one, has ever felt so much like home.

But this does.

He does.

This kiss holds the whole world. He kisses me like he already knows everything about me. Like he already loves me.

It is late. It was a long day. I let him lead me into the house, up the stairs. I slip out of my dress and into his bed. We disappear into each other, a summer's worth of racing hearts colliding. Being next to him, wrapped up in him, held by him is somehow more intimate than everything else we do. Afterward we lie there and we talk, whispering into the dark, laughing, our hands running lightly over all our newfound places, waists and foreheads and napes of necks. I have wanted to touch him for so long, and now it feels like it's all I've ever done.

Chapter 31

Dress Rehearsal, two days until Opening Night

I usually wake up with men in a panic. Do they want me there? Do I want to be there? Should I slip out before we have to find out? Needing no one and nothing got me all the way through my twenties and early thirties. I've liked people before, a lot. I've liked people maniacally, frantically, on a desperate level that I would have told you felt like love.

It wasn't love.

It was anxiety.

Waking up next to Will is the most ease I have felt with another person maybe ever. Before I have opened my eyes, his arm is around my waist. There are things I want. I want his hands to move up to graze my breasts, or down, down, down, where I could disappear into him entirely, but he rests where he is, pulling me closer but not too close. He kisses my shoulder.

"I'm glad you're here," he whispers.

"Me too."

He slips away and is back a few minutes later with coffee. He gets back in bed with me. "So, how do I rank?"

"I beg your pardon?"

"Compared to the last man you slept with in my bed."

I laugh out loud. "Theo didn't even spoon me," I say. "You're the clear winner."

"Good."

I look over at him. His hair is a mess, he's unshaven. He's a much looser version of himself. I like it. "You look great. I like you like this," I say. He shakes his head. "No, I mean it," I say. I sit up and take a sip. "This coffee's perfect."

"I'm glad."

"So, um. What happens now?" I ask.

"What do you mean?"

"Well, I just . . . We have rehearsal tonight. How do we behave?"

He leans backs against the pillow and looks at me. "How do you want to behave?"

"Very badly," I say, in my sexiest voice. He raises an eyebrow but doesn't flinch. I sit back. "No, but seriously, do we . . . Are we . . . ?"

"Do we hold hands publicly?" He smirks.

"Yeah?"

"You don't want to?"

"No," I say. Why do I feel shy? "I do. I really do."

"Okay, so?"

"I'm worried people are going to—"

He puts a finger very gently to my lips. "Hey. We're adults. We don't need to be a big deal about it. We don't need to make out onstage, but we don't need to hide it. We don't need a game plan. Don't overthink it. It's a good thing. Let's just enjoy it."

"Huh." It did not occur to me that I could simply enjoy anything. "But what do we say when . . ."

He kisses me. "It's no one's business."

Will and I walk into the dress rehearsal together. I'm expecting all heads to turn, like the prom scene in a teen movie, or at least for the fairies to notice. I feel like it's obvious. I feel completely lit up, like there are big Vegas flashing arrows above our heads, pointing toward each other. But no. We walk into the dressing room and are immediately swept up in a frenzy of costumes, curling irons, clouds of hair spray, communal makeup.

There are two changing rooms and one large hair and makeup area. I am used to my own section of a makeup trailer, at least, but now we have six mirrors with thirty people. Bailey and I get our own to share. My mother takes a whole one to herself, the corner spot, to remind everyone of her role here. There are people everywhere, costume ladies on the ground with pins in their mouths. Suddenly, with costumes on, it feels real. It feels like a surprise that we are these characters, that we are really doing this. I'd forgotten what the hype felt like. Maybe I am aglow from last night, or maybe I'm getting swept up in it, but I can't help but smile as I look around. Will's fingers graze mine, catch them, and squeeze before he is accosted by one of the wardrobe assistants, who needs him for a final measurement.

The lovers are dressed all in shades of white and cream, beige for the men, layers that come off as we spiral into the fairy magic, so that by the end, we are in light, gauzy shifts similar to the fairies'. I like my costumes: I am in a cream chiffon slip with ribbons under my bust and waist, my hair undone, and I'm barefoot. Fairy Helena. Bailey is in a similar thing, hers with a higher neck and a lower back, lace instead of ribbon, and we cause a little bit of a stir when we come out in them. Theo wolf whistles, and I immediately look over at Will, who raises his eyebrow ever so slightly and twitches his lips. After we run the cues for our last scene before the wedding, he grabs my hand backstage and pulls me into a dark corner behind the curtains.

"That dress," he says, almost in a growl, "is barely a dress . . ."

"Oh, thanks." I smile into the dark. "You like it?"

"So very much," he murmurs into my hair. His breath on my neck sends a shiver across my whole body.

"Remind me why I'm not supposed to take it off?" I whisper, tilting my face up so he can hear me. Our faces are nearly touching. One inch forward and my mouth would be on his. Our hands find each other, winding our fingers together. I want this man. I want this. I want . . . Someone pushes past us on the other side of the curtain, pressing us closer together, and I spring back.

"Something about putting on a play?" He steps away, giving my hands back to me.

"Fuck the play."

Dress rehearsals are stressful: There is no stopping, there is only survival. Sally has made a big chart both backstage and in the dressing room with the order of the scenes, but still there is much frantic whispering backstage about what's next, as always happens backstage.

Our scenes go well. I am almost late entering because Will is standing on the other side of the stage in the wings, smiling at me, and I am remembering the feel of his mouth on my mouth and his hands in my hair. Luckily Glory is behind me and pushes me onstage. I need to pull it together.

There is a bit of a stretch where we don't come onstage for a while. Will pulls me into the same corner as before, draws me in close, and kisses me deeply, his hands in my hair, and it's a world away from yesterday. Today I already know what he tastes like and how there is a spot at the base of his neck that I now own. We pull back, breathless, slipping out from our corner just in time for our cue.

It isn't until we are onstage that I notice my lipstick on Will's face. He sees my face, smudged in the same way, as does everyone, and that's it. We're busted. There's a nervous titter from the few people in the audience, and in the darkness, I hear my father clear his throat.

We press on until intermission, where we stop for the first round of notes. My father runs through some missed cues, reminders to project voices and enunciate. He has a few notes for Sally about light levels and things.

"And, ahem, could my daughter and her, ahem, associate kindly rectify their makeup situation before returning to the stage." He does not look up from his notebook, but I hear a touch of mirth in his voice as everyone bursts into laughter and then applause. Will stands and pulls me up with him, and we bow, and I feel cracked open in a way that feels new and open and good.

Barb, I can't help but notice, does not join the applause.

"So." Theo squeezes in beside me in the dressing room. "Does that mean . . . ?" He glances at Will. "I mean, obviously, you were making out backstage, but what's going on?"

I tell him about last night. "I mean, we like each other. We can't seem to stop touching each other." I shrug.

"Bullshit."

"What do you mean?"

"This is more."

"I don't know what it is." I glance up to Will onstage; he's chatting with the mechanicals and laughing. Everyone loves this guy. "It feels . . ." I exhale slowly. "It feels very scary. And also good."

"Tell me about the sex."

I elbow him. "No comment," I say.

He stares at me, delighted. "Hussy!"

"I'm not telling you." I turn to him. "It was nice. Okay?"

"Nice," says Theo.

"Okay, ugh, Theo, it was amazing."

"There we go!"

"Like, otherworldly."

"Excellent!"

"Is he, like, does he do this a lot? Like, how casual do you think this is?"

Theo laughs. "No, Mira. Trust me. He likes you." I look at him, surprised. "No, I just mean, we are old friends, I know he . . ." He stops himself.

"What?" I grab his arm. "Did he say something about me?"

He laughs again. He takes my hand. "I will just say this: He got a front-row seat to your last relationship." He's not wrong. "And I think he just wants this one—this thing—to be different." I sigh.

"Why does it all feel so complicated?" I ask. "Theo, I like him so much."

Theo leans over and kisses the top of my head. "Maybe it feels complicated because it's real?" I think about that. "Maybe this is just a real, good thing."

After notes we have a small break. Everyone has brought snacks, and I'm about to join the picnic when my father calls me over with a wave.

"Yes, Father."

"Is it any and all iterations of Demetrius that you enjoy, or is young Will . . . an upgrade?" He's smiling, but there's a tone of warning.

"Is that your business?" I arch an eyebrow.

He sits back in his seat. "For the next week, my dear, yes, it is. This show has been rattled enough by . . ." He stops before he says something shitty about my sex life, but I know where it's going.

"I'm a big girl," I say. "Also, a professional." I start back to the dressing room.

"You never saw Maggie Smith with lipstick all over her face," he calls after me. Like he has ever worked with Maggie Smith. Legend.

"I'll take the comparison," I say. "Thank you."

Chapter 32

I'm annoyed by the interaction with my father. I feel a little deflated. I look around for Will, but he's surrounded by the fairies, and I get the sense that he is getting a similar talking-to. Pulling him away from them will start a whole other thing. I feel a headache coming on. Too much coffee, not enough water.

I root around in my bag for an Advil but don't have any. My parents keep some in the office. It's locked, but I have the key chain my parents gave me with the house and theater keys. The lights are out down the back hallway. I turn the key in the lock and flick on the light . . . and gasp at the scene in front of me: my mother, flat on the desk, moaning, with Arthur between her legs, pants around his ankles, his tiny pale ass pumping away.

I shriek, and he jumps up, fumbling for his glasses as my mother throws her gown over her knees, sitting up.

"What are you doing!" she screeches at me. "No one is supposed to be in here!"

"I had a headache."

"Get out!" she barks at me, her eyes wild and frantic. "Get out!" I stand there for a moment longer than necessary, staring her down. "What, you're judging me? When you nearly ruined the show with all your drama?" Her face is twisted. In the corner, Arthur makes a show of adjusting himself. I have a feeling that my intrusion has added to the thrill for him.

"I don't know what this is," I say evenly. "And I actually don't care." I pause. Where does my father fit into this? Clearly not at all. Do I tell him? "But make no mistake, Mother, I am not the person putting the show at risk." I turn to leave. "Arthur, your dick is out."

I shut the door behind me and take the key from the door.

Will finds me at the far end of the hallway. He slips his arm around my waist and kisses my cheek.

"Hey! I was looking for you." He catches my expression. "What's wrong?"

"Um." I debate not telling him, but there's no way I can tell no one. "I just found Arthur inside . . . my mother." I will the image to leave me, but it's probably branded there for life.

"Oh, wow," says Will. He glances at the office door. "In there?" I nod.

"And then *she* tried to slut-shame *me*." I sigh so heavily it's practically a growl. "Fuck. What do I do? Do I tell my dad? Do I just pretend that didn't happen? *Ugh.*"

Will can't help but chuckle. "Gotta give it to them, on a thirty-minute break between acts . . ." He sees my face. "Sorry." He puts his hands on my shoulders. "Right now, you should eat something . . ."

"Ew. I'll never eat again." The memory makes me gag.

"Fair. But we have a show to finish. We have, like, ten minutes before break is over. Do nothing. Just get through act two, and then we'll figure this out." I smile at "we." I lean my head against his chest.

"I'm traumatized."

"Poor baby." He pats my head. "Let's get out of here." He throws his arm over my shoulder, and we get the hell out.

Act 2 opens with Titania and Bottom in their love nest: I am not looking forward to watching my mother and Arthur in action after the preview I just got. The lights are in blackout, and it isn't until the lights come up, and I feel in my pocket not one but two keys to the office, that I realize what I've done.

"Titania and Bottom," calls Sally, in her dress rehearsal voice. "Wynnie, Arthur?" Silence. "Does anyone have eyes on them?" Everyone looks around. Across the stage, Will catches my face, eyebrows raised. We race backstage.

"Shit! I think I locked them in!" I whisper. "There was already a key in the door . . . Mom must have left hers in it accidentally. I was distracted when I left and . . ."

"You took it?"

I nod urgently. We run down the back staircase together, around the corner, and down the hall to the office door, but we are too late. We arrive just in time to see my father use his own key, turn the lock, and open the door. I watch him step inside. I see Arthur scurry out a moment later. My father slams the door. Arthur meets us in the hallway. He looks incredibly awkward.

"I. Uh. We . . . You see . . ." he stammers like a child. "Good show!" he bursts out, and slips away back up the stairs. I hear my father's voice; he knows exactly what's going on. I turn to head back upstairs. I don't need to hear this.

I catch Sally in the theater.

"Where are they?" she asks. She's flustered. We are behind schedule.

"Um. They are detained?" I say. "Something came up."

She sighs and shakes her head. "He found them, didn't he?"

"You knew about this!"

She sighs heavily. "I can't discuss this with you." She storms off toward the office.

Theo jogs up to me. "Hey, what's going on? People are getting restless." He wiggles his fingers in a cute way, but I grab his hands.

"Theo. The show is fucked."

He laughs.

"You can't tell anyone." He mimes zipping his mouth, locking his mouth, swallowing the key, re-zipping his mouth. Actors. "I caught my mom and Arthur." He looks at me blankly. "Like . . ." I can't even say it. "Sexually."

Theo nods. "Yeah," he says. He avoids my eyes.

"Wait, *you* knew too?" I look around. "Does everyone know?!" He shrugs. "Why didn't you tell me?"

"Do you think your life would have been better with this information?" he asks.

I can scarcely remember life before this information. But he's right.

"You had enough going on this summer," he says. I think back to the party at Nick's cottage, my mother's tinkling laugh as she rubbed Arthur's bald head. I thought she was being ironic. Apparently not.

"Fair," I say. "So, who knew?"

"Sally told me. She's been so stressed, keeping it a secret."

"How long has it been going on?"

"Since the party, for sure. Maybe longer?"

"Ugh." I slump into a seat. "Here I thought I was going to be the one to let it all come crumbling down." I laugh to myself. "To that end, this is a relief."

"Lord, what fools these mortals be!"

"Jesus, Theo, not now."

Another theater superstition is that a bad dress rehearsal means that the opening will go well. To that end, my parents are really taking one for the team. We can hear them screaming at each other all the way from the office. I go to the back doors and pull them shut, but I sit on the other side of them so only I can hear.

"—that you've done this again! I told you last time—"

"—why do you even care? You don't notice anything—"

"I didn't want him to come this summer, and YOU insisted—"

"I thought it was over this time!"

"I saw this coming a mile away—"

"How could you? All you care about is the show—"

"All either of us care about is the show."

"Thou drivest me past the bounds of maiden's patience!"

"Don't you quote my play at me!"

"It's our play, Ross, *our play*."

The shouting turns to loud, angry talking, and I can't tell what they are saying. Finally, I hear the door open, and they come up the stairs. They see me and stop suddenly.

"You told him!" my mother shrieks.

"You knew?" My father's face is a tempest in and of itself.

I stare at them in disbelief. "Are you two serious right now? You have an entire cast and crew waiting for you." My mother looks aghast that I have dared to speak. "Mom, I did not tell him. Dad, I did not know. I found out five minutes before you." I stand up and face them. "I could not be less interested in your personal lives, but this show is opening in two days, so pull your shit together and get in there." They look at me, stunned. I hold the door open. "Please."

Act 2 is a hot mess. My mother is robotic, pretending to make love to Arthur in donkey ears. Every time she is onstage, my father leaves the room completely. The fairies get turned around and keep jumping lines in their scene with Arthur. If I didn't know better, I'd think they were doing it on purpose to throw him. In the big lovers' quarrel scene, I accidentally clip Bailey on the side of the head doing a fake slap, and Max trips and grabs the closest thing to steady himself, which is a whole wall of greenery, which comes down with a loud rip. I can hear Sally sighing backstage as she tries to call the show. Whoever is on lights is a cue behind, so sometimes we are delivering lines into darkness. I am relieved when the wedding comes and we can just sit there until it's all over.

After, my father runs through notes, but they are rushed and he skips parts. He pointedly ignores my mother.

"Any questions?" he asks at the end, closing his script with finality.

"Don't you have any notes for me?" asks my mother.

"I do," he says, looking over the top of his glasses. "If you could conduct your infidelity outside of my production, I'd be much obliged."

In the back row, one of the high school kids says, "Oh, snap."

My father likes to do an inspirational speech at this point in the week, but tonight he says, "Get some rest, people. Big week," and walks out. I feel for him.

My mother passes me on the way out. "You might want to stay somewhere else tonight."

"No shit," I say. I know that what we heard downstairs today was simply the prologue for my parents' fight, which will resume the second they get home.

Will comes up behind me. "My place?"

"Oh, yes. Please."

Chapter 33

"Do you want to talk about it?" Will asks on the drive home.

"I'm just trying to forget." I shake my head in an attempt to dislodge the vision of my mother spread eagle with Arthur between her legs.

"Aside from what you saw . . . I'm sure it's upsetting. Seeing your parents like that." He pauses. "And they were kind of shitty to you."

"They were angry at each other," I say. "Anyway, I don't care what they do. It's not like we have this tight family bond."

It's funny, it never occurred to me that my parents have a marriage. It was always me against them. In my mind, they were this impenetrable unit: living together, working together. Their lives revolved around theater in such a bubble that even I, their child, felt peripheral to it. It occurs to me now that they might also only be peripheral to each other.

"They didn't really want a child." I've never said it out loud. "I think they were trying to be normal people, and it seemed, I don't know, like an interesting character choice. *Oh, what if we were parents.* But they never really . . . took to me. They involved me in their shows, and people liked that, so I became a useful prop. But it's like, offstage, in real life, at home, we were all just . . . there. But all kind of doing our own thing."

"That's a little sad."

"I mean, I didn't really know it was," I say. "Until recently." I glance over at him. His eyes are on the road, but he grabs my hand and brings it to his lips.

"You haven't been loved well."

"Maybe not."

"Challenge accepted." He kisses my hand again firmly. My heart clenches a little at the idea of being loved at all.

"You're pretty good on these drives home," I say. He laughs. "Except we aren't going home. I'm taking shelter in your barn from my crazy parents."

"I was thinking I'd let you stay in the house."

"Oh, wow."

"In my room, even." He pulls into the driveway.

"This is so generous."

"Yeah, well . . ." I look at him, laughing, his eyes crinkled at the corners, and something sparks, like I can see it all for the first time, this, him, me, what it could all be. What it could all mean if I let it.

He stops and we get out. I come around the truck and grab his shirt, pulling him toward me. I kiss him with a new urgency that surprises me. He hesitates, then wraps his arms around me, pulling me in. I slide a hand up the back of his shirt, and he runs his hands through my hair, then down my body, crumpling the hem of my dress as his hands rise.

"You're sure?" he asks, pulling away, his breath hot on my neck. "You've been through a lot today."

"Yes," I whisper. "Yes, yes, yes."

Chapter 34

One day until Opening Night

The next morning with Will is even better. As soon as I stir, he reaches for me, kissing my forehead gently, then my mouth when I tilt it up to his. I feel him, hard against my leg, and this time I slide my hand down freely. Something has unlocked, a new ease between us. I bury myself in him. It's real, whatever it is, it's so real, and I haven't felt that maybe ever.

After, Will makes coffee and strawberry pancakes. We sit in the sunlit kitchen, a sweet, hazy filter on everything. I'm wearing a button-down flannel shirt he gave me, big woolly socks, and a pair of his boxer briefs, and I feel sexier and more myself than I have ever felt. I inhale the pancakes like they're oxygen, and Will watches me, pleased.

"You were hungry."

"These are amazing," I say. "I've never had pancakes."

"What?" He's shocked. "What do you . . . I . . . How is that possible?"

"My parents don't cook," I say. "They do grazing boards. And then, you know." I gesture at my body. "Carbs."

"Uh-huh," he says, looking away.

"What?"

"Is that a thing you've worried about? I mean, obviously I think you are perfect, so . . ."

I laugh. "I'm a TV actor. Yes. It's very much something I've worried about." I spear another strawberry. "In the past." He's eyeing me carefully. "It's not great, I know. It's a thing I'd like to change." It's not until I say it that I realize it. I have been hungry for years. I have been out in the desert, starved for nourishment, for art, for love. "You know *The Velveteen Rabbit?*" I ask him.

"The kids' book, yeah? Remind me."

"Well, basically there's this toy rabbit, and the love of the child who owns it turns it into a real rabbit, or something. It's about becoming a version of yourself that is fully realized. Just—real."

"Are you a real rabbit, Mira?"

"Any day now." I smile. "But really, it's like, I don't know, the city, the show, the money, the people."

"The men." He winks.

"Sure. Just a lot of things that are all the things you're supposed to want. But they kind of . . . reduced me?"

He smiles. "You're safe now, city girl. I've got you."

"Yeah." Something about that unsettles me, but I smile.

Our phones ping at the same time. I read the email that has just come through.

"Oh, shit."

My father has called an emergency rehearsal. He has BIG NEWS, his email proclaims. I was really hoping our one day off before opening could be spent in bed, maybe a bath, maybe some lazy afternoon sex. Running lines by the fire on a bearskin rug. But no. We are to report to the theater POSTHASTE!

At the theater everyone looks around nervously. Several people look notably pissed, being here on their day off. My father bursts into the room. He clearly hasn't slept or bathed. He is carrying two mugs of coffee, which, I learn, are both for him, and not his first of the day.

"Thank you for coming." His energy is frenetic. "I would like to announce that after twenty-nine years, Tempest will be closing its doors. *Midsummer's* will be our last show." Around me, people are looking at each other in shock. "As such"—he takes a large pull from his coffee mug, and it occurs to me that it's probably not coffee—"in the absence of any further input from our producer"—I look around, realizing my mother is noticeably absent—"I have decided to up the ante, as it were. We happen to have a little disposable income, as we had enthusiastic donors this year, although Mr. Nolan is no longer with us." There is a general gasp from the group.

"He's alive." Sally steps in. "Calm down."

"Quite," says my father. "As such," he tries again, "I am adding a few production elements." He then proceeds to tell us, animatedly, how there will be dry ice, how fog colors will be added as the lovers become more entangled under Puck's spells. There will be flowers that fall from the sky at certain points in the fairy scenes. "I am presently installing hydraulics under the risers so they move, bringing the lovers together naturally. We will have to review some blocking, *and*"—he rubs his hands together—"there will be fireworks."

"I hope he only means emotional ones," mutters Theo next to me.

"I have a feeling not."

"At the end of the play, after the mechanicals' play at the wedding, and before Puck's monologue, there will be fireworks." He explains how they will shoot up, then shows us, running around onstage, how they will explode.

Beside him, Sally adds in safety details, deadpan, but I can see her panic.

When he is finished speaking, my father goes to refill his "coffee" and everyone takes their places for the top of the show. I run up to Sally.

"Sally, what do we do? He's lost his mind."

She sighs heavily. "Yup." She takes a sip of coffee, which also might not be coffee. "He can't be stopped."

"Have you tried?"

"I've been here since seven a.m., trying." She takes another long drink.

"Right, shit, sorry."

She is quiet for a moment. "Your mother doesn't know." She looks at me meaningfully. "He won't let me tell her. He's hoping to . . . surprise her with the, er, updates."

"You can't just text her?"

"He hid my phone."

"That's insane behavior."

"Yeah, well." She shrugs. She pauses for a moment. "This happens every year, the Arthur thing. A flirtation, anyway. And every year, your dad threatens to shut down the theater, and every year, your mom acts like it's no big deal." She sighs. "So, we're actually right on schedule. But . . . I would say that this time seems worse. Much worse."

"Oh, Lord. Okay." I pick up my phone to call my mother. There's no answer. I text her.

You need to get to the theater. 911.

She writes back:

There's no rehearsal today.

THERE IS NOW, I reply. GET HERE

My mother waltzes in twenty minutes later with Arthur trembling on her arm. She marches up to my father.

"Ross, you've lost your mind. What are you thinking, bringing all these people here? They have a show tomorrow."

"I'm fixing it!" he bellows. "It's shit! I'm making it better."

"It's not a shitty show." She looks beatifically at her rapt audience. "It's a beautiful show. Everyone has worked very hard!"

"It's my last show. I'm done with this. I'm done with your games. I quit."

"Oh, Roscoe, what do you mean, you quit?"

"I QUIT!"

"My love, why don't you go home and"—she leans in and sniffs him—"sober up. And we'll tidy everything up here and all have a nice rest and come back tomorrow fresh. Mmm?"

"No!" my father shouts. "Stop trying to placate me, woman!" He waves his arms angrily, not seeing the young stagehand walking behind him with the pyro flash box. My father knocks it out of his hand, activating the pyro with a loud bang. A huge white cloud of smoke goes up ten feet in the air. A few people scream, especially my mother.

"Stop acting like a maniac—you've completely lost your mind!"

And then someone yells the magic word: *"Fire!"* The bottom of the backdrop is indeed smoking.

My father staggers back, smoke billowing all around him. He falls into the backdrop, which comes down with a crash and immediately bursts into flames.

"Darling!" shrieks my mother, rushing toward him.

The quick-thinking stagehand has grabbed a fire extinguisher, but my mother's scream startles him. He drops it with a hard thud, setting off another explosion of fine white powder in every direction. The fire is out, but my dad lies crumpled on the stage.

"Call 911!" someone screams, but Sally is already on it. We wait in stunned silence until they come.

My dad will be fine. He's shaken and took a bad fall when he stumbled back, and he has some superficial burns, but the paramedics take him in for a once-over anyway. The scrim is in shreds, and the beautiful, layered forest art is burned to shit. The fire extinguisher has left a fine dust over absolutely everything. The stage is in shambles.

The show, it would appear, is ruined.

People are crying. A few sit stunned; a few just leave. Sally sits with her head in her hands. I join her. I put my hand on her shoulder.

"Never," she says. "Never, in forty-six productions, never have I dealt with so. Much. Shit." Her voice cracks bitterly on the last word. Whatever calm she mustered this morning is long gone. "I—I can't. I'm . . ."

"I know," I say. "I don't blame you. They are absolute assholes." She laughs a little. "Listen. What do you want to do?"

"I don't know."

"Well, technically, it's your show now. We open tomorrow." She looks at me in horror. The adage that the director hands over the show to the stage manager upon opening doesn't usually entail so much damage control.

"We have no set. We have no stage. We have no curtains. We have no director. We have no Titania."

"She'll be back." My mother won't pass up this plum role for anything. I'm racking my brain for ideas. "Do we cancel?" She shrugs. "Can we postpone?"

Sally sighs. "People have bought tickets. We're sold out tomorrow. And if we cancel"—she looks around the room—"it would be such a disappointment." She sighs again. "Your family . . ."

"I know." I sigh. "We're such assholes. We ruin everything."

"No." She looks at me, surprised. "Your family has done so much for this town, for the arts. It can't end like this."

"Oh." We sit there in silence for a moment.

There is a fantasy version, the Hallmark-movie version, where I figure out how to fix everything, where I save the show, the town, the whole world—all without breaking a sweat or messing up my hair. But right now, all I see is chaos.

The kid who dropped the extinguisher comes up to us, head bent. "Sally. I'm so sorry."

"It's okay, hon. Shit happens."

"Um, right. Um, Sally, I hope it's okay, but I called a few of my buddies to come help clean up." He nods toward the stage, where a group of teenagers is already arriving with brooms and cleaning supplies. Before Sally can even reply, one of the mechanicals appears.

"Sally, the backdrop artist is a friend. I called her, she's coming over . . . She says if we can get some helpers to cut the pieces out, we can do a quick, simpler version of the installation."

"Oh, wow," says Sally. "Okay. Yes, thank you!"

I'm frantically googling how to replace a scrim in twenty-four hours. It's not possible. "It says we can stretch muslin over a frame? Hopefully the trees hide the seams?" She nods, thinking. "Can we get that much muslin?"

"I'll call around," she says.

Will appears beside me. "How hard is it to build a large frame for a makeshift scrim?" I ask.

"Are we saving the day?"

"We are going to try."

"Okay, people." Sally leaps to her feet. "We have a lot of work to do."

It isn't easy. We do not fix everything. By the end of it, we are covered in sweat and dirt and paint. But eight hours later, we have cleaned up, and we have four giant flats covered in stretched muslin, painted in a gentle green wash. We have rebuilt the art installation. The artist found some fabric with a slight shimmer that is actually better than the original, and it catches the light in a way that brings the magic levels up significantly. A couple of high school girls spend all day getting fake flowers at every dollar store and removing their petals to rain down on Titania, and we decide to keep the dry ice, the two best ideas in my father's fever dream.

I order pizza for everyone—my parents can pay me back later. Eight hours later, our set is a new, humbler, heart-filled version of itself. We are reset, we are exhausted, filthy, and sore, but the show is still on. I feel foolish for even doubting. But the show must go on.

What surprises me most is the urgency I felt today, my desire to save this thing that three months ago I nearly turned down. It is a new feeling—community, investment. It has been so long since I cared this much about anything.

Chapter 35

August
Opening Night

A good daughter would check on her parents after their trip to the hospital. I'm trying to be a good daughter these days. Also, I'm not letting one more thing go wrong in this show. I show up on their front porch the next morning with coffee and pastries from Has Beans. I'm going to give them a talking-to. I'm going to call them out on their shit. I'm going to tell them that their drama is affecting everyone, that they are acting like assholes, yes, both of them, and that enough is enough. I'm going to save the family, I'm going to save the show and the theater and the whole company, and I'm going to be a goddamn hero.

I stand on the porch, half expecting to still hear screaming from inside. I knock, but there is no answer, just like my texts and phone calls this morning. I use my key and let myself in.

The house is silent. Worryingly silent. I find a box on the counter with a note:

You'll feel better soon. xo Glory

I read it again, thinking I'm misreading. I peek inside the box. Brownies. I sniff them. Oh, Glory. Oh, shit.

I move cautiously up the stairs. I'm not sure what I'm expecting, but the closer I get, the more nervous I am. Their bedroom door is ajar. I peek carefully around the corner, and there they are, sprawled on the bed, wrapped in each other's arms, naked except for (thank God) a sheet. I look closer. Are they dead? Did they die together, like in *The Notebook*? I take a step forward. My mother lets out a small, contented sigh, and they nestle further into each other. I jump back and slip out the door and run down the stairs before they wake up.

I leave the coffees and pastries on the counter, but then rethink it and take them with me. Better that they never know I was there.

Opening night feels almost incidental after the drama yesterday. I arrive at the theater early. The crew has done final cleanup, and full order has been restored. The dressing room is not the frenzy of costumes and hair spray from the night of the dress rehearsal; rather, it is calm and quiet. Someone has made an indie playlist, someone else has brought trays of fruit and cookies, and there is a general air of quiet purpose. It's like a page has been turned: The energy is, indeed, different. I put very little stock in last night's witchcraft, but whatever this is, I'll take it.

My parents arrive together, hand in hand. Whatever tempest possessed them seems to have passed. They make a brief stop in the dressing room and wish the cast a good show, thanking everyone for their teamwork yesterday, assuring us that they are both fine. It's a little off the mark—their focus should be on us—but it is brief and congenial and contributes to the general air of peaceful fortitude.

Some people do flowers and gifts on opening night (I always do mine on closing), and there is a small collection of cards at my spot on the counter. There is one from Theo:

Happy Opening, Mirabel!
Can't believe we're here again. What a joy to share this

*stage—and life—with you. I'm so proud of you and the
lovely performance you are about to give.
Much love, T*

There's a text from my *Listings* friend, Nisha:

Girl, I'm so sorry, not going to make it, schedule is madness, but
sending you so much love! You're going to kill it!

I'm a little disappointed, but I know how it is. People in the city can
barely fathom life outside of the city. I don't bother reminding her that
the run is for two weeks. Somehow, it doesn't seem to matter.

There's an ostentatious spray of roses from Nick, with a card.

*I'm sorry. Truly.
xo N
P.S. I'd say "break a leg" but . . .*

That makes me laugh.

There's a hand-tied posy of wildflowers in a mason jar and a note
card attached.

Thou art as wise as thou art beautiful . . .

Will. I smile to myself.

I try to take it all in. It really hits me, sitting here in this room of
friendly chaos, that so much has been missing in my life. I put so much
energy into getting away, making it, but it has been so long since I actually
considered what I left. There was only one version of my future that I was
willing to accept, and I did what so few people do: I got there. But what
did it really bring me?

Everyone is abuzz before curtain. People are doing their weird little rituals: stretching and prayers and mantras. Bailey makes everyone pass around a crystal that is supposed to be grounding. I have a little time before I go onstage, so I wait out in the hall. Will squeezes my hand in passing. I can tell he's a little nervous. Theo hugs me; he is practically bouncing with excitement. He has always been that way. I wonder if he does that in professional shows. I bet he does.

That magic moment happens, when the audience instinctively quiets themselves: It's time. The house lights go down, and we are all suspended in darkness. And then, the opening notes of the first sound cue, the lights come up, and this thing that has been ours for so long, this thing we built, has now begun.

I watch Will, Max, and Bailey in their first scene. I can't stop smiling, watching Will. There's such a particular buzz watching someone onstage and knowing they are yours. The realization strikes me: *He is, isn't he? Mine. Do I want that? Does he? Do I even need to ask?*

I move back into the corner to focus, to gather myself before my cue. I have no ritual, so I just close my eyes and put my hand on my heart and breathe. I'm not sure why. It just calms me. *Find your breath.* I am listening. I am readying myself. I am dropping back into the place where I'm scorned and frustrated and unloved. I let Mira drop down and Helena rise. My cue comes.

"Call you me fair?" I enter, and off we go.

It goes well. Not perfectly, but incredibly well, considering that the set was on fire yesterday. A couple of late cues, dropped lines, but also a few moments of real alchemy. The fight scene with the four lovers is the best we've ever done, and when we awaken from the "dream," when Will kisses me onstage under the warm stage lights, I feel my whole world coalesce. Everything in me pulls tightly together, and it feels so sweet.

We get a standing ovation, the bonus of being a novelty act in a small town, and after, when the curtains close, everyone starts hugging and high-fiving and saying kind things about each other. Will takes me in his arms and kisses me long and hard in front of everyone, and I don't even mind.

There are few highs that top coming offstage after a good show, knowing you did well, you got certain laughs, you hit your marks, and that you get to do it again. After we have changed, we go out into the main hall, where family and friends are gathered. There is applause when Theo and I walk out, and people come up and congratulate us.

"I remember the two of you in *Romeo and Juliet*," says an older woman I don't know. "*Ooooh*, the chemistry. It was so tragic. Tell me, why did the two of you never get together?" I look at Theo, unsure what to say.

"Well, I'm gay." He smiles. "But if there was one gal in the world for me, it would be this one." He gives me a side squeeze, and the lady pats my arm disappointedly and walks off. I am turning to head back to the dressing room when I hear a squeal behind me.

"OHMYGOD, Miranda!" Sweet holy Jesus. It's Kelsie and seven more Kelsies. I put on my most shrill smile before turning around.

"Kelsie! You made it!"

"I so did! Miranda, this is my book club! Girls, this is Miranda, we went to high school together!" They all squeal at me in sync.

"Hello." I wave lamely. "Thank you so much for coming."

"We saw you on TV," says one of them, leaning in as though this is an exclusive shared experience between us.

"Oh, yeah, I . . . I'm on . . . it."

"Okay, so, your play . . . I didn't understand the language," says Kelsie, "but I thought you were, like, so good. That play would make a really cute rom-com. We are a romance book club." The Kelsies all nod enthusiastically. Of course they are. "And that guy you hook up with, OMG, he's so sexy!"

"He owns the cider place," another Kelsie whispers to me.

"Yeah, I know, we . . ." It's like their eyebrows are telepathic, like they know what I'm about to say. They lean in together, wide-eyed.

"We, uh, went there a few times after rehearsal." If there was ever an opportunity to flex in front of my high school nightmare, this is it, but I don't feel the need. Maybe I'm growing. They nod disappointedly. They were hoping we were sleeping together. I smile to myself.

After, we go to the pub for one celebratory drink; we do have three more shows this week.

"I wonder if I should sleep at my parents'," I say to Will at the pub. "Now that they are . . . stabilized." In truth, my parents seem to be enjoying a renaissance following their near demise: I caught them kissing twice before and after the show. I'm certain they would appreciate the privacy.

"Why?" asks Will. "I mean, you're totally welcome to stay with me." He looks at me closely. "You don't want to?"

I look down the table toward my parents, who are holding hands while sharing a martini with two straws. "Of course I want to," I say. "I just . . . I don't know . . . it's been . . . what, three nights in a row . . . and I really appreciated it . . . I just . . ." What? I don't even know.

"Hey, there's no pressure at all," he says casually, but I can see he's hurt. "You need space, I get it."

"Is it just all too fast?" I blurt out.

"Hey, you don't need to move in," he says. "Unless you want to." He winks. I drop my head. "Oh, hey, listen, Mira, we can totally slow it down. I just thought . . . things seem to be going really well . . ."

"They are."

"So?"

"So that's . . . that makes me nervous."

"Okay." He takes my hand and kisses it. "So, a night in your own bed might just be what you need?"

"I think . . . yes?" I feel stupid. I look at my hand in his, his easy smile. I think about how I climbed on top of him this morning, his cry, his breath on my neck. "Or . . . no?" I shrug. "Aren't you tired of me? Don't you want your place to yourself?"

He shakes his head and takes a sip of beer. "Don't do that," he says. "Own your choice. I've told you I am happy to have you spend the night. And I understand if you don't. Don't make it more complicated." He gives that half smile, and I know something vital has shifted. This man sees right through me.

"Well, now I feel dumb for being weird." I steal a sip of his beer, trying to be cute. "Okay, ugh, fine, if you insist. I will come to your bed." I smile hopefully.

"Lovely." He nods curtly. "I look forward to it." Just then, Sally sits down next to us and starts chatting about what a good audience it was, and we move on.

I drive myself to his house after. The door is unlocked, and I let myself in. He has run a bath upstairs and poured me a glass of the magic cider.

"Let's get one thing straight," he says later in the bath, his legs wrapped around me, my whole weight resting against him. "I want you. I want you here. As often as you want. Okay?" He rubs his fingers along my jaw, dropping a kiss on the side of my head.

"Okay." I am quiet for a long moment. "Why do you even like me?"

I feel him laugh behind me. "What? How can you ask me that?"

"Well, I'm just kind of a shit."

"You are." He kisses my head again. "I think you've been underestimated . . . and unappreciated for so long by everyone around you that you can't even see yourself clearly."

"Huh. Wow."

He holds me tighter. "You are wildly talented. Fiercely intelligent. Scathingly witty. Sexy as hell." I try to laugh it off. "No, you are, Mira. You're remarkable. You're brave in a way that most people aren't. You have succeeded in a way that most people can't. And under the scathing wit, and I promise not to tell anyone this, you are kind and compassionate and insightful."

"Wow," I say again. "You're . . . good too."

"I never said you were great at expressing your emotions."

"Fair," I say. I lift one of his hands to my lips. "Thank you, sweet Will."

"So, we're clear now?"

"Yes." I say. "Completely."

Chapter 36

Once the show is open, a deep calm sets in. We got here. It's good. People like it. Nothing else needs to burn down. Audiences infuse the whole show with new energy: All this time we have performed only for each other. Now there are reactions, now there is laughter. Now there are collective inhales and shared discoveries. Now it's a play.

The run is two weeks: Thursday to Sunday, twice, with a three-day break in between. The first week is a little frenetic as we figure out last-minute tech changes in real time, but it's a happy relief to finally be in motion. We sell out each show and, after, greet people in the lobby. It's sweet to see the excitement. Glory's whole aquafit class has come out to see her. They let out a wild cheer when she appears in the lobby, sashaying like she's Vivien Leigh. The older guy who plays Wall has a flock of grandchildren pressing flowers into his arms. My first thought is cynical—it's a lot of fuss for such a tiny role—but I watch as he hugs them with tears in his eyes, and I wonder if maybe I have it wrong.

Will has to work most days between shows, but I have been hanging out at his place, lingering in bed or the bath, taking walks in the orchard, venturing out to the back vegetable garden and making simple salads with my findings. It's quiet in the mornings, and I like to sit in the window nook in the upstairs bedroom and watch the sun rise. I could never fully see it in the city. Here, there is wide-open sky. When the cidery opens and people trickle in, it builds to a roar by midafternoon and the place is buzzing. It is, I'm starting to realize, really successful. Will's cider is on tap in many local bars, and I know he's talking to someone about selling bottles more widely, provincially, even. I like to watch him down there: He's the boss, but he helps out the servers, stops to chat, brings a cold pint to whomever is playing guitar in the corner. He is attentive, aware; he sees everyone and is beloved for it.

When our first week of the run ends, we have three days off. Despite my quiet daytimes, doing the show each night is exhausting, and I am looking forward to some deep rest before we open again for four more shows. Will and I have another canoe ride planned, a "paddle," he calls it, and I am actually looking forward to it. We spent the first day as planned: The cidery is closed, and we sleep in, watch movies in bed, go for a long walk down a trail off a side road, and it's lovely. It's easy. We are good together. I like him.

We wake up the next morning to a rattling on the roof, and Will jumps out of bed and looks out the window. "Fuck!"

I sit up in bed. "What?"

"Hail." He peers farther out.

"It's August!"

"It happens." He starts to pull his clothes on. Outside is a veritable tempest, rain and hail and howling wind. Hailstones bounce off every surface, and I can already see the branches flailing in the wind. "I've gotta go."

I sit there in bed, not sure what to do. He clearly has farm things to do. I don't know about farm things. Should I stay? Should I leave? I don't want to be in his way. It's not my farm. Not my orchard. Somehow this storm is challenging my whole identity. What am I doing in this man's bed? I look out the window, and he is already out there in giant rubber boots and a raincoat. There is a storm, and he has run into it. That's who he is. There is a storm, and I am cowering in bed. What does that say about me?

Five minutes later, I find him in the barn, hitching a trailer to the small tractor. I am sleeping with a man who owns multiple tractors. I'm half soaked just from walking from the house to the barn, the giant raincoat I found in his hall closet hanging on me.

"Hey."

He looks up, surprised. "What are you doing?"

"Um, I mean, it felt rude to leave you in a storm by yourself, so . . ."

"Thanks." He's smiling, but I see he's stressed.

"What's happening?"

"I'm about to lose a ton of my crop, that's what."

"What's going to happen?"

"The apples aren't ready." He rubs his face. It's not time to ask him about the ins and outs of apple farming. I know harvest is in the fall, and I know the apples on the trees are bitter, a lesson I learned the hard way when I plucked one on one of my walks, taking a bite, then spitting it out instantly. "They have low sugar, which yields low alcohol . . ."

"Which yields bad cider?"

"Yup."

"What do we do?"

"You don't need to do this, Mira, honestly." The idea of going back in and running a bath is very appealing right now.

"No. Tell me what you need." The rain sounds like thunder on the steel barn roof.

"Okay, well, the wind and hail are knocking the apples off the tree. I need to collect what I can, as fast as I can, before the hail damages them. I can find a way to use them later."

I jump in the trailer, and he fires up the tractor, pulling us out of the barn and into the rain. Mud flies up and splatters us as we barrel through the wet orchard. Will stops when we are among the trees and hops out, points at the fallen apples, and starts gathering the good ones and tossing them into the trailer. It's too loud to talk, and I am already soaked, but the air is surprisingly warm underneath the wind and the rain. It's uncomfortable; I'm dirty and wet, but as we make our way up and down the rows of trees, as the trailer starts to fill with salvaged apples, a sort of satisfaction starts to set in, a strange sense of purpose. I'm gathering fallen apples in a storm, in the hope that Will can still make something from them, and I barely even know how cider is made, but I know I'm helping, I know being here is good, I know working next to Will feels good. I know he steadies something in me.

We work for hours, taking a couple of quick breaks for food and dry socks. We save several loads of apples, bringing them back to the barn to sweat in large bins before Will presses whatever juice he can from them later, something about starches and sugars. Then we head back out in the rain for more. It's awful out, and I'm sure Will is worried about the crop, about the damage. I'm sure this has implications on how his whole next year is going to go financially, but he just keeps working. There is no outburst, there is no meltdown. In my line of work, that's surprising.

When the wind and rain have finally subsided and we have gotten as much of the crop off the ground as we can, when the hail has melted into the mud and the sun has even ventured out, we collapse inside. My body feels wrung out, and my brain is empty, but I feel clear—proud, even. We shower together, shivering, not speaking, other than the kisses Will drops onto my bare shoulder. "Thank you, thank you, thank you."

Will makes a fire in the woodstove and we bundle up. I throw a frozen pizza in the oven, and we find a mindless murder mystery, then lean into each other, some sweet, new, easy thing landing in us.

Over the next couple of days, I venture out more when the cidery is open. I run flights of cider out to the picnic tables and light the little candle lanterns on the indoor tables. I chat with the customers. It's nice, the moving, not thinking too hard, having casual, pleasant interactions with people who are gone in an hour. I get to know Mark and Jenny, the bartenders, even lingering for a drink with them after we close.

I keep meaning to leave, but I like it here. It's this or my parents' house, and the more time I spend here, with Will, the less I want anything else. The more plausible it seems that I could just . . . stay.

And that absolutely terrifies me.

Chapter 37

Week two, Opening Night

Our second week's opening is much more subdued than the first. Now we are tired, we are a little pleased with ourselves that the show is going so well, and we are cocky. There are always mishaps at this point; the first show is like a rehearsal as we settle back in and let live theater humble us.

I'm leaving in a week. That's the plan, anyway. I have no job. There's still the offer of *Listings* . . . I haven't officially rejected it yet. Jay keeps calling and I keep ignoring him. But the longer I am removed from that world, the less I want to return. The city holds less for me now. I've been thinking about trying to move back from TV to theater. There is an amazing theater scene in the city, so much good work happening. Theo even told me he has a director friend coming from Stratford this weekend. I could talk to her. And the glaring option that I barely know what to do with: Stay. Stay here in North Lake. Be with Will and . . . what? Live with my parents? Live with him? Do community theater for the rest of my life, after everything I have achieved? Pour cider?

I avoid the topic, but two days before we close, Will brings it up after breakfast.

"So, what's next for you?" he asks as casually as if he's asking what I want for dinner. I am quiet. I knew it was coming. He's not wrong to bring it up. "Not to sound all needy, I just noticed the show was closing this week."

"You just noticed, huh?"

"Yeah." His tone is casual, but he catches my eye and everything is there. "I'm just going to say it: On my end, nothing needs to change, whether you go back to the city or not. Distance doesn't bother me."

I have compartmentalized this relationship so much that it barely exists outside the context of the play. Maybe that's why I have allowed myself to let go as much as I have. But any mention of the future and I slam shut.

"I don't know," I say. "I haven't really thought about it."

His eyes go blank. "You haven't thought about it." He turns away.

"I mean, I really enjoy you."

"You enjoy me."

"Stop repeating what I'm saying." I take his hand. "It makes me nervous."

He pulls his hand back. "Well, good," he says. "I mean, Jesus, Mira, I'm not saying we should get married." My eyes widen. "I'm just saying this is a good thing, there's something here that feels very real." He looks straight into my eyes. I look away. "And I'd like to have you in my life. If you want that. And I think I'm asking very little of you. I'm leaving things as open and easy as I can, but come on, it's not unreasonable to wonder where this is going."

I say nothing. "I don't know." Finally I say, "I . . . yes, I really like you too." He looks so young, standing in front of me. He is still so much that sweet seventeen-year-old who drove me home. "It's just complicated."

"No." His voice is short. "You have been living in a bubble; you don't know 'complicated.' You have no idea what 'complicated' is. You don't see that you have total freedom. You have opportunity and options, and I am telling you I'm here for all of it. And you're playing head games." He stares at me hard and, when I still say nothing, turns away.

"I'm sorry," I whisper. "I don't . . . I don't know how to do this."

"Do what?"

I sigh. "Can't we just enjoy right now and figure the rest out after the show?"

"The show's done in two days."

"Can we just . . . put a pin in this? For now? I just . . . I need to figure things out."

I hate this expression on his face. I know I'm the unreasonable one. "Please."

He turns away and starts loading the dishwasher. "Sure, Mira. Whatever works for you." I stand there for a minute, but it's clear the conversation is over. I can let myself out.

"I'll see you at the theater," I say.

It's the first time in days we haven't spent the whole day together, that we haven't arrived together. I go to my parents' house and sit in my room. It has become home again over the summer—my clothes are slung over furniture, my makeup covers the dresser. There's a stack of books by the bed I meant to read and never got to. But having spent so many nights away from it makes it feel foreign again. I go over my lines for something to do, but I know them inside out. I'm good that way. How can I know my way around a stage, a script, a character with such confidence, but I don't know how to talk to a man? I don't know how to have a relationship, if that's even what this is.

Onstage, I am really able to lean into Helena's I'm-an-unlovable-piece-of-shit-ness. In our last real scene, before the lovers wake up and get married and live happily ever after, we each enter individually, lost and delirious in the woods, each collapsing on the forest floor. It's a tiny scene—six lines—but tonight the lines nearly break me:

"*O weary night, abate thy hours . . . steal me awhile from my own company.*" I am supposed to fall asleep onstage next to Will, not knowing he's there. Most nights, he runs a finger down my spine, invisible to the audience. In the blackout, we are supposed to move closer so as to wake up entwined; Lysander and Hermia, the same. Tonight, he doesn't touch me. From the audience, we would indeed look entwined, but we are most definitely not.

He doesn't hug me after the show, and doesn't come out for drinks, claiming a headache. He is friendly and congenial as ever to everyone and makes no show of frustration toward me. But if you were looking, and I am, you would notice a subtle shift between us.

"Dude," says Theo at the pub. "What the hell is going on with you two?"

"What are you talking about?" I feign surprise, but Theo, like everyone else these days, apparently, sees right through me.

"Trouble in paradise," he says. Not a question. "What happened?"

I tell him everything. I tell him my confusion, my theory that I don't know how to love. "Bullshit," he says.

"No, but actually, Theo, look at my life. I have these weird parents who barely notice me, unless I can fill a spot on their stage. And, like, their marriage isn't exactly a perfect example. I have never had a relationship longer than six months, despite my best efforts. Honestly, these days, *you* are my best relationship . . ."

"And you ghosted me for the better part of ten years," he says.

"Yeah, I'm sorry about that." Theo gives me a look. "I really am."

"Why was that, Mirabel?" he asks.

"What do you mean?"

He stares at me for a long moment. "We were best friends."

"I was in love with you." Why is he doing this? "You broke my heart."

"Yeah, I'm gay," he says a little sharply. "You need to forgive me for that."

"Whoa, Theo."

"That doesn't mean I didn't love you too." He softens a little. "Don't still love you."

I'm quiet for a long moment. "For a long time I wondered if you were the love of my life."

He leans back and sighs. "Ah, buddy. What love? What life?"

"What do you mean?"

"What version of love? What version of life? Can't we be the loves of each other's lives in this beautiful friendship? Why does the meaning end at romance? Why this idea that there is only one? Don't be so finite. It's very boring."

I take this in. "I didn't think it mattered. I didn't think *I* mattered," I say. "You got so successful, and I . . . and I was embarrassed."

"I don't care about that. Like, at all."

"I do, Theo. I felt like a failure. And then when I got successful, it felt weird to reach out. Like too much time had passed."

"You didn't think you mattered." He shakes his head. I shrug. I finish my drink. "Mirabel. You matter a lot. You broke my heart too." I look up at him, surprised. "You did. I missed you so much. I thought you just didn't like me anymore."

I grab his hands. "Oh, no! That's so sad!"

"Well, yeah." He shrugs. He means it. I really hurt him.

I get up and slip into his side of the booth. I pull him toward me. "I'm so sorry, Theo." He mock-resists me, but I pull him closer. "You're the most amazing person I've ever met, and it just never made sense to me that you actually wanted to be my friend." I pull away. "I thought I was just your North Lake friend, and when you got out in the world, you would realize I am just . . . whatever. I don't know."

"So you pulled out first," he says, before realizing what he's just said. We look at each other and burst out laughing.

"Oh, God." I laugh, wiping tears away. "Why am I so fucked up?"

"Maybe because the first person you ever really loved couldn't love you back the way you needed me to?" He nudges me gently.

I brush it off. "That's giving yourself a lot of credit," I say, still laughing a little, but it stings in exactly the right place for me to know he could be right. "That definitely might have been true in the past, but . . . I feel like it's not an excuse."

He pulls me in close. "You are loved, Mirabel. And lovable." He kisses the top of my head. "But it's up to you to accept that." I know he's right. I just don't know how to begin to do that. Especially this time, with Will, when the stakes are climbing sky high.

Chapter 38

Closing Night

Closing night is my favorite. Some people love opening, but by closing, the wrinkles are ironed out, and there is an even greater sense of occasion, of momentum. The show is tighter. This is the last time we will ever do this. This thing we have labored over will soon evaporate. There is a set strike scheduled for tomorrow. All are expected to come help, so we will all still see each other then. But there is a bittersweetness in ending that heightens everything. After the show is a cast party at my parents' house. We spent the day preparing a makeshift bar, placing all the flowers we have acquired over the run into vases, giving a vaguely funereal vibe, which isn't totally off the mark. My parents have decided to spend the money they saved on pyro on food and an open bar, which thrilled the cast. Despite all their hijinks, the community does love them.

We get to the theater early. I have written a few cards to Max and Bailey, Theo, Sally . . . I had a sexy little present for Will planned, an embroidered framed quote from the play—*"But I shall do thee mischief in the woods"*—but I chickened out, given our current status, which is unknown, and bought him a nice bottle of whiskey instead.

He comes up behind me while I'm doing my makeup. He lays a hand tentatively on my arm.

"Hi."

"Hi." Our eyes meet in the mirror. I place my hand over his.

"We should talk," he says.

"Yes," I say. "Maybe after?" He deflates a little. "After the show?"

He nods. "Last one."

"Yeah."

"Let's make it good."

We make it great. People get a little silly on closing: Everything is bigger, louder, and some people go over the top, like Arthur, whose donkey sounds have escalated beyond shrill. The play feels like a frenzy in a wonderful way. It goes in slow motion and also at high speed.

"I can't believe it's the last time!" weeps the woman who plays the lion, pacing backstage. "We'll never say these lines again!"

I don't bother reminding her that most of her lines are roars. I am surprised by how much crying there is at the end, the hugs, the big declarations of love. People are kind; they say nice things about me, my acting. There are a few shots fired at Nick, which I smile at and brush off. It's over. This all-consuming thing that occupied my whole summer, that I uprooted my life for, is done. Taking off my costume, soaked wet with sweat, my own and everyone else's, I feel a surprising pang of sentimentality. When no one is looking, I stash my flower crown from the wedding scene in my bag. A souvenir.

After we have done the requisite meet and greet after the show, after we have cleared away our personal belongings and returned our costumes to the racks, we change into party clothes. I have an excellent dress for the occasion: a long, gauzy cream sundress with layered ruffles at the bottom, a smocked bodice, a halter tie, and a completely open back. It's like if a Shakespearean forest fairy was attending a garden party on a summer's eve. Which, tonight, she is. I shake out my hair, a little longer now, loose and wavy from being pinned back onstage. I feel happily drained, anxious about things with Will, glad the whole thing is over, and also a little sad. I take a last look around the theater. I'll be back tomorrow morning for strike, but the thing we built is over. The house lights are up, and the fairy magic wafted out the door with the last audience member.

The party is just getting started as I arrive. People are trickling in, some still heavily made up, some with scrubbed faces. I feel buzzed and anxious. It's the end, and suddenly I have this larger need to make a lasting impression, to connect with people. I was so cold when I got here, so certain I was an afterthought. Now these people feel like family.

Compared to the party at Nick's cottage with costumes and catering, the cast party is a humble affair, even with my parents' open bar. I grab a glass of wine and start to circle around. It's a relief to know that I don't need to worry about Glory's baking. There is a case of Will's special Midsummer's Cider at the bar, but I can't bring myself to drink it. I try to chat with everyone; people are in a good mood, and there is sort of a collective happy exhale. The only person who looks down is Arthur: He is sitting off to the side, staring miserably into his drink while the sound guy talks his ear off about some solo motorcycle road trip he took in 1987.

I see Will across the room. I try to catch his eye, but he is standing with the fairies with his arm slung over Barb's shoulder. Theo appears by my side.

"Good show, Mirabel." He clinks glasses with me.

"Good show."

"Look at us, all grown up and openly drinking in front of your parents in their living room."

I laugh. "Largely because of them."

"Not untrue." He follows my gaze across the room. "Will Reed is looking extra delicious this evening." It's true. He is freshly showered, damp hair curling on his forehead, wearing jeans and a plain black T-shirt.

"It's so unfairly effortless for men," I say.

"Speak for yourself," says Theo. He glances at me. "So what's the deal with you two?"

I take a large sip of wine. "I'm not sure. I haven't stayed over in two nights. He has been friendly but distant. But tonight, onstage, he held my hand in the sexy way."

"There's a sexy way to hold hands?"

"Um, duh, yes." I look back over at Will, and this time he catches my eye. He tilts his head toward the door and holds up a bottle of the magic cider. "I think I'm being summoned."

Theo catches my hand before I leave. "Remember, Mirabel. You are allowed to be loved," he whispers before releasing me. *"She will find him by starlight . . ."*

"The play is over, Theodore," I say, but I smile.

Will and I walk in silence toward the back gazebo. One of my parents, in a burst of whimsy, has added fairy lights, as well as small spirals of solar lights throughout the garden. The backyard looks like a fairyland. Will's hand grazes mine as we walk. I don't move, and he moves it away.

We sit next to each other on the swing facing the house, not touching. He hands me the bottle, and I take a swig. It's a little warm.

"Show's over," he says finally.

"Yeah."

"Hard to believe."

"Yeah," I say. "Totally."

We say nothing for a while. We have gotten really good at a comfortable silence, but this isn't it.

"I'm going crazy, Mira," he finally says. "Talk to me."

I lean back against the swing and stare at the sky. It's a perfectly clear night, mild and starry. I take a breath. "You know what the problem with Helena and Demetrius is?" He looks at me sideways. "Lysander and Hermia: They are in love from the get-go, right? Puck's fairy magic casts the spell on Lysander accidentally, he falls in love with Helena, Puck realizes his mistake, and casts the spell on Demetrius too."

"Um, I mean, this is the plot of the play we just did . . ."

"Right, but here's what's always bothered me: Lysander wakes up from the spell and sees clearly that he loves Hermia as he always has."

"Right."

"But Demetrius . . . what, he just suddenly loves Helena? After rejecting her all this time?"

"Mira, what exactly are you getting at?"

"How does she know it's real? What if he is still under the spell, and what? Is he just going to stay that way? Is she doomed to a life of false love with someone who doesn't know he's been drugged by a fairy?"

Will looks up at the sky too, as though I am looking for the answers up there, as though he can help me find it. "For what it's worth, for my performance, I thought that he woke up from the spell, like Lysander, but that the love for Helena was reawakened. That he saw what was right in front of him, that his love was real." He glances at me. "I know we're doing a metaphor, but I can't tell where you're headed."

"I like you," I say softly. "So much." He reaches for my hand, and that small contact nearly undoes me. "I just wonder . . . I don't know what I'm doing. Or what I want. Or who I even am." I close my eyes. The cider is starting to burn a little in my chest. "Is this thing with us real, or is it just what happens when you play lovers? Is it just . . . fairy magic?"

"I see," he says.

"It's all feeling very complicated."

"Okay," he says slowly. "And I'm going to tell you again that that's okay. I just . . . and I'm really not trying to put pressure on you, I just feel like . . . at this point in things, an idea of what's next is, like, basic communication."

"That sounds very unromantic."

"I . . . No, that came out . . . For fuck's sake, I'm just asking for—"

"Basic communication," I repeat.

"Well . . ."

"I just can't answer it. I can tell you I like you. I can tell you that being with you feels amazing." I sigh. He softens a little beside me. "I can tell you it feels like it's gotten kind of serious, really fast."

"It's showtime," he says.

"Huh?"

"We spent every day together, nearly, for three months. It's not regular dating, it's showtime."

"Yes, I know showtime," I say. "It's just not the most sustainable relationship model."

He exhales hard. "You don't get it, do you?"

"Get what?"

He turns to me and puts his hands on my face. "I'm falling in love with you." He stares at me hard. "And I can't even tell if you're going to answer my calls." His face is close to mine, and I don't know what to say, so I kiss him, long and deeply.

"I am," I say softly when we come up for air. "Okay?" His face melts into that smile, and he kisses me again, pulling me into his lap.

"How dare you wear that dress," he murmurs into my hair, sliding his hands under the flimsy back straps.

"You like?"

"It's criminal," he says. "I love." He pulls back and looks in my eyes, smiling, then pulls me close again, kissing me with more urgency, his hand sliding around my back toward my breast, and . . .

"Oh, children!" Theo calls from the back deck. "It's speech time." Will takes my hand, squeezes it, and pulls me up. We run up the lawn toward Theo.

"Naughty. Naughty," he says, patting us each on our bottoms as we pass him. "Good?" he whispers to me once Will is past.

"I think so?" I smile and slip inside, but an old, familiar dread is already churning inside me. The instinct to flee.

For the rest of the party, Will is attached to my side, one hand around my waist, his hands grazing the lines where the dress meets my skin. "I miss you," he whispers in my ear when we have a moment alone. "Come home with me."

I'm a little drunk and very tired. "Tomorrow?" I say. "After strike? I'm so tired."

"Sure, yeah, okay." He nods, gives me a squeeze, but I can see he is disappointed.

When the party ends and people hug goodbye, as though we won't all see each other tomorrow, Will pulls me into a corner and kisses me intensely. "Tomorrow," he says.

"Tomorrow." I avoid his eyes.

"Then it's not just showtime. It's not fairy magic," he says. "It's just you and me, real life."

"Whatever that is." I laugh it off, but my voice catches.

He leans his forehead against mine, his hands gently holding my chin. "I'm not just falling," he whispers. "I have fallen." He kisses me. I kiss him back, but doubt has already started to calcify in my chest.

I fall asleep immediately, but my dreams are restless. I dream I am lost in the woods, like that night at Nick's cottage, but this time the trees grab at me, trying to pin me down, hold me tight. I wake up with a start, gasping, my heart racing, my veins coursing with fear. Panic. I put my hand on my chest and try to steady my breath. It will pass. It always passes. I do this every time. I jump ship before it sinks. But this time there is no reason to worry: Will is steady, he wants this. He wants me. I have never had someone want me completely without conditions or reservations. I have never let anyone this close. He must be wrong. He must not know that I don't begin to deserve him. I can't bear the moment he finds out, some moment when I feel safe and loved and secure and am blindsided again. There is only one way to save my heart.

I don't realize I'm crying until it's running down my neck. I don't know what I want. I don't know what to do, but I need to do something.

By six a.m. I have packed my things and am on the highway, headed back for the city.

Chapter 39

Strike

My apartment is cold. My subletter moved out last week. She has left the place immaculate, which is a relief. Stepping into it feels unfamiliar, like it no longer belongs to me. Or it belongs to another me, one who no longer exists. I look around: It is a nice place. The kitchen is white and shiny. The bathroom is white and shiny. The bed, the walls, the throw cushions all soft neutrals. It looks like a real estate stage: no personal effects, no pictures or trinkets or even a dish with miscellaneous keys and coins. It looks minimal, vaguely feminine, and uninhabited. There is no sign of me.

The thought that kept me spinning all night, that kept my foot on the gas on the long drive back to the city, was this exact thing. I'm not sure who I am, and I don't know what I want. I have been living in a bubble, and it has burst, and without the protection of the play, of the fantasy world it lent me, where do I even belong?

I did the only thing I ever wanted to do. I wanted to be an actor, I came to the city, I studied, I hustled, I did a million auditions, and I became a professional actor. The sheer fact of this is epic in itself: That doesn't happen. I got a role on something that has run for six years. A small role. A boring role. A role that largely depended on my being a certain level of conventionally attractive. A role that, no one would ever admit, depended on my staying very thin. A role that let me own a home in an expensive city and not have to worry a ton about money. I mostly ate out, and very little at that. I mostly wasn't home. I had long shooting days, and whenever there was a break in shooting, I would hop on a plane with my show friends and drink in the sunshine and starve myself till midafternoon each day to make up for it. I didn't really read. I didn't really see my parents, and that was their fault, right? My parents didn't know me either. They certainly weren't proud of my success on television; they were almost embarrassed that I had gone for something so basic.

Love wasn't a thing. I knew I didn't want kids, and I wasn't even sure about marriage. Frankly, I wasn't even that interested in a partner of any kind. I had no trouble finding sex, dating someone for a few months, for the fun part, and sure, sometimes they caught feelings, but I never did.

I never did. What does that say about me? I never did because I was dating guys as shallow and vapid as I was. You can get pretty far on sex and premieres and eating at cool restaurants. You can really believe that you are that busy, that life is that full. You can get pretty far on false starts. I ran so far from that teenage girl who was wide open, who was so desperate for life to happen to her, who was so desperate to fall in love. And then Nick opened something up. Nick reminded me why I kept men at bay. I got hurt. I was almost willing to abandon myself for him. Being vulnerable has not served me well. Opening my heart has proven dangerous.

And now there's Will.

How dare he fall in love with me! How dare he even suggest that there was love here? I have built a whole life around not needing anyone. I have shown them all—my parents, my hometown, the theater community, Theo, even—that I didn't need them. I rose above all of it.

But I'm not happy. I haven't been happy in years.

At least, I haven't been relaxed in the way that I was this summer. I haven't been creative in any real way. And I've never just let someone land in my life the way Will has. To a normal person, this might be a happy revelation: I met a beautiful man who is kind and true and talented, and he sees through all my shit and he loves me!

What's wrong with him? Why would someone do that?

The more I turn it over in my tangled brain, the more I know it can't be real. He is not to be trusted: He doesn't know me. How could he possibly know me if I don't know myself? How could he love me? He's a romantic, I can't fault him for that. He wants it to be real, he wants it to be true. It was a summer romance. A showmance. It's the oldest story in the book. The intensity of a show, the frequency and proximity of a theatrical production, and the simple fact that you hold this person onstage, you breathe them in, you have to convincingly portray love. And in the moment, if you are doing a good job, you have to believe it a little bit, yourself, also. You need to, for the purpose of the show, be a little in love with each other, at least onstage, and so often, so, so often, this gets confused.

That's all it is.

Will is an amateur. He doesn't know that when you step offstage, you need to turn the love off. It's my fault: I was out of my element. I was distracted. I was confused. It was all just a dream, a lovely golden summer dream, but I snapped out of it, and I got out before anyone got hurt.

That last part, I know, remains to be seen. The last part is the lie that kept me from turning the car around. If I'm honest, I know we both got hurt.

I'm home. I'm back in my own world. I am exhausted from the drive and the restless night and the love and the theater. I collapse into my own crisp white bed and sleep.

When I wake up, it's almost dark. I check the time. Five p.m. I look around, confused, before remembering that I am home, this is my room, my bed. I look at my phone. I'm expecting a couple of texts. I expect my parents to be pissed that I left in the night, Will, probably. I know I have some explaining to do. What I am not expecting is for my phone to have blown up.

There are three missed calls from my parents. Texts from Sally, Max, Barb, all asking if I am okay. Twelve missed calls from Theo. One text from Will:

You're gone, aren't you?

I stare at it for a moment, and then reply:

I'm sorry.

These two lines, and a whole summer ended. I stare at my words. They are a nothing response. Usually when something ends, I feel relief. Even with Nick, when it ended, it felt like coming up for air, like I was safe. This doesn't feel safe. This feels like shit.

My phone lights up: Theo calling again. I take a breath. Better him than anyone else, I guess.

"Hey."

"What the fuck, Miranda?" He only calls me that when he's pissed. It's been Mirabel since day one. I say nothing. "People are worried about you."

"I left a note for my parents."

"Bullshit," he says. "You missed strike."

"I'm sure I wasn't missed at strike." In our large cast, with friends and neighbors helping, it probably took two hours.

"You were," he says. "Because you are a part of the group, and you just bailed. People wanted to say goodbye to you. No one knew you were leaving . . . People are upset."

"I'm sorry. I had to get back." Silence. "Something came up."

"What came up?"

"Just . . . business."

"For such a good actor, you're a pretty bad liar," he says. There is another long pause. "What happened?"

My heart is racing. All the certainty I fell asleep with is gone. Everything feels like a complete mess.

"He said he loves me, or, he's falling, has fallen . . . I don't know."

"Okay, so?" says Theo.

"So, what? It's too much! It's too soon."

"I mean, showtime . . ."

"No! The show is a fantasy—it's not real life." I sigh.

"And what exactly is your real life, Mira? You are so privileged. You have so many options . . ."

"I am unemployed and . . ."

"You're avoiding real life," he says. "I love you." He pauses. "But what you did was selfish. In so many ways. To so many people."

"It's not personal, Theo—"

"No." He stops me. "It is. It's incredibly personal to me that someone who I love so much is being such an asshole. It's personal that you have ghosted me *again*. It's incredibly personal that you are just tossing away a man who is one of my closest friends. And if you can't see that he's the best thing to happen to you in a long, long time, then I don't know what to tell you."

"I don't want to hurt him . . ."

"Then don't! Grow up. For fuck's sake, Miranda." I can hear him sigh heavily over the line. "You left me." There is a break in his voice that chills me to my core. "You left me again, and you didn't say goodbye."

"I'm sorry. Theo, I honestly had no idea I would upset you this much."

"I have too much else going on in my life right now to be dicked around by you again."

"Theo, I—"

"Goodbye, Miranda." He hangs up.

There is a particular burn to shame when you know unequivocally that you're in the wrong. I feel it like a vise around my shoulders, a weighty clenching. I know at any moment I could let it all go, I could admit my errors, I could call Theo back, I could get in the car and drive back home. But the only thing worse than abandoning literally everyone in my life without a word would be having to face them again.

It's a lot easier to just be an asshole. Right?

I haven't eaten since the party. I put on some city clothes: a cute black jumpsuit I never wore this summer because it was too fashion-y. I throw my gold hoops back on and a red lip. I step out into the city street, expecting a cinematic night scene: *She's back, Toronto! Miranda Belmont survived summer in the sticks and she has returned!* Sometimes the city really delivers: the lights glitter, you can see the sunset through the skyscrapers, the sidewalks seem to part like the Red Sea. It can feel like you are the only one in a crowd of hundreds. You are the star of your own sitcom.

But tonight, I am jostled on the sidewalk before I've barely left my doorstep. It's garbage day tomorrow, so businesses have overflowing bins out front, reeking with flies everywhere. A group of teenagers push past me in a cloud of bubblegum-scented vape smoke, and when I go to dodge them, I step in dog shit in my little leather flip-flops. I stand still, the shame vise tightening. I deserve this. I turn and go back inside my building, throw my shoes down the garbage chute, and wash my feet about six times.

I'm back, and Toronto doesn't give a shit. Well, just the one.

I text my parents an apology, then turn off my phone. I spend $200 on grocery delivery, the bulk of which is wine. I pull down the blinds, literally and figuratively, and indulge in a forty-eight-hour hiatus from planet Earth. It's nice. Wine makes my head not think. I try to watch luxury real estate shows to numb my brain. They remind me too much of *Listings*, so I have to resort to a hard binge of British murder mysteries. I have to stop because those remind me of Will. I am genuinely exhausted. Most of all, under everything, I am so sad. If I let myself say it, I am heartbroken.

Chapter 40

On my third day back, I take a shower, take a breath, and call Jay.

"Miranda!" His voice always seems to be oozing. "How was Shakespeare in the Park? I have to say, I'm surprised to hear from you."

"It wasn't in the park . . . Never mind." I take a breath. "Listen. Jay. Some things changed and I am available after all." There is a pause. "For the job." I never did get back to him on that. I ignored his calls and he finally gave up.

His inhale is almost a whistle. He laughs. "You've really grown a pair of balls, Belmont."

"Lucky me."

"Ha! I'm not going to lie, I want to say no because you really pissed me off with the radio silence. But . . ." I can practically hear the wheels turning. "I will admit that I probably deserved it considering how things went when you left." I say nothing. "And between you and me, Nolan isn't really bringing it at the moment. I mean, I get it, the guy's in a wheelchair, but also, I mean, it's not a good look. It's boring television."

"Nothing worse than boring television."

"Right? You get it. And it actually tested pretty well, the idea of you in a lead." He pauses, I think so I can thank him. I don't. "Uh, yeah. So, let me just confirm with the execs, but, I mean, it's going to be a yes. I'll have the PA shoot you a call sheet, and we'll see you Monday."

"Okay," I say. "Thanks, Jay."

"Glad you called," he says, and hangs up.

I sit there with the phone in my hand, my heart racing. I was hoping I'd feel calmer, but instead I feel light and twitchy. Today is Saturday. Two more days. I put on proper footwear this time and go for a walk. I live just off Queen Street, one of the main streets in Toronto that goes all the way across the city. I walk and walk, I pass bars I have been to with friends, chic little cocktail places with dim lighting, I pass my favorite Thai takeout, a hole-in-the-wall place where I used to buy a plate of seven-dollar noodles that would last me three days. I pass a couple of small indie theaters that I did theater workshops and play readings in, back in the day. I pass bars I had bad dates in, the small park I once made out with a guy in, in my twenties, then ghosted him. Queen Street is a tour of my youth, a microcosm of everything and everyone I wanted to be and became. It's all jumbled in there together.

Toronto has been home for ten years. It is so familiar to me. I feel more city girl than small-town girl. I used to, anyway. I've been gone three months, the longest I've ever been out of the city since moving here, and for all the chic spots and amazing food and interesting people and general coolness, it also feels claustrophobic now. I have less patience for people pushing past me in the street, for the constant sirens, the endless honking. You can see straight down whatever street you're on, but you can never really see the unobstructed sky. I am surprised by a pang of homesickness. I thought I was already home.

I text a few friends that I am back in town. There are wildly enthusiastic emojis, but only a couple of people take me up on my suggestion of drinks at our favorite spot. I put on a black dress, do my makeup the way I always did, put on strappy shoes, but when I catch a glance of myself in the mirror, I don't seem like myself. I look like everyone else. My dress feels too tight, and my skin can't breathe. I look good, sure. I look like Miranda Belmont but not Mirabel.

At the bar, my friends ask about my time away, and I find myself editing the tale, focusing on the drama of Nick. I don't mention Will, because he is mine. I don't want to share him. One friend braces us for a big dramatic announcement, which is that she is finally getting fillers, and the other girls treat this with the seriousness of any major life decision. I stare into my drink and wonder what I'm doing there.

On Monday, I go back to set. It's the first week back for everyone, so my presence is a small blip that is only vaguely out of place amid all the other hugs and catch-ups. I am truly glad to see some people. There are good people everywhere, but it's also all business. Nisha shrieks when I pop my head into her dressing room, leaping up to hug me.

"Mira! I'm so glad to see you! I didn't believe it when I saw your name on the call sheet! Is it real? You're real? You're really back? Oh my God, I missed you!" She's sweet, and she means it, and I hug her back, but it feels different. We barely spoke all summer. She didn't come to the show. And it's fine. I think I thought we were closer, and like all parts of this job, I was just a little wrong. "Nick Nolan is such an asshole, I can't believe he followed you! Oh my God."

Two months ago, I would have sat with Nisha for hours and agonized over every detail, every twist and turn in my Nick drama. We would have had a bottle of wine each, and I would have felt empowered, vindicated in voicing it all to her, power that would slowly wane again in Nick's presence.

"Yeah," I say. "It was some summer." I can tell she wants all the gossip, but, I have realized, she hasn't earned it. And that's okay. "We'll catch up soon," I say. "Dinner?"

"Absolutely!" she says. "I want to hear everything."

I have a new, bigger dressing room. There is a thin envelope with the large bonus check I negotiated for upon my return. There are flowers from the execs on the counter, and a script and a schedule in side-by-side folders. I have a flash of the *Midsummer's* script laid out on my bedroom desk, the bud vase my mother left there. I flip through the script. Was it always this shitty? I know I've spent three months reading Shakespeare, but this is barely literate. Jay walks into the room.

"Belmont!" he booms. "Good to see . . ." He stops and looks me up and down. "Jesus, Miranda."

"Um, what, Jay?" But I already know, and I hate myself for not realizing before he did. I gained weight this summer. I knew I did, but I wasn't worrying about it. I was eating properly for the first time in years.

"You're looking . . . robust." He runs his hands over his face, like this is the literal last thing on planet Earth that he has time for. "Okay, it's fine. So, listen, I'm just going to send someone from wardrobe down here for an update." I blink at him. "So about how quickly do you think you could, you know . . ."

"What, Jay?"

"Well, you know, camera adds ten pounds, and now . . ." He switches tactics. "Listen, we just want consistency, right? Maybe we write in a pregnancy or something. You're not pregnant, are you?"

"I'm sure you're not allowed to ask me that."

"Yeah, sure, totally. But, like . . . are you?"

I am getting that same tight feeling I had on the phone. I close my eyes and take a breath. When I open them, Jay has left. Seconds later, an apologetic wardrobe assistant asks to take my measurements. I stand there while she writes down numbers. She is sweet. She is new.

"What's the damage?" I ask, annoyed.

"Oh, I mean, honestly, it's not that bad," she says, then catches herself. "You look great." She touches my arm. "Like, actually, really great." She smiles at me, she means it. I'm grateful. "You're up, like, an inch and a half all over. Seriously, no big deal, we just need to go up a size in your costumes. Easy." Out in the hall, I can hear Jay on the phone.

"Blown up like a goddamn dough boy," he says. "Could be pregnant, she won't say . . . No, of course I didn't ask her, fuck, feminism, et cetera. I didn't want her back at all, you know. This is Nolan trying to cover his ass." The wardrobe assistant looks up at me, alarmed, and shuts the door. She drops her eyes to the floor.

I step back. "You know what? Actually, we're done here."

"Oh!" she chirps. "I literally just need, like, two more . . ."

"No." I open the door. "I'm done." She scurries out anxiously.

I march down the hall into Jay's office, where he is speed-eating nicotine gum.

"Kill me," I say.

He looks at me, confused. "What the fuck, Belmont."

"I'm asking you—I'm telling you—to kill me off. Do whatever you need to do. I'm not doing this."

He makes a show of popping another piece of gum into his mouth and chewing it slowly. "You're out?" he snarls.

"I'm out. I remembered that I can't work for you."

"This is so unprofessional." He is already texting the execs.

"Not as unprofessional as firing me because your star told you to, or asking me if I'm pregnant because I finally dared to nourish myself," I snap. "I could go on, you know. I have seen a lot of shit here, and I have an excellent memory." I stare him down. He knows. Years of sexist comments, sexual comments, overtly offensive jokes. I'm so done. "I know you think it's a joke, how I spent my summer, but I loved it. I got to work with people who actually cared. I got to be creatively engaged. I got to work with a script that wasn't riddled with clichés and plot holes."

"You won't work in this town again," he sneers.

I can't help it, I laugh. "That a line from your shitty script?"

"How dare you—"

"I don't care, Jay. Being here for literally an hour has reminded me how much I hate it here. This show is garbage—you know that, right? I'm honestly not sure how it's still on air. Being here, seeing you, it's reminded me how much of my life I have wasted in this world, starving myself in all kinds of ways. I'm a classically trained actor! I'm playing a secretary! What the fuck! I'm out. I'm done."

"You'll have to return the bonus," he says, sudden desperation in his voice. "How do I explain this to—"

"I don't care. You did this to yourself. You ignored me every time I asked for more story, more lines, and I gave you six years, and you just disposed of me because Nick Nolan told you to. And we both know that if I went public with that, you'd be really fucked. So I'm keeping the bonus, and we'll call it even." He looks at me, wide-eyed. "Fuck you, Jay. Goodbye."

A few people are huddled around the door and quickly disperse as I exit. They look at me, eyes shining. No one says anything for a moment, then a crew guy high-fives me, and some girl I've never seen with a clipboard leans in. "You're my hero," she whispers.

I step out into the parking lot and hand in my pass to the security guard, who looks at me like I'm crazy but takes it.

Chapter 41

My parents call. I sigh deeply before accepting the call. It has been a week since I left North Lake, and here I am again, jobless, loveless, directionless.

"Hello? Is it on? Darling, can you hear us?"

"You mean see you."

"It's both, darling. Can you hear us and see us?" Their faces are very close to the screen.

"Back up," I say.

"We haven't even said anything!" My mother is, as ever, indignant.

"Back up from the screen," I say. "I can see your tonsils."

"Rude," huffs my mother, but they both lean back and come into clear view. "Oh! Oh, I see." She leans in again. "Oh, you don't look well, darling. You—"

"Yes, I know, I gained weight."

My mother shakes her head. "No . . ."

"Well, she has, Wynnie." My father, blunt as ever. "But it suits her."

"I was going to say you look tired," says my mother. "Your glow is gone."

"Is there another reason for this call?" I ask. "Or is this just a routine assessment of my appearance?"

"No." I can see my mother is trying. "No, we wanted to say that we . . . Well, we just wanted to see how you were. You left so suddenly." I wait for the slew of accusations headed my way, but they don't come.

"We missed you at strike," my father says.

"Yes," I say impatiently, "I know, I was expected to be there. I'm sorry, okay?" My parents look at each other. "Theo already gave me shit and told me how disappointing I am, so if that's what this is . . ."

"It's not," says my father. "Quite the opposite, in fact." They glance at each other again. "We didn't get a chance to thank you." He clears his throat awkwardly. "You were a great help this summer, with all the, uh, casting . . . adjustments. You showed a lot of leadership." My mother nudges him. "And your performance . . . was truly lovely."

"We are very proud of you, darling," says my mother. "It was very special for us to do that show with our daughter."

I'm a little stunned. This is as great a display of affection as I've ever had from them. "Oh," I say. "Thank you." We sit in a brief awkward silence as I hold the fact that this might actually be a nice family phone call. "Me too," I say awkwardly, a little too late.

"So," my mother presses on, "there's something we would like to discuss with you."

"Are you getting a divorce?" I blurt out, surprising myself with how much like a child I sound. "Are you really ending Tempest?"

They look at each other and chuckle. "Not as it were," my father says. "This play—"

My mother cuts him off. "This play nearly broke us, and that was very much my fault."

"It was a mutual effort," my father adds, patting her arm. "It was a long time coming and brought up some, ah, dynamics that required, er, addressing."

"But it also brought us back together," says my mother. For once, she sounds completely sincere. "We have decided to take a break from the theater. It's been our greatest joy—"

"Uh, aside from you," adds my father a split second too late. We all know, deep down, that it's not completely true.

"But it's such a constant worry," says my mother. "It takes all our time. We love it, but we need a break. We need to spend some time together, just us, to reconnect. To rest. And we were wondering, well, noticing . . ."

"Are you coming back or not?" blurts my father. "You don't really mean to stay there in the city?"

I have given them no reason at all to think otherwise, but it's not until this question is put so bluntly to me that I know my answer. "No," I say. "I'm not staying." A small gateway of relief opens in me.

"Well, thank goodness for that," my mother says. She and my father eye each other. "That's good news."

"So, uh, what did you want to ask me?" I ask.

"Well, as we said, we need a break. Three shows a year is a lot. We feel that our life in recent years has revolved around the theater, and we would like to open our life up a little . . . We have decided to do some traveling over the winter and . . ."

"We wanted to offer you the winter show." My mother beams. "To direct it. You can even choose it, pending board approval." We all know that the board is just the two of them. "You could cast it—it would be your show, completely."

"Huh," I say. I am not repelled by the idea. "I mean, it's an idea, for sure." My life, my future, is so amorphous these days that the idea of anything concrete feels almost terrifying. Especially something that could be so loaded. "That's only, like, three months of the year, though," I say. "What would I do with myself? I need work."

"There's a teaching job at the university, the acting class," says my father. "I'm friends with the dean—I know it's open." I don't love the idea that my entire future could be choreographed by nepotism. Which is rich for someone who used to work in television.

"Yeah," I say. "Maybe. I mean, yes. I would need to figure some things out." I am deliberately vague, peeking through a door to the future. The idea is foreign, but it also appeals to me.

"Well, think about it," says my father.

"Oh," says my mother. "You heard about Barb." She says this like an obvious fact.

"No." My chest tightens.

"Oh! We thought you would have been speaking with Will," she says lightly, and my stomach drops in shame. "Barb had a stroke."

My stomach drops. Will. "Oh, God, is she okay?"

"She's in the hospital. It was just two days ago, so I think it's hard to say what's next . . ."

"Is she—is he . . . I haven't talked to Will." I haven't said his name out loud in a week, but it surges in me like a giant wave.

"Oh!" They are surprised. "We thought the two of you . . ."

"We were." I realize with sudden clarity that any chance of bringing that back to present tense depends on my next move. "We are. I've got to go, guys, but, um, I'll see you soon."

"All right, dear. Think about—"

"I'm coming home."

Chapter 42

As I drive north again, the summer swirls through me. My parents, the theater. Reuniting with Theo, Nick surfacing and his dramatic exit, the play, the people, the community, the many, many ways they inspired me. And Will. Of course, Will. The boy who drove me home. The man who pulled me out of the lake. He just kept saving me. It's nice to be saved, but I don't want to be someone who always needs saving. But there he is, anyway, continuously drawing me back in, back to myself, back to reality. And all I've done in return is run away.

I texted my parents and told them I'll be home for dinner. My mother is ordering a celebratory meal, but first I need to fix my whole life.

I pull into the cidery. It's busy, one of the last golden days of summer. I guess I had some romantic reunion in mind: The place would be silent, dusk, maybe, and I would wander up the lane in some diaphanous skirt and a winsome hat, and I'd see him, he would see me, he would run to me, all would be forgiven, forgotten, but no. The parking lot is full, and there are clusters of people gathered at picnic tables and a local girl with a guitar singing in the corner. I look around at this thing he built, this safe, charming place where people are gathered, relaxed, together. The whole vibe is exactly him. Casual. Unpretentious. Genuine.

I imagine walking in there, awkwardly approaching the bar and asking for him, waiting in the entrance while people enter and order drinks. It's not what I imagined. And what if he doesn't come? What if he hears I'm here and won't see me? I wouldn't blame him. It occurs to me that he might not even be here, he might be with Barb at the hospital, if she's even still—

A car pulls up. The window rolls down and a white head peeks out. "Couldn't stay away, huh?"

"Barb!" Tears rise quickly, surprising me. I rush around her car to hug her. "I thought—my parents said you had a stroke!"

She laughs. "I had low blood sugar. Broken telephone and all that."

"So, you aren't . . ."

"Not dying today, dear." She looks me up and down. "You look terrible."

"Jeez, Barb." I glance again toward the cidery, and she follows my gaze.

"He's not here," she says.

"Ah, okay, yeah . . . I get it."

"He's in the back orchard." She points down the laneway past the house and the cidery.

"Oh," I say. "Do you think . . . Does he even . . . ?"

Barb looks over her glasses at me. "He'll want to see you, sure." I feel a small flicker of hope.

"I'm so sorry I left like that," I say in a rush. "I've behaved so badly, I . . ."

"That boy is my heart," she says.

"I know," I say. "He is mine too."

"Well, go get him!"

I walk down the lane to the far edge of the orchard, where the newer trees are. Dozens of saplings, roots wrapped in burlap, are laid out in neat rows on the ground. There he is, digging.

"What are you doing?" I say without thinking, though the shovel, work gloves, and dirt all over him make the answer pretty obvious. He stands up and looks at me, holding his hand over his eyes like a visor.

"Is it you?"

"Hi." I take a step toward him. It all feels so stark in the daylight.

"You're here." He is blank in that way when I first met him, unreadable. His face is completely neutral, his tone pleasant but unrevealing.

"I, um . . . Can we talk?"

He shrugs. "Sure." I take a few more hesitant steps toward him, but he doesn't move.

"I heard about Barb." He doesn't blink. "My parents . . . their flair for the dramatic . . . they said she had a stroke."

"A stroke? No, she had a blood sugar thing."

"Yeah, I know. I, uh, saw her." I pause. "She sent me here."

He raises his eyebrows slightly. "So you came back to North Lake because of my grandma?"

"Well, not just her, but, I mean, they made it sound like she was at death's door."

"They do that," he says, and only in that moment do I really realize that my parents have played me. They have bullshitted me back home.

"They sure do." He doesn't reply but wipes his forehead with his sleeve. "So, what are you doing?" I ask.

"Planting. The storm took a lot of trees down, so I'm replacing them. Need a little new life around here." He keeps digging. I think of that night in the storm, how frantic it felt, how willing I was to save anything he loved. "It's later than I'd like, depends on what kind of winter we have for the root system to develop. But I need something in before winter." He glances up at me. "Never mind."

I take a step toward him. "Will, I'm so sorry." He stops. He jams the shovel in the dirt.

"Why did you leave?" There is the finest break in his voice. "Is it because I said . . . ?"

"You scared the shit out of me." I sigh. "It was so much, so fast. It was so soon after Nick and—"

Will snorts. "You're going to compare this"—he gestures between us—"you and I, to that guy?"

"No . . .Yes, because it messed with me. He hurt me, and then suddenly there's you and it's all so perfect, and nothing ever has been, and . . ."

"Who says it couldn't be?" he says. I take another step toward him.

"Well, at this point . . . you," I say.

Will is quiet for a moment. "Mira, I've already lost the person closest to me." I want so badly to interrupt him. "I think it has made me more open to life. To love." He looks at me pointedly. "But it also has shown me how precious time is."

"I know. I get it." He doesn't want his time wasted.

"No, you don't." He turns back to his shovel, hacking at the ground.

"I'm sorry," I say again. "I don't want to lose you."

He stops suddenly. "I'm not afraid of losing you." He looks up at me sharply. "I've already lost my soulmate. It was the worst thing of my life, and I don't have a lot of time for people who don't get that. I survived it. I can survive you."

"I don't want you to." I step forward. "Will, please."

"I'm not going to beg you or chase you, Mira. And I'm not going to spend any more time trying to convince you why you and I—"

"You and I what?" I say, a small shred of hope in my voice.

"Fuck it." He throws his shovel to the ground. "We're supposed to be together, Mira."

"We are?"

"Yeah." He shoves his hands in his pockets, defeated. "I've felt that all summer."

"I have known for . . . less time," I say. "But you're right. We are."

He finally looks at me, and I see the hope in him too. "How do I know you won't run away again?"

"Well, I'm moving back here, for starters."

"You are?"

"Yeah. I have a few options here now." He raises an eyebrow. "Creative options, I mean! Just the one option for . . ."

"For what?" He steps toward me.

"For you. For this. For whatever this is or could be."

"What do you want it to be?" We are so close, I can smell the earth on him.

"Everything," I say softly. I reach for his face. He catches my hand in his.

"I don't need promises," he says gently. "I know I came on too strong. What I told you—"

"Did you mean it?" I interrupt him.

"Yeah," he says. "Of course I meant it." He searches my face. "If you're not there yet, it doesn't mean . . . We can slow down. The show is over. It's just real life now."

"Real life." I smile. "Whatever that is."

"Whatever that is."

"So you still like me?"

"I more than like you, you know that."

"I more than like you too," I say. "Lots more."

"This is feeling very high school."

"I love you, Will Reed. Now kiss me."

He laughs and grabs my face and kisses me like we never stopped. It feels real. It feels like home. I had my first kiss under an apple tree, and here I am again. We pull apart and he starts laughing. "Oh, God, your face."

"What?"

"It's covered in dirt now. I'm sorry."

I wrap my arms around him, burying myself in his arms. "So you think this can be salvaged?" I ask.

"Our . . . love?"

"This orchard. How much damage did the storm do? Can you fix it?"

He pulls away from me and looks at it, then back at me. "I'll die trying," he says.

"Well, then," I say. "Let me help." I pick up a shovel and stick it in the earth, my best Scarlett O'Hara pose. He laughs.

"Sounds good, let's go." He grabs some tool and starts lifting the earth. He glances over, noticing I haven't moved.

I pause and clear my throat. "Yeah, that was more of a symbolic gesture . . . I don't actually know how this thing works."

"You can't work a shovel?"

"I know Shakespeare," I say. "I have other skills."

"Yeah, you do." He laughs. "I know this is where I abandon everything and we make love among the trees or whatever. But it's going to rain tomorrow, and I need to get these in."

"Gotcha," I say. "Farm life!"

"This is where you start digging, Belmont." He eyes me. "You said you're staying . . . so stay."

This is a test. This is like the canoe. The apples in the storm. This is where I am supposed to roll up my sleeves and prove my love by planting baby apple trees.

And so I do.

We won't know if the trees take until spring. Sometimes the answers need to gestate. Will has hours of work left.

"Meet me at home?"

I smile. I nod. I kiss him. "Okay."

But first, I have a stop to make.

I pull up to the house where I spent so much of my youth, running lines and practicing kissing. It always struck me as such a cheerful house, white with red shutters, a spray of ferns hanging from every corner. I see his mom, Annie, on the porch, wrapped in a blanket, and when the man next to her stands up, I see that it's Max, not Theo. He sees me pull up across the street, waves, and calls into the house.

Theo steps onto the porch, my beautiful friend, with a blanket and a cup of tea, which he hands to his mother. He sees me and stands there on the steps, his face blank. I raise my hand tentatively and give a half smile. I don't know how I will be received. He comes down the steps and waits at the curb as I cross the street.

"You're covered in dirt," he calls as I come toward him.

"I was digging a tree."

"As one does. Dare I ask if it was an apple tree? At a cidery?"

"I only do apple trees."

"So you and Will are . . . ?"

"Yes."

"Attagirl."

"Theo." I take a big breath. "You were right about everything. I'm selfish. I treat people like shit, and I've abandoned you over and over, and I am starting to understand why, but that doesn't excuse—"

He cuts me off with a tight, fierce hug, lifting me off the ground.

"There you are," he says when he sets me down, his eyes full.

"Here I am." I take his hands. "I'm sorry."

"The course of true love never did run smooth." He smiles and my insides loosen in relief. We are our own kind of love story.

I take a breath. "So I was thinking maybe *Private Lives.*"

"For what?"

"It might be a nice show for us. For the fall slot at the theater . . . I bet my parents would go for it. Well, if you're still in town?"

Theo glances back at the porch, at his mother. "Yeah, I might be . . . For Noël Coward with the right gal, I could almost guarantee it." His face crinkles into a big smile. "I'd love that, Mirabel. I think 1930s Paris would look good on us."

"I think it would."

I stay for tea with Annie and Max, then make my way home, which, I have learned, is an apple orchard down a dirt road with fairy lights and my own real love. I drive through my hometown, past my high school, past the theater, where I spent so many hours this summer, so many hours of my whole life. The idea of directing or teaching acting scares me, but they are slowly sparking, taking shape in my mind. The idea of the next show, a new show, another chance to act with Theo, thrills me. I text my parents to cancel dinner. They'll understand. This is all their fault anyway. I think of the chaos that brought me here, right back where I started. I think of the play. I wonder if there wasn't a little fairy magic there after all.

To act, that is, to act well, you need to simulate realness, even when you are wearing someone else's clothes, speaking words in a voice that isn't your own. A good actor can translate all the artful trappings of life and present them as reality. A good actor knows how to find her light and knows the boundaries of the stage in the dark. A good actor forgets the audience and also plays to them. I have been acting for years, but am only starting to realize that I've been doing it all wrong. I have been so afraid of reality that I have simulated it, hiding in a big city, in a role that required zero creativity, in relationships that held no risk. I have been so afraid of the cracks in life, of real life getting in. But that's where real life is. This summer, my hometown, my family, my best friend, who refuses to let me self-sabotage, and Will, who dares to love me in spite of myself . . . They have cracked me open. They have shown me the beauty in my realness. They have shown me that life, real life, needs an audience too. We are here to witness each other. We are here to grow together. We are here to love each other. Yes, sometimes we get a little lost in the woods. We chase the wrong people and take the wrong paths. Sometimes magic potions, or accidental brownies, make us do things we normally wouldn't, but sometimes they help the truth spill out. Sometimes we don't know who we are or what we want; our minds aren't our own. But we end up where we need to. Eventually, if you're lucky, you awaken from the dream and let the realness of daylight draw you home.

The End

or

(Fifteen weeks until opening night . . .)

Acknowledgments

Kind of like theater, it takes a community to publish a book! I am so grateful to so many people.

To my agent, Carly Watters: Thank you for your incredible support, generosity, patience, and general awesomeness. You are so gifted at what you do, and I can't imagine a better partner in this. I am so lucky to have you in my life. Thanks also to Mireya Chiriboga and the team at P.S. Literary for your efforts and support.

Thank you to my editor Emily Friedenrich, for guiding me so gently through my debut. Thank you for keeping the fairy magic alive and bringing such heart to this process. Thank you to my developmental editor, Karen Brown, for your wise insights and for engaging so deeply and generously with me to get the story just right. Your encouragement and support have meant so much. Thanks to everyone at Lake Union / Amazon Publishing for making this experience so easy. Special thanks to production manager Liz Gluck, copyeditor Michelle Hope, proofreader Kellie Osborne, cold reader Jessica Poore, art director Jo O'Neill, and cover designer Zoe Norvell.

Thank you to my beta readers: Carley, Nadene du Plooy, and Jessica Christon. Your early feedback was invaluable, and I am very grateful for your insights. Thank you to my brothers, Denny Stokes and Eric Robillard, for sharing your professional expertise in helping me figure out the theatrical fire. Thank you, Devin Stokes (no relation!), and the folks at Two Blokes Cider for clarifying aspects of cider-making. Any errors are my own.

I was lucky to play Helena in a production of *A Midsummer Night's Dream* in my twenties, which informed aspects of this book, and which remains one of my favorite theater experiences of my life. Shout-out to my friends and family from that production, especially our brilliant directors, Annette Stokes and Michael Serres.

The "secret garden" is inspired by Sweetman's Garden in my hometown, North Bay, Ontario. It has always been a sacred place to me (and yes, I kissed some boys there!). Thank you to the advocates and volunteers who protect and maintain this treasured community greenspace.

Thank you to my friends and family: I have been inordinately blessed with an abundance of good ones. Thank you for loving me, for reminding me who I am, and for your great support of my writing and my life. It's hard to express how bolstering a walk, a karaoke night, a phone call, a cup of tea, a check-in can be in the midst of a very solitary art form. Suffice to say it adds up to a very rich life, and I am so grateful for the people in it. Denny, Rose, and Meg: really nice to meet you!

Thank you to my parents for the ways you each model a creative life, and for instilling the value of this in me. Thank you for taking me to the "libwaywy," for reading to me, and for driving me to all those play rehearsals even though you knew I was really a writer. I love you.

Thank you, Scott, for your bottomless support, enthusiasm, and patience for a wife who is part hermit, part goblin, for understanding and encouraging me, and for all the ways you hold me in our life together. I love you and I like you.

About the Author

Photo © 2025 Scott Murdoch

Lara Stokes studied theater and creative writing at York University, where she was the recipient of the bpNichol Award and the Judith Eve Gewertz Award. Her work has appeared in *The Danforth Review* and the *Ottawa Arts Review*, among others. Born and raised in Northern Ontario, she now lives in Kawartha Lakes, Ontario. For more information, visit www.larastokeswriter.com.